FINDING GEORGE WASHINGTON

A Time Travel Tale

Bill Zarchy

Roving Camera Press
Albany, California

Finding George Washington:
A Time Travel Tale
By Bill Zarchy

Published by Roving Camera Press
2020 Trade Paperback Edition
Copyright © 2020 Bill Zarchy

Cover photos by Bill Zarchy, including photograph of the painting *Washington After the Battle of Princeton* (1779) by Charles Willson Peale at the Smithsonian National Museum of American History, Washington.

findinggeorgewashington.com
billzarchy.com

ISBN-10: 0-9849191-2-0
ISBN-13: 978-0-9849191-2-3

For my dear Susan,
life partner, pandemic pal,
best of wives and best of women,
who never ceases to amaze me,
and brings love, beauty, and music
into our lives
every day of the year.

Contents

Part One: Finding   1
1.   Aurora   3
2.   Riding Machines   8
3.   Nevada   10
4.   Crux   15
5.   Matt   20
6.   Plumbing   24
7.   Restless   26
8.   Guest   30
9.   Earth   36
10.   Tour   38
11.   Return   45
12.   Plantation   50
13.   Bondage   52
14.   Manumission   56
15.   Expert   61
16.   Excellency   66
17.   Turning Point   69
18.   Challenge   73
19.   Money   78
20.   Weeds   81
21.   Ballpark   85
22.   Dogs   91
23.   Kiss   95
24.   Fog   98
25.   FBI   102
26.   Oreck   107
27.   Dentures   112
28.   Natural   117
29.   Pierre   121
30.   Einstein   128
31.   Paranoia   136

32. Extras   142
33. Foresight   144
34. Complicated   149
35. Dead Drop   155
36. Spycraft   158
37. Corrida   162
38. Impatient   169
39. Plan   172

Part Two: Fleeing   179
40. Flight   181
41. Mendo   185
42. Ganja   189
43. Sailboat   194
44. Dark Star   197
45. Dozer   202
46. Shakes   207
47. Warning   212
48. Dream   217
49. Davis   223
50. Zephyr   226
51. Winnemucca   232
52. Fitz   237
53. Burden   241
54. Rockies   247
55. 199   251
56. Diversion   255
57. Siding   259
58. Nurse   264
59. Rerouting   270
60. Chicago   278
61. Phone Call   282
62. Lake Shore   287
63. Lifers   291

64. Blown 296
65. Luggage 303
66. Phils 309
67. Independence 315
68. Series 320
69. Bum 324
70. HQ 328
71. Bakelite 333
72. Saddle 337
73. Ballerinos 341
74. Patsy 346
75. TVD 349

Part Three: Forgetting 355
76. Parade 357
77. Replay 359
78. Liberty 363
79. Fiona 369
80. Epilogue 374

Author's Note: Why Washington? 378
Acknowledgements 381
Book List 383
About the Author 386

PART ONE
Finding

"Baseball provides us with a family album older and deeper, by many generations, than all but a relative handful of Americans can claim for their own lineage ... the charm of baseball today is in good measure its echo of a bygone age; and ... it is gratifying to think we have something lighthearted in common with the harsh lives of our forefathers, going back to the nation's earliest period and likely beyond ... It is no creation myth to report that the Father of Our Country played a bat-and-ball game called *wicket*, now vanished but long concurrent with baseball, with the troops at Valley Forge."

—John Thorn, *Baseball in the Garden of Eden: The Secret History of the Early Game*

Chapter One
AURORA

A new freeze gripped the valley, and a few inches of virgin white covered the now-frozen ruts in the roads. When the soldiers first arrived at this winter encampment two months before, rain and cold had compounded the misery of the men. Lately it had been freezing and snowing, making the hardened ground easier to traverse than the sleety, slippery mud had been.

A small farmhouse made of tan and brown fieldstone sat in flat bottomland near the creek. The back door opened and a splash of warm light lit the new snow. From inside came the sounds of a party—a fiddle, laughter, and high-energy conversation. A tall man in a heavy cloak and three-cornered hat stepped off the small porch at the rear of the house and into the cold. A sentry snapped to attention.

"Just getting some air, lad, stand easy," the General said. "No need to follow." He trudged off north, away from the house, enjoying the brisk chill.

Ah, he thought, *it's fine to have my dear wife here with me these past couple of weeks! She and the other wives provide such a boost to the morale and hopefulness of the men. It's worth a wee party to celebrate the difference they make ... and my birthday.*

The dreadful winter weather and the spread of disease had cost him one-fourth of his army in the early going, but at last there were signs of hope. Foraging for food was still a daily struggle, but now the men were finally housed in hundreds of hastily constructed wooden huts. The eager effervescence of the Marquis de Lafayette for the past half year; the appearance of the Polish nobleman Pulaski a few months before; the continued loyalty of so many of the troops; the imminent arrival any day now of the Prussian Baron von Steuben; and the General's wife coming to stay with him during the winter encampment—all these events gave him hope.

Perhaps we have survived a low point. And moved beyond it.

The snow had stopped some time before, and now the night was crisp and clear, stars twinkling above the snowy landscape. As he reached the top of a small hill overlooking the Schuylkill River, the sky lit up. A faint green glow on the horizon grew and grew. Great shimmering swaths of chartreuse and mauve dove and dodged across the heavens to the north. He had heard of the aurora borealis from Franklin, but he hadn't known it could be seen as far south as Pennsylvania.

The General watched as the Northern Lights spread, shimmered, and swirled through the sky like the smoke from God's own cigar, now rising, now dipping, now twirling and pulsing.

Though soldiers often considered the aurora a bad

omen, at that moment it thrilled him. To the east, he could see the glow of sentry fires of some of the closer regiments, the troops hunkered down for the night. A short distance to the south, the men of his personal guard occupied their own group of makeshift huts within sight of the farmhouse.

It's cold. I should get back before Patsy and the staff begin to miss me.

He paused and took a deep breath of the night air. He was a durable and determined man who had survived cold and wintry weather during his early life as a surveyor and, later, as a British officer. He would show his Continental Army troops that the cold didn't bother him, that staying strong was a state of mind. Certainly they had it worse than he did, but they respected that he had refused to move out of his tent into the stone farmhouse until his men moved out of their tattered shelters into log huts.

The fluid, ethereal display of light in the skies danced and pulsated. Before he could climb down the hill and head back toward the farmhouse, the ground under his feet began to shake and rumble, providing a steady, geological drumbeat to accompany the green and red light in the sky. The terrain rolled. He lost his footing on the ice, just at a point where a crisp moonbeam seemed to hit the patch of turf he was crossing. The earth came up to meet him, and he banged his head on the frozen ground. Woozy and lightheaded, teetering on the edge of consciousness, he felt a great sadness, felt the bones in his body melt in the shard of moonlight, even as, in his remaining awareness, he realized the moon was not out that evening. He felt his body scooped off the ground, as if by a vengeful wind, then tumbled in a heap onto something hard and unyielding that swept him along at a great rate of speed. All went dark.

The General awoke some time later, lying on a cold steel floor in a large rectangular room. A few bits of light poked in through cracks in the walls, but not enough to see very well. His head ached, and the light hurt his eyes. He looked about for a moment, then fell unconscious again.

Later, through his delirium, he heard footsteps and whispering and felt hands on his body, inspecting his face, then propping him up, not unkindly, and giving him water.

He started to regain consciousness when he felt the room begin to move. Was this another earthquake? What was happening? Was someone else in there with him? His head still hurt. The movement made him nauseous. He seemed to be in a large box made of steel or iron, a dungeon, perhaps. He took inventory. *I appear to be intact,* he thought, *other than a persistent headache and a new layer of grime. Still have my hat, shoes, cape, and sword. But what has happened? Did someone assist me? Have the British captured me? Where is this dungeon and how can it be moving? And where, oh where, is it going?*

Though he could not see outside, the steel box did seem to be moving rapidly, first steadily for a while, then swaying as if turning or swooping in curves. As he began to explore his surroundings—first on his knees, then standing—he realized the bitter cold of Valley Forge was gone.

On one side of the box he saw a large, wooden door, which refused to slide open. The box also contained a number of wooden crates, a few dozen barrels, and lots of smaller boxes made of some type of thick, printed paper.

In a corner he found his benefactors, two men of the road who cheerfully shared the steel box with him.

"They'll open that damned door sometime soon," the one with the beard like Methuselah said, revealing a gap-toothed smile. "We'll be able to hop off somewhere when they slow down."

His companion wore a filthy, tattered, collarless shirt, a picture of a bird with a lute or guitar and the word "Woodstock" emblazoned across his chest.

The two men also shared their water and bits of food.

"There's always more food to be found," said the beard. "People just leave it about. So careless."

The General was aghast to be eating stolen food, but there was little enough, and he had no alternative. He lost track of time.

Chapter Two
RIDING MACHINES

On the third or fourth day, the General woke up to discover the door ajar and the men of the road gone. He pushed the door open and looked outside. A rural landscape rolled by at a great rate of speed, faster than a galloping horse. He leaned far out of the door and surveyed his ride. The steel box was a wheeled conveyance, a type of carriage in a long, connected caravan of similar boxes, no doubt used to transport goods. As the caravan curved around, he could see it traveled on a roadbed of stone, wood, and steel rails stretching toward the horizon in both directions.

The rails often paralleled roads, rolling through fertile land, past fields, farmhouses, and barns built in an unfamiliar style. Tall poles strung with wires lined the roads, connecting to each house they passed. Soon the houses grew closer together as the caravan approached a town or city. The General noticed water off to his right, a bay or the ocean. It was late in the day, and the sun would soon set over the water. *Sunset over the ocean? Where in the name of Providence am I?*

To his left, a shiny black road was crammed with brightly painted types of carriages, unconnected, each large enough for several occupants. Each carriage had glass windows, solid black wheels, and—most confounding of all—no horses. No obvious signs of propulsion at all. Some of the carriages roared loudly and emitted a thin, foul-smelling smoke.

Riding machines. Very fast riding machines and large cargo-box carriages on the smooth, hard road surface.

A long, mournful whistle came from the front of the General's box caravan. Coming into a more populated area, it began to slow down.

Time to get away.

The box slowed to a crawl, and he hopped off, his body stiff from days of cramped inactivity. On one side, the road with the crazy riding machines. On the other, a swamp. He chose the swamp.

Chapter Three
NEVADA

Point Isabel, August 16, 2014

Vada, come!"

I watched as she swam a little farther out in the Bay, scooped up a second tennis ball in her cavernous mouth, then turned back to me.

"Good girl!"

The wind picked up, blowing in from the ocean. The sun sank, and it turned cold. In the distance, a fog bank skulked ominously offshore. I could hear a freight train approaching.

Fresh air! It was great to get outdoors. Enough video games already.

An eighty-eight-pound bundle of muscle, a whip tail, and unbridled enthusiasm, the love child of a chance encounter between a Boxer with a big head and a sleek black Lab with a huge tongue, Nevada had no trouble paddling back toward shore. She climbed up the rocks, dropped one tennis ball at my feet, and shook cold Bay water all over me.

As the shake engulfed her, I tried to grab a second tennis ball out of her mouth, but she pulled away with a playful toss of her head. It was our usual version of parallel play. I was playing Go Fetch, and she was playing Keep Away.

In a typical trick of the weather, the City was still vividly backlit with an orange glow, while the fog began to pour furiously through the Golden Gate and across the Bay toward us. I took off my dark glasses, twisted the ball out of Nevada's mouth, and flung it as far as I could, away from the water. The ball soared out of sight, over a small hill, and around the corner of this park on the east side of San Francisco Bay, where dogs ran free and their people desperately tried to keep up. Ah, the joys of being owned by a puppy, especially a large, frisky six-year-old! She scampered after the ball.

The fog engulfed us in chilly pea soup. Nevada stopped and looked around, startled by the sudden change in the weather, then ran out of view behind the hill. The wind slackened. The ocean smell turned dank and musty.

I lumbered over the hill after Nevada. This far side of the park was nearly empty. I looked east, away from the Bay, toward the marshland. Rush-hour traffic zipped along in both directions against the backdrop of the East Bay hills. Next to the freeway, the freight train crept along, heading south toward Oakland. One boxcar door was ajar.

As I watched, someone grabbed the door from the inside, slid it open a couple of feet, then dropped to the ground outside the train. The figure, who appeared at first to be a tall woman with a long ponytail, stumbled, took one look at the freeway traffic next to the railroad, then began to wade through the marsh, directly toward me. From a distance, she appeared to wear a funny hat and a uniform with brass buttons and gold epaulets, like the ones we had worn in marching band.

Nevada brought me both balls, then gleefully resumed her game of Keep Away. We quickened our steps and turned back toward the parking lot. It was getting cold.

In a mellifluous baritone with a vaguely British accent, the woman in the band uniform called to me through the fog.

"Excuse me, young man. What manner of place would this be?"

I realized the woman was actually a man with long reddish-brown hair, graying at the temples. As he approached, walking with a slight limp, his muddy uniform seemed more military than musical. From a bygone era, it consisted of a blue cutaway jacket with tails, off-white breeches and vest, high boots, a long, dark cape lined in red, and a sword and scabbard attached to the belt.

And the hat! Broad-brimmed, tricornered, the kind of thing you might find on a Revolutionary War officer. In some parts of the Bay Area, this outfit wouldn't get a second look. After all, people wore panda and giraffe hats to baseball games. The annual Bay to Breakers race drew entrants dressed as centipedes, the Jamaican bobsled team, cartoon characters, and Tarzan with bright-green glasses and a real snake around his shoulders. Cosplay enjoyed huge popularity. Everyone loved dress-up, and Halloween was practically a national holiday. Tellers at the bank near my parents' home in Berkeley dressed as funky ghosts, ghouls, or witches with green skin, missing teeth, and crooked hats.

"I say, young man, what manner of place?" He looked warily at Nevada, as she ran over and performed a ceremonial shake in front of him, then nuzzled at his hand.

"This is Point Isabel. It's a park, a public park. A dog park."

He looked dubiously out across the Bay, where we could still make out the skyline of the City through the thickening fog. "And what city is that yonder?"

"That's San Francisco. But don't call it Frisco. Natives like me hate that."

"Natives?"

"Yeah, I was born in New York, but I've lived in California since I was three. After ten years, you automatically become a native Californian."

No smile in reaction to this glib patter.

"California. I have heard tell of this island, seen it on old Spanish maps. And those structures across the water, are they bridges to that city?"

"Yup."

He turned back toward me. I saw confusion in his eyes.

"But where is my army?" I heard a quiet clickety-click sound as he talked.

"Army?"

"Yes, the Continental Army. I must get back to my men."

I started to edge away cautiously. A witch in a bank was one thing. A big guy with a sword who thought he had lost his army was quite another.

"Look, buddy, I don't know what you need, but I've gotta get home. Nevada, let's go!"

I had hoped my sharp call would alert her to possible danger, but she continued to nuzzle the stranger's hand. Some watchdog.

"Nevada, come!"

She looked up at me for a moment, then stuck her big black snout in his crotch. He barely noticed, his dignity somehow uncompromised.

13

"I pray thee, help me. I fear I have become separated from my troops, and I must find them again. If we can weather the storms this winter, perhaps we can rally in the spring and muster an offensive against the British."

Winter storms? It's August, and California's in the middle of a drought. This guy doesn't know that?

"Listen, that's really not my problem, mister."

"General."

"Okay, General. I gotta go."

Chapter Four
CRUX

He seemed worried, concerned but not panicky, as I tried to walk away from him.

"So you choose not to assist me in returning to Valley Forge?" He spoke quietly. The clicking continued, barely audible.

I should have just left. But the guy seemed sincere and not dangerous, despite the sword. And there was something about him, something that made me want to trust him. Besides, the fog was dense now, the park dark, windy and cold, a few miles from anywhere. I hated to leave him out there. Maybe I could drop him somewhere in Berkeley. He'd fit right in with the crazies on Telegraph Avenue, though he was pretty dirty, even for that crowd.

"Got a way into town? Know someone with a car?"

"Car?"

"You know, man, a horseless carriage? A set of wheels to get you back to Berkeley, or wherever it is you're staying? Like one of those?" I pointed toward the freeway beyond the marshland. Traffic sped by in unrelenting fury, headlights slicing through the gathering gloom. Amtrak's Coast Starlight train rushed passengers along on its daily run from L.A. to Seattle.

The General stared at the cars and trucks and train and shuddered without comprehension. "Young man, here is the crux of the dilemma. I know not where I am, nor how I have come to be here. And what has happened to the winter?"

Despite this ridiculous story, he maintained a stately presence. I headed back toward the parking lot, and he fell into stride beside me.

"So when did you see your men last?" I asked, humoring him.

"I believe it has been several days now. I left the headquarters house one evening after dinner. We had staged a small party with my aides to celebrate my birthday and the recent arrival of my wife, Patsy. I stepped away to get some air and planned to walk to the nearby encampment of my personal guard. But the snow had stopped earlier in the evening, the skies were clear, and the aurora borealis was visible."

"The Northern Lights? Awesome!"

"Yes, quite. I might have lost my way. At one point, the wind rose with a fierce howl, and the earth seemed to tremble for several seconds."

"An earthquake?"

He ignored the question. "I slipped on the icy path and fell, and I suppose I lost consciousness."

What a story!

"I awoke after a time, trapped in a huge, moving, steel box, the door locked."

"Boxcar."

He looked at me curiously.

16

"I watched you jump from that boxcar."

"Yes. I still feel a bit dizzy from my fall. There were other men in the box … car. They helped take care of me, gave me water and food. I must have been in there for days. A short time ago I discovered my companions were gone and the door had been unlocked. When the box slowed down, I made my escape, into the swampland. Then I noticed your dog and waded toward the shoreline."

He peered off into the gloomy dusk toward the Bay Bridge and the lights of the City.

"But where is Valley Forge?"

"In Pennsylvania?"

"Exactly!" he thundered. "So you know it? Is it far?" An excited clicking accompanied his words. I looked closely. He rarely smiled and barely opened his mouth as he talked, but I could see his teeth appeared to be loose, brown and uneven. Not something an actor could throw together for a casual costume.

This guy thinks he's George Washington, I thought, *and something about him makes me want to indulge him.*

"Valley Forge is very far away, General. Listen, I don't know how you got here, but it's nearly dark, and it's cold and I've got to get home. Come on, we're almost back at the parking lot."

"Parking lot?"

"I'm guessing you don't have a ride."

He flashed me a look of kindly condescension and responded carefully. "I have no carriage, horseless or otherwise. And my steed Blueskin is at the camp with my army."

"Of course he is. Can I drop you in town? Perhaps you can find your men tomorrow, when it's light out."

"Yes, thank you for your assistance, young man."

"My name is Tim. Timothy Morrison."

"And I am General Washington. As you are probably aware."

"George Washington."

"Indeed."

"Sure, whatever."

He glared at me coldly. But he needed my help.

My battered econobox was the only car left in the lot. He gaped at it. "What kind of infernal contrivance is that?"

"It's my ride, General. Toyota Corolla. Best-selling car in the world." I opened the door and motioned for him to get in. "Dude, you ride shotgun."

"Shotgun?"

"The passenger seat. Next to me."

My Revolutionary War history was starting to come back. I recalled the Continental Army's struggle to survive during their winter at Valley Forge. But how could the Father of Our Country have walked away from his army, stepped through a door into the twenty-first century, and somehow ended up at a dog park on the California coast? Ridiculous. Yet part of me wanted to believe him. I recalled reading that Washington had false teeth made of wood. Maybe the teeth on this guy made me trust him.

Reluctantly, but with a certain grace, he folded his long frame into the front seat of the Corolla, tucking the scabbarded sword in next to his leg. Nevada hopped into the back. The General jumped when I started the motor.

"What beast roars like that?"

"A hundred horses, trapped under the hood in front," I said. "They propel the car."

He looked skeptical. "I have known many horses, but I have never met a horse that roared. And they must be very

18

small indeed! How do you feed them?"

"There are no animals, General. It's a machine, like a clock, with the power of many horses. But you don't wind it like a clock, you burn a fuel. I'll show it to you later. Where are you staying?"

"If we are not near Valley Forge, then I have no billet at present."

George—if that was actually his name—held on for dear life as we drove into Berkeley, marveling at the smooth, black roads, ducking and cringing as other infernal contrivances overtook and passed us, and exclaiming over the straight, paved streets and neat rows of houses. From the back seat, Nevada, man's best friend, licked him on the neck and ear.

Chapter Five
MATT

Berkeley, August 16, 2014

I parked in the driveway, let the General into our kitchen, and texted Matt next door.

Come over

I knew he was playing *Halo* in his room.

Busy, he responded.

Dude, u gotta come see this

Later

I knew that "later" meant "soon." LaMatthew Johnson had been my best friend since middle school, since he had moved onto our block and we discovered our mutual love of video games, the Giants, and a red-haired girl in math class whose name I could no longer remember. Matt was working at Taco Bell that summer, while allegedly researching his graduate thesis.

I'd been living at home for a while, waiting to return to grad school, my fellowship money delayed. At first I relished having time off. But my lazy punting on a half-hearted job search fooled no one. The house was empty, my folks in Italy on sabbatical. Except for Matt, all my high school friends were gone.

I had borrowed Matt's copy of *Independence*, the epic game set during colonial times. Two years old, ancient for a video game. The main character had dealings with General George Washington during the Revolution.

And now I might have him in my house.

Ha! Who am I kidding?

He sat at the kitchen table, staring suspiciously at the appliances around him. Nevada lay on her back snoozing on the floor, tuckered out from her outing, her legs dream-sprinting in the air as she chased a mental squirrel.

"Want a Coke or a brew?"

The General looked blank.

"Libation, sir?"

"Yes, thank you."

I opened the fridge, and he examined it with wonder, marveling at the packaged foods inside. He held up his hands and felt the cold air coming from the stainless-steel box.

"What manner of magic is this?"

"General, if you are who you say you are—and I'm not convinced of that, sir—but if you are, then you're going to find many magical changes."

"Eh?"

"More than two hundred years have passed. It's now 2014. Valley Forge happened a long time ago, in 1770-something."

Stony silence. Bewilderment.

"How is that possible?"

"I don't know. Also, we are very far from Valley Forge, nearly 3,000 miles, on the *west* coast of North America. Close to the Pacific Ocean."

He looked perplexed. "West coast? I can see that everything appears different. As I said, I have heard mention of the island of California, but thought it just a myth."

My pocket vibrated, spewing heavy-metal rock.

I was used to this ringtone and the accompanying tingle near my groin, but my guest freaked at the sound.

"What is that clatter?"

"It's music, General."

"Hmmm."

Text from Matt: *OMW*.

A minute later he came in the kitchen door. I introduced him to the General.

"Matty, this is George. I found him at Point Isabel."

The General looked surprised at this informality, but he nodded politely.

"LaMatthew, sir. Pleasure to meet you. Excellent costume. Timmy, I think I'm gonna be Boba Fett again for Halloween."

"I don't think this is a costume. This dude might really be George Washington. For reals!"

The General—tall, muscular, and pale—drew himself up to his full height, suddenly regal. Matt—short, roly-poly, and chocolate-brown—gaped in confusion.

"Whaaaat? Timmy, I dunno …"

George told Matt about Valley Forge, the snowstorm, the shaking of the ground, his purported leap in time and space. I watched Matt's face turn from sneering mockery to furrowed-brow doubt. Apparently, this story seemed far-fetched even to someone who had just fought an interstellar war on his PlayStation. Yet there was something about George. Either he was a great actor, or he was, indeed, for reals. I wanted to believe him.

Matt looked dubious, then stricken. "How can this be true? If this is George Washington …"

"I know, right? How is this possible? And yet, I really think it could be. I don't know how, but call me crazy. I mean, it can't be."

"Well," Matt gulped, "if this is George Washington, then he's a slaver. He owns other humans. They are property, chattel, compelled to work for him, for no pay. He buys and sells people. He could own my family."

"He's the Father of Our Country. I think."

"A slave owner nonetheless. An oppressor of African Americans. And he's got a sword."

Surprised, the General looked down at Matty, sternly at first. His expression slowly dissolved into a kindly, avuncular look. The clicking of his teeth was audible as he spoke. "Are you a slave?" he asked with hesitation. "Or a freed man?"

Matt didn't know what to say. He backed up a couple of steps. The guy in front of us looked like a young George Washington. But I knew some woman in Russia had undergone surgery to enhance her resemblance to a Barbie doll. Was this fellow a magnificent actor who looked a lot like Washington, or was the first president of the United States indeed sitting in my kitchen, sipping a can of Miller Lite?

Chapter Six
PLUMBING

Matt got very quiet for a while. The General sat back, bone-weary, enjoying the rest. He then examined his drink.

"Beer, you say?" he grinned tightly. "Very watery, isn't it?"

We quickly ran out of things to say. He marveled at the cans.

"Such bright, beautiful metal! They appear to be made of gold and silver."

"Not."

After a while, inevitability reared its ugly head.

"Young man?"

"Please call me Tim, General."

"Timothy. Could you kindly direct me to the privy?"

"Sure. But I'd better show you how to use it. It's all changed since your day."

"That won't be necessary."

"Well, there are plumbing devices to learn."

"Plumbing?"

I took him on a tour of the bathroom. I was sure that, even in wartime, the General had always washed from a basin filled with warm water by servants. He had probably never seen running water in a sink, much less a shower.

At the basin, he gleefully grasped the left lever and twisted, then stuck his hand under the tap.

"Oh my! It's warm. No, it's hot! Who heats this water and puts it into this pipe?"

"The water comes from a tank, where it's kept hot by burning a fuel. Here's where you sit, General." I showed him how to lift the lid and the seat and mentioned the protocol of closing the seat after use. He eyed the toilet suspiciously.

"And this little magic lever on the side blows water through and makes it all go away," I added.

"Where?"

"Where what?"

"Where does it go?"

"Just … away."

"Is it magic, Timothy? Like the cold box?"

"No sir, just technology."

"Eh?"

"Invention. Science."

He was curious, yet his shoulders slumped with each new revelation, his apparent displacement in time and space beginning to weigh on him. He needed help.

He looked at me with a tight smile. "I fear I must rest. I hate to impose, but is there somewhere I could lay my weary head?"

I smiled. "I know just the place."

"And perhaps something to wear that is a bit less formal than my current attire?" He looked down at his high boots and filthy wartime clothing.

Chapter Seven
RESTLESS

My sister was away at college. I sprawled in a chair in her room and stared at a dollar bill. The guy on the currency peering back at me seemed to be carved out of a block of marble, uncomfortable in his own skin, lower jaw bulged out, lips compressed, and bored with having to sit for the artist. His mushroom-shaped white hair and tight, toothached expression resembled an older, glummer version of the powerful, vigorous man now snuggling under my sister's old Hello Kitty quilt and surrounded by Beanie Babies. Nevada napped at the foot of the bed.

I pulled out my phone to search for images of Washington. The variety of ways in which he was depicted amazed me. Of course, he had died long before the advent of photography, but many artists had painted his portrait, over several decades. Sometimes he looked old and tired, sometimes young and vigorous, usually white-haired and distinguished. One thing was clear, though: the face of the younger man in my sister's bed looked more oval than the older face on the dollar bill, his jaw longer, his mouth more relaxed.

George stirred, pushed aside two especially ugly Beanie Babies, opened his eyes, and stretched his long legs. He wore a bright-orange Giants T-shirt that said "The Freak" on the front and "Lincecum 55" on the back. His military uniform sat in a pile on my sister's school desk, sword leaning against the wall.

"Thank you, Timothy, for your hospitality. This is considerably more luxurious than the common soldiers endure in our encampment, and much warmer. I am so very tired and must rest." He nestled deeper into the covers.

"Must rest ... so much has happened ... must find my army ..."

He drifted off to sleep. I drew the quilt up over him a bit higher, realizing as I leaned close that I would have to teach George how to use the shower in the morning. After months of encampments—or perhaps, after months sleeping in doorways in San Francisco—he smelled like a soldier. In wide-eyed, mouthless innocence, Hello Kitty, her pink bow at a jaunty angle, waved up at us from the quilt.

Matt dozed in my living room, a PlayStation controller in one hand.

"What now?" I asked, after shaking him awake.

"Damned if I know. Need sleep."

He went home muttering, still unnerved by his encounter with a possible slave owner.

And I had just tucked in George Washington—or whoever he was. While he slept like a baby, I couldn't get to sleep.

What now, indeed? Why did I bring him home? Should I be taking this guy to a loony bin, or to the police? Hello 911, I've just found George Washington at the dog park. Where do we drop off ex-presidents? You know, ones who died 200 years ago? Of course this is an emergency!

I tossed for several hours.

If this is George, and he stays here in his future, who will lead the Revolutionary Army after Valley Forge? Can the revolt of the colonies succeed without him? Are we stuck with a permanent houseguest from the eighteenth century?

By morning, I was convinced of one thing: if this was George, we had to get him back to his own time. America had to win its War of Independence. I couldn't imagine the consequences if we didn't, but every option I contemplated seemed sinister.

And I didn't even believe in time travel!

That morning, without comment, I handed George a dollar bill. He accepted it with two hands and gaped at his image, silent for a long while.

"This looks like me. I appear quite old here," he said eventually.

I recalled that the image on the dollar was based on the Gilbert Stuart portrait, painted years after the Revolution. It helped that I had been a history major.

"The United States of America? We were, or will be, victorious in our Revolution against the Crown? The colonies are able to unite? Why is my visage on the currency? Will I be … did I become … the new king of America?" He found it difficult to know what tense to use. My present was his future.

"No, sir, you were the first *president* of the United States," I said. "You led the thirteen colonies to defeat the British, a new government was formed, and you refused to be king. Instead, you were elected president under a new constitution. Since your time, the United States has expanded across North America. There are now fifty states. California is one. And by the way, it's not an island."

Matt came over to hang. We were still hesitant to believe that we really had George Washington in our midst. Part of me was tempted to accept that this tall guy with the ponytail was our first president, but it made no sense.

Sure, I like sci-fi movies, but I've always felt that one thing happens after another. Time is a continuum and time travel a temporal paradox. Right?

If it was true, we had to convince our guest that he had been propelled more than two centuries into his future and to the opposite end of the continent, that he was now displaced in time and space from the only world he knew.

I had an idea.

"General, would you allow us to see your teeth?"

"No!"

Matty looked at me, then back at George. "They're made of wood, right? Your dentures?"

George looked mortified and said nothing.

"Perhaps we could establish your identity for certain if we could see your dentures. Every American school kid learns that Washington had dentures made of wood."

George's apple cheeks flushed redder against his pale skin, and his blue eyes flashed with anger. But his voice stayed calm and measured.

"Every student knows of my dentures? That is a private affair. One I do not wish to discuss. I know who I am. The matter is closed."

Chapter Eight
GUEST

Berkeley, August 17, 2014

George turned toward the TV.

"What in the world is that? A magical looking glass?"

"I suppose you could say that."

He watched the screen intently.

"Is this some manner of ball game? How is it played?"

"It's baseball in San Francisco. The Giants against the Pirates. That's Posey now. Posey's a big star."

"Posey? Star? I see nothing floral nor stellar. Your giants do not seem much larger than their opponents. Are the others truly pirates? Will they attempt to steal the ball and kidnap the giants for ransom?"

"No, they hit the ball with the bats and run around the bases. This is a game, an entertainment for the amusement of spectators. Some are watching right there at the field, in person. Some are watching from afar, like us."

"Ah, it resembles *wicket* and other ball games I have seen in Philadelphia."

He checked out the players' uniforms.

"Why, some are wearing breeches, as in my day," he said. "And some have those long pants you boys wear. What is the difference?"

"It's just a style preference. Each player can choose whichever suits him. There really is no difference, though a few years ago, a Giants player insisted that wearing the old-fashioned knee-length breeches, or knickers, made him appear to run faster."

George thought about this gravely, then decided it was funny and laughed in a dignified, serious way, lips pressed together in a sort of smile.

My Giants had started the season with a bang, winning forty-two and losing twenty-one. They peaked around the time my folks left town in early June, but they had tanked in the weeks since then. Now they were in second place behind the Dodgers, their long-time rivals.

I tried to explain this to George.

"So many games? How often do they play?"

"Every day."

"Ah. And they won twice as many games as they lost?"

"Yup, until my folks left. Since then, they've been terrible, losing most of their games."

"Because your parents have departed?"

I knew there was no connection, but I still liked to blame them.

Though Matt and I weren't sure what to do with George, he was good company and an appreciative guest. So he stayed at my house, first for a few days, then weeks.

He was curious about everything. He loved to learn how things worked. My Aunt Rachel had told me that Washington was an innovative and scientific farmer and gardener, and the first American to compost on a large scale! Later in his life, he had managed a number of diverse, often profitable industries at his Mount Vernon estate: whiskey distillery, blacksmith shop, fishery, spinning and weaving enterprises, and food production. All with slave labor, of course.

But he had never seen electric lights, paved roads, steel bridges, tall buildings, cars, planes, trains, urban sprawl, phones, TV, computers. In his day, even simple machines like the cotton gin and steam trains were still in the future. Horses and coaches were the main means of speedy transportation. Candles and oil lamps lit homes. Unless you were rich, your house was dark and shadowy.

He loved our era and immersed himself in our modern lifestyle. To George, all electronic devices with screens were looking glasses. iPhone, iPad, laptop, plasma TV. He appreciated that they came in various sizes and might let you play music, watch shows, view the news, or converse with others. He loved screening movies on our flat-screen TV and understood, most of the time, that it was fiction, actors putting on a play, telling a story. He didn't understand "live" TV and how that was different from playing DVDs or streaming movies from Netflix or Amazon. In his day, all artistic performance was live.

After a while, he had a hazy understanding of how the car worked. He knew we were burning a fuel to provide the propulsion, but he didn't grasp the realities of the internal combustion engine and insisted there must be steam in the process somewhere.

He knew electricity was a kind of energy that came out of wall outlets, and that it was something like lightning. He knew that it powered our lights, and he knew that some of the looking-glass devices had to be plugged in.

Like most people, he didn't understand or care about what was happening inside a smart phone, tablet, or computer. I tried to explain that our devices had small mechanical brains inside, that they usually used some kind of memory storage, and that they connected to the world through wireless and wired transmission. But of course he didn't understand any of those words. For all George knew or cared, Wi-Fi was a Tahitian goddess and transistors a rebellious army. It was all magic to him, a useful kind of sorcery.

I had never thought of George Washington as a playful person, until I loaded some games onto my sister's old iPod Touch, gave it to George, and showed him how to use it. He soon became addicted to Candy Crush.

"It's a puzzle game," I said lamely. "It's good practice for, uh, judging spatial relationships among various, uh, unrooted bodies of matter."

Lame! It was a game about managing a flood of falling gumdrops.

"I do so enjoy attempting to line up the various colors of jelly, striped candy, licorice, chocolate, and fruity morsels," George said, "till I achieve several in a row and they all tumble to the bottom."

I swear, I thought he had lost his mind, but it did occupy his time for a while.

The third day he binged on Candy Crush, I snatched away the iPod angrily.

"Hey! You've got to learn how to mute … the … damn … insipid … repetitious … monotonous … soul-sucking … MUSIC! It's all middle, no beginning, no end, no resolution. And if I have to listen to the guy with the three-testicle voice saying 'Sweet!' or 'Tasty!' or 'Delicious!' one more time, I will commit a violent act with your sword!"

I couldn't stay in the same house if George wouldn't keep the damn thing muted. He seemed content to keep playing, lining up the candies, dropping them down, and trying desperately to clear all the jelly. For about a week. Then, in an epiphany of sudden disgust, he bubbled over with frustration. He flung the iPod down onto the bed, as if he had just realized he was holding poison ivy, and exploded in frustration.

"This is a nonsensical pastime, a complete waste of my time! I cannot believe that I am spending hours—nay, days—consumed by a looking-glass game involving sweetmeats!"

I turned him on to Angry Birds instead, and he enjoyed the challenge of knocking down the defenses constructed by the evil pigs.

"It's quite similar to shooting artillery, in a way," he said. "You can adjust the angle and the elevation, and, to some extent, the power of the charge. There is definitely a certain amount of skill involved."

He adored the Monument Valley game on my iPad, which let him solve architectural puzzles containing crazy geometric figures. A little person in a pointed hat has to elude bothersome crows as he attempts to climb to the tops of various towers. The player turns cranks to pivot and adjust a variety of stairways, walkways, ladders, and building parts. The game messes with perspective with clever visual tricks. The little person steps out onto a walkway, which pivots, and a horizontal walk becomes a vertical wall. An M.C. Escher print come to life. George was good at visualizing in three dimensions, and he quickly mastered the swipes and other finger gestures on the iPad.

Despite the diversions, George was eager to get back to his army. He brought it up often, but we had no idea how to proceed.

"I am missing my destiny," he told us with quiet intensity one evening.

George couldn't quite grasp air travel. He had seen planes in the sky, but not close up, so he hadn't yet figured out the scale. I explained that planes were huge metal containers with hundreds aboard that hurtled through the heavens. I'm sure he thought I was pulling his leg.

He didn't email or text, because, of course, he didn't know anyone in our century besides Matt and me. We thought it prudent to keep him under wraps, so social media were out of the question. George Washington on Facebook? Preposterous. And the idea of tweeting out "Hey, I've got *the* Founding Father crashing at my place" had no appeal whatsoever.

Our neighborhood Safeway intrigued him. He had seen few packaged foods before, so the variety and quality of readily available consumer products blew his mind. He examined a grocery cart closely, appreciated that the fold-up shelf had leg holes for youngsters, tut-tutted over the exotic product choices on the shelves. He seemed most at home among the meats and the produce. He was a farmer, after all, and fresh food was his business. But he knew nothing of pineapples, coconuts, cake mixes, Hamburger Helper, Tapatío salsa, dried pasta, aluminum foil, or canned tuna. He loved to walk the aisles, reading the labels excitedly, in his own reserved way, and he enjoyed trying new foods. Bagels and lox tickled his palate, and he explored all varieties of espresso in the first couple of weeks.

Mostly, though, he discovered that he loved Mexican food. Burritos, enchiladas, and especially chimichangas, though the fried tortillas were difficult for him to chew.

Chapter Nine
EARTH

Berkeley, August 19, 2014

I showed George Google Earth on my laptop. As a young man, he had been a surveyor, mapping countless square miles of western Virginia and Ohio for wealthy clients and politicians. He loved maps.

We started with a bare satellite view high above Valley Forge, looking down at the verdant countryside of the National Historical Park, surrounded on three sides by suburban development. Slowly I added all the elements that transformed what we saw from a bird's-eye view to a well-annotated map: light-green borders, white town labels, yellow roads, local place names, bright-green parks, blue bodies of water.

He was fascinated, and he was impressed that I could zoom in on the map. I typed "Washington's Headquarters, Valley Forge" into the search box, which brought us closer to a particular area of the park, so close we could see stands of trees.

"What is that, Timothy?" he asked, pointing to a gray area with shiny colored rectangles.

"A parking lot. Those are cars. This is present day. That's where visitors leave their cars when they come to visit the farmhouse you used as your headquarters."

We tracked due west from the parking lot and found the tan stone house that had been his temporary home and base of operations during the winter encampment. I clicked a button on Google Earth to show a photo of the house.

"There it is!" he said. "The home of Farmer Potts. We have rented the house for the winter, and the farmer and his family moved in with relatives."

We went back to the map.

"The night I left Valley Forge, I walked away from the house and proceeded north up a small hill to watch the aurora borealis. I had planned to continue east from here to the huts of my personal guard, who, by design, had encamped quite close to our headquarters. Over here, south of the parking."

I explained that the Google Earth view was made up of millions of individual images taken from a satellite, a machine that orbited the earth and sent us pictures. Through the air.

"How can they be up so high, looking down?" He snorted. That was as preposterous an idea as people cruising around in giant flying machines.

Chapter Ten
TOUR

Berkeley, August 22, 2014

Matt and I decided to take George on a tour of Berkeley, wearing some of my clothes.

Even now, in his mid-forties, he was athletically built: tall, leggy, with powerful broad shoulders. Add to that his reddish-brown graying ponytail and gray-blue eyes, he cut quite a figure in my jeans, old pair of Nikes, and World of Warcraft T-shirt.

Visually, he fit right into the scene. Emotionally, he was struggling to grasp the magnitude of what had happened. Where he was. And when he was.

We drove up University Avenue toward downtown Berkeley. The hustle and bustle overwhelmed him, especially the noisy, infernal transportation contraptions. His genuine fear and wonder toward the cars and buses made him more believable and helped me to accept his story.

We parked, and the three of us walked through the Cal Berkeley campus. I was pretty sure Washington had little formal education.

"Is this a place of learning?" he asked. "I have visited the College of William and Mary in Williamsburg, and this place exudes a similar feeling. Though I have never seen buildings with so much glass."

He enjoyed strolling among the eucalyptus trees and breathing in deeply the exotically scented air. The campus was a calm refuge, far from the cars and cacophony of downtown.

We walked across a huge lawn, and Matt, a Cal grad, guided us into the Doe Library. Under an elaborately carved ceiling and lit by a tall bank of windows, a twenty-four-foot-long painting sprawled across one wall of the reading room: *Washington Rallying the Troops at the Battle of Monmouth*. My Aunt Rachel, a librarian and former teacher, had prepped us for this visit.

The painting depicted a battle scene, dominated by General George Washington charging in from the right on a brown horse, his curved battle sword raised to the sky. General Charles Lee, whom Washington has just relieved of command for cowardice, sulks on a white horse. The chaos of war surrounds them: cannons firing, soldiers attacking, wounded men dying, a dog fleeing in panic.

"Is that supposed to be me?" George asked. "Not a great likeness, I would say. And why am I riding a bay horse?"

"This picture was painted many years after the war, General, by Emanuel Leutze," I told him. "I'm sure he made up some of the details. It's the same guy who painted *Washington Crossing the Delaware*."

"Crossing to the Battle of Trenton? You know of this conflict?"

"Yes. The Christmas night battle."

"Ah, of course. But what horse appears in this painting? My preferred battle steed is Blueskin, whose coat is iron-gray, almost blue. My favorite hunting horse as well. I do also own a bay, named Nelson. But what battle is this?"

I didn't know how much to tell him. The Battle of Monmouth was still in his future, his near future. Perhaps this wasn't a good idea. I was stymied.

"And these other officers? This one looks like Hamilton, and that one like Lafayette. Is that General Lee? And this one here in the metal helmet? Who is he?"

"That's Baron von Steuben, the Prussian officer. You don't recognize him?"

"I have never met the man, though his arrival at Valley Forge has been eagerly anticipated. Timothy, what battle is this?" he asked again.

I knew from Aunt Rachel that the Battle of Monmouth Courthouse had occurred during the spring after Valley Forge, that Washington had dressed down General Lee in uncharacteristically colorful language for calling a retreat, and that von Steuben had been there. The Colonial Army had sent the Brits packing, largely because of their training from von Steuben. But now I understood why George didn't recognize him.

A cold dread engulfed me, a tightness between my shoulder blades and a knot in the pit of my stomach. This time-travel stuff was new to me, but it felt all wrong to be showing someone from the past a depiction of something in his own future. Especially his immediate future.

Do I want George to know the outcome of this battle, that the American victory depended on military training from someone he has yet to meet? What if he alters something about the training, the encampment, the battle plans—anything—because he already knows the outcome of the battle? And what if changing his plans then affects the results?

And why should I care?

Matt and I hurried him out of there. Clearly it had been a bad idea to show him the painting.

Outside, Cal students, many dressed like George, walked by on their way to class. Several young women overtook and passed us on a tree-lined path between buildings. Two wore short shorts over tanned, muscular legs. One wore a tight tank top, with no obvious interior support. Little was left to the imagination. George stopped and stared.

"Who would they be?" he whispered huskily. "Are these ... hussies? I have heard such ladies of the evening exist in cities."

"Nope, they're just coeds," Matt said. "Women students."

"Women are allowed to study here?" George asked, stopping to think about that. "But why do they dress this way? More specifically, why do they wear so little if they are not immoral creatures?"

"It's the style, General. They're just college kids. Many of them dress like that."

"I am beginning to realize that either I am enduring a long, complex, and highly imaginative dream, or I am indeed in another world."

"It's the same world, George. Just 3,000 miles west and 200-plus years later."

We walked along, engrossed in thought, watching the diverse group of students bustle around us.

"And Negroes? They study here too?" He took a sidelong glance at Matt. "They are not slaves, but freedmen?"

"Listen, General, we need to have a talk," Matt said.

"Many years after you were president, the slaves were freed in our country."

"All the slaves?"

"Yes."

"But who was left to work the fields? Surely no plantation could profit without slave labor."

"The transition was very difficult. The nation was splintered by a bitter civil war."

"Because of slavery?"

"Yes. The Southern states didn't want to give up their slaves. They felt that this decision should be left to individual states. All the Northern states had already banned slavery. Most of the slave states tried to secede from the Union to form their own nation."

George was shocked to hear that the Union he was helping to craft would one day fall apart.

"The Northern states refused to let them leave," Matt continued. "A four-year war broke out among the states. Well over half a million Americans were killed on both sides, but the North won and the slaves were freed. No one should be able to buy or sell another person."

George's face softened. "I have recently begun to understand that sentiment. My wife's cousin sold some Negroes, and it appeared to me quite cruel to divide up families, selling them to different owners."

"Of course it is!" said Matt. "Now, in our time, Negroes—we say African Americans—can work for money, own property, vote, hold political office. They are full citizens, with all the inalienable rights they were denied for so long. In fact, the president of the United States right now is African American."

That got George's attention. He was silent for a long

time.

We headed over to Telegraph Avenue. The street was crammed with middle-aged Saturday shoppers, college kids in board shorts and flip-flops, old hippies in tie-dyes and broad-brimmed leather hats, urban cowboys in fringed buckskin jackets, and a dirty, bewhiskered Captain America. A girl in a black tutu danced on a corner with a guy in a pink leotard. I realized that in his own clothes George probably could have blended with the crowd.

Street vendors peddled political buttons, handmade jewelry, bumper stickers, leather wallets and belts, used books, smoking supplies, snow globes, and T-shirts that said "Cannabis Club," "Save Water, Drink Beer," "Free the Jackson Five," "You Lost Me at Hello," "Jesus Saves, Moses Invests," and "In Case of Emergency, Gimme Head."

Two young women in tight jeans attracted George's attention as they glided by, giggling over some joke. George veered off and began to follow. I quickstepped to keep up, finally grabbing his arm before he talked with them.

"My apologies, Timothy. I must keep in mind that my wife has come to stay in our encampment at Valley Forge. I am indeed fortunate."

"Yeah, what's up with that? You called her Patsy. Everyone know Washington's wife was named Martha."

"Yes, her given name is Martha. Patsy is her pet name within the family."

I pulled out my phone and googled Martha Washington. He was right. Her nickname was Patsy.

"Regardless," George went on, "I have never seen two women as attractively garbed, let alone two so young and comely. I wished merely to engage them in conversation."

"I don't think that's such a good idea, George."

"Perhaps not. But I'd prefer you address me as General. Must you be so informal?"

"I think you should get used to it. Informality is common in our society, and I don't want to call you General when we are out in public. I don't think we should let anyone else know that George Washington is skulking about the streets of Berkeley in the early years of the twenty-first century. It's too crazy an idea."

"Ah, then you do believe me?"

"I'm getting there, George," I responded, amazed at myself. "I'm getting there."

We headed home to watch the Giants game. They were in D.C., playing the Nationals.

"It is, indeed, shocking," George said, "to see 'Washington' emblazoned across their tunics. What, pray tell, does their name mean? Are they a national team? Are they in fact named after … me? Please explain."

We hesitated, since the building of Washington, D.C., was still decades ahead for the General. Matt took this one on.

"Many years in your future, after the Revolution, the United States will build a new capital city and name it after you. Because it's the national capital, many years after that, they will name their baseball team the Nationals."

This was a bit much for George to absorb. He said nothing, remaining thoughtful for quite a while. The Giants eventually drubbed the Nats 10-3, their fifth victory in six games. They were starting to perk up again.

Chapter Eleven
RETURN

Point Isabel, August 25, 2014

George stayed on at my house. We weren't sure what else to do with him, and he enjoyed the warm weather and our modern conveniences.

Matt and I had always watched a lot of games together, and George was becoming a baseball fan. The Giants were still in second place, four-and-a-half games behind the Dodgers.

About a week after Nevada and I found George, we took him back to the dog park.

Matty came along, eager to see where I had discovered the General. Just in case he was transported back to his own time, George wore the full band uniform—which we had scrubbed and brushed and polished and divested of its muddy coating—and paraded along the shore with impressive military bearing. Nevada was our cover for the dog park, but George's garb and manner still drew a few stares.

It was late in the day, not too many people around.

We returned to the secluded stretch on the back side of the island.

"How did you first see him?" Matt asked.

"I threw the ball for Nevada, followed her around here, and looked toward the hills. A freight train passed, and I saw George slide open the boxcar door, then hop out onto the ground."

"He jumped from the train?"

"It was traveling slowly. He did stumble as he landed."

George began to strut up and down, and I noticed again that he limped slightly.

We hoped to find a virtual door, a temporal tunnel, a passage or portal back to the Revolution, but we had no idea what to look for. At one point, George pulled out his sword and began to swing it about. Not in a threatening, slashing, stabbing way, like a Viking marauder engaged in hand-to-hand combat, but in a heroic circle above his head, then pointed forward, like the painting we had seen of the Battle of Monmouth, where he led his troops onward into battle on a fierce, foaming steed. A silent solo dance of leadership and bravery. George had no steed, of course, but Nevada followed him around, wagging and jumping joyfully at the sword work, which she took personally as a form of play.

Nevada had been a service dog, trained to assist my Uncle Chuck, my dad's blind brother. Sadly, he had passed away a few months earlier of a heart attack. Freed of her service harness, Nevada enjoyed romping at the park, but I'm sure she still wondered where Chuck was.

The whole thing felt a bit incongruous. George looked impressive in his full regalia, but I was glad we were away from the other dog walkers. That sword definitely made me nervous.

Nothing happened. No time portal, no physical dislocation. The sun set, and it grew darker and colder. Matt stared at the train track.

"Let's get out of here," he said with a gleam in his eye. "I've got an idea."

We headed back to my house. Matt pulled up Google Earth again on my laptop. He prodded George to tell him more about what happened that night under the aurora.

George frowned. "At first I was groggy from my fall and all was in darkness. I thought perhaps I had been captured by the British and imprisoned in some dungeon. As I grew more lucid, the box in which I had awakened began to lurch and shake, and I realized that it was moving. Only later did I learn the car was hooked up to many others.

"It is clear to me now that I have come a long, long way from Valley Forge. I have read of English companies building rail lines similar to that one, with wooden tracks and horse-drawn carriages, but I have never seen one. But here, what force is used to pull those long lines of carriages and boxes that have been linked together?"

"A large carriage with an engine," said Matt.

"Powered by steam? I have read of Newcomen's engine in Scotland and Watt's work in England. But I was unaware that a steam engine had ever been used for propulsion."

"It's powered by a fuel made from petroleum, a black oily sludge that comes out of the ground in certain places. The same fuel that powers the horses in my car."

That puzzled him. I haven't yet shown him my Corolla's horses, and what horse would devour oily sludge?

"So, General," Matt said. "There was no railroad at Valley Forge during your encampment, correct?"

"I have never before seen such a train of carriages, let

alone the type of moving box in which I was confined."

"That's what I thought," Matt replied. "Think about this: many years after the Revolution, a railroad was built that passed near the farmhouse where you stayed. The track is still in use there now."

We both stared at him. *How does he know that?*

A faint memory stirred in me.

"You grew up in Philly!"

"Right," Matt said. "Till we moved out here. Every school kid in Pennsylvania has gone on field trips to Valley Forge."

"Aha!"

"Yup. Look at this."

The three of us huddled over the computer screen.

"Right here, on a hill up behind the farmhouse that Washington used as his headquarters, there's a railroad station and train track."

Sure enough. I hadn't noticed it before, but it was plain to see now.

"Passenger service to Valley Forge ended many years ago," Matt went on, "and the station is now a museum. But they run freight trains through there all the time."

"With boxcars."

"Exactly. General, I think you fell through some kind of a gateway in time that sits right where the train track is now. As you passed through it, by some quirk of fate, perhaps, a train came by—in 2014. A freight train passing is a lengthy event, not a momentary coincidence. Most trains have dozens of cars, sometimes a hundred or more. You happened to end up in a boxcar. 237 years later."

This made sense to me. The gateway in time was probably back in Pennsylvania. But what to do? Clearly we were out of our league.

"We know nothing about time travel. We really need to consult an expert," I muttered.

Matt brightened up. "I know who! Let's go see one of my old profs."

He shot off an email to his former undergrad faculty adviser, and we waited for a response.

Chapter Twelve
PLANTATION

Mount Vernon

The General approached the mansion from the west. He floated up the serpentine path, around the bowling green, and through the north colonnade, until he could see the lush Potomac River valley. He glided toward the inviting shade of the columned piazza on the east side, then soared up near the cupola for a better view of the boat traffic on the river. Eventually he floated down toward the broad lawn, stopping to hover, two feet off the ground.

The mansion had a preternatural glow, golden and haloed, inside and out. Bathed in the warm rays of a setting sun, yet lit also from within by the light of a dozen fireplaces.

Patsy and the children must be within, he thought. *I shall expect them to enter the piazza in the near future, as soon as the sun takes its leave. Some of the slaves are weeding and harvesting vegetables in the upper garden now, and others are in the kitchen preparing the evening meal.*

In the stable, one of the servants curried the General's

horse.

But how can Blueskin be here at Mount Vernon, when I have just left him at Valley Forge? All is not as it appears.

He floated near the ceiling of the stable, absorbing the olfactory smorgasbord that accompanied the presence of horses: powerful, sweaty bodies, leather saddles and bridles, and manure mixed with straw. He took a deep breath and drank in the beloved aromas.

In the distance, he heard voices. *Perhaps Patsy and the children? Ah, the genteel murmurings of a Virginia plantation family!*

He focused on the voices and was shocked to discover it was not his family at all, but the two young lads in California. As consciousness snuck in, the vision of Mount Vernon began to slip away. His last glimpse of the mansion was an uphill view from near the compost dung heap.

Chapter Thirteen
BONDAGE

Berkeley, August 27, 2014

Matt was intense and insistent.

"I don't care what you say. Or who he is. Slavery is immoral and impossible to defend, on any level."

I couldn't disagree. "Of course. I just want you to remember that George was a product of his times. As we are of ours. Their values were different back then."

"I know. But I still call *Bullshit!* It is wrong to own other people. Period. The Washingtons owned many other families. How can anything be right about that?"

"Well, we know from history that most of the other Founding Fathers owned slaves as well. George was not the only one, by far."

"Still immoral!"

I heard a banging on the wall.

"Gentlemen, please!" George called out. He left my sister's room and found Matt and me on the stair landing, frustrated.

"General, sorry to wake you," Matt said, "but this situation distresses me!"

"What situation?"

"You. You are clearly a good person, with only the highest morals and goals for your young country. To a point."

"Yes."

"Yet, in your era, your nation—our nation—was afflicted with a terrible cancer. A horrific blight on our history and our legacy. That one segment of our population could keep another group in chains, in permanent, inherited bondage."

George stood silently at first, a grave expression frozen on his face.

"Quite so."

"I mean, doesn't it bother you? Don't you want complete freedom for your country?"

"For all peoples?"

"Yes."

"Including indentured servants?"

"Yes. Indenture is a form of slavery that often lasts a lifetime, with offspring added to an original limited contract. How can you live with yourself?"

Long silence.

Matt continued.

"Why, sir, is there no mention of slavery in the Declaration of Independence? How could you and your fellow delegates pledge to fight for inalienable rights, for life, liberty, and the pursuit of happiness, and systematically exclude a third of the population?"

George looked away, lost in thought. I wondered how he could rationalize the plantation system of colonial Virginia. Our values were as different as if he came from Mars.

"Don't you see the evil in this practice, especially in the

power of an owner to split up families?"

George turned to Matt and met his eyes gravely. "As I said, I have seen this at slave auctions, and the palpable misery and anguish among slave families about to be separated is visceral and raw."

"Then how can you condone it?"

"I do not. I attempt to keep the slave families at Mount Vernon intact, to the extent that I can. Though I was brought up to be indifferent to the conditions under which they live."

"And you keep buying and selling people, slowly increasing your holdings in hereditary human bondage. As your slaves procreate, their children are likewise enslaved for life, and your property grows in value."

"LaMatthew, understand that, as much as possible, I insist my overseers avoid use of the lash."

"Yet you possess human chattel. You might treat them kindly, but the fact remains that they are your property, to dispose of as you see fit."

"In those terms, please be aware that they are a major economic asset to any plantation. One of the main assets of Mount Vernon, one of the primary holdings, is its workforce."

"So?"

"This is not an easy situation to change. I was in the field with the Continental Army and did not attend the debate over the Declaration of Independence, but apparently Jefferson had written a passage condemning the practice of slavery—"

"Jefferson, ha! Another slaver!"

"—which was voted down by most of the Southern states. I fear the delegates may never have declared independence and created the Union when they did, without that concession."

"Perhaps, but it will fall apart decades later anyway, when the Southern states secede from the Union."

Chapter Fourteen
MANUMISSION

George looked crestfallen.

"We are doing the best we can. A flawed early Union, with the united strength and will to break away from the British, is better than a group of separate colonies divided over slavery. What would you have us do?"

"Free the slaves," said Matt.

"All of them? Complete manumission?"

"What's that?"

"Complete emancipation."

"Yes, General. That's what should happen."

"That will never do," George said. "Freeing all the slaves would leave Mount Vernon without a labor force. And leave the Washingtons very poor, indeed. Land poor. And there are other concerns. It is not a simple problem. If I were to free my slaves, what would they do? Where would they go? They have no education, no training."

"Then build them schools, give them jobs and homes."

"They have jobs and homes now."

"But not their *liberty*. They yearn for their freedom *from you*, the same way you and Jefferson and Adams and Hamilton pine to be free of England and King George."

That stopped the conversation for a while. Putting the plight of his slaves on the same ground as his own struggle against the mother country seemed to be something George had not allowed himself to consider.

"How came your people here, LaMatthew?"

"What do you mean?"

"Your name, LaMatthew. Is that a French name, like Lafayette? Are you descended from African slaves, or did your family come to America some other way?"

"On my father's side, our ancestors, who became known as the Johnsons, were kidnapped in Africa and forced to emigrate to South Carolina in the early 1800s. They were Black."

"Yes?"

"And my mom's parents, the Lefkowitches, came from Poland during the Nazi era."

"Nazi?"

"A subject for another day, General. Mom's people moved to New York during the 1930s. They were White. And Jewish. So, yes. I am descended from slaves. And the Jews have long been a persecuted people as well."

George gasped quietly. "Intermarriage! Blacks with Whites, Christians with Jews. The social fabric of this nation has indeed been woven in ways I could never have contemplated."

He looked thoughtful.

"There is another complication, LaMatthew. I do not own all the slaves at Mount Vernon."

"What do you mean?"

"There are, at this moment, over 100 slaves at Mount Vernon. Or at least there were at the time I left … that era. How odd, not to know what 'this moment' means!"

"And?"

"Approximately one half belong to me. The others belong to the estate of Patsy's first husband, Daniel Custis, who died suddenly at a young age, without a will and testament. Under the laws of Virginia, I can administer his estate, but I cannot sell the assets. In addition, by law, freeing slaves is illegal in Virginia. Even if I wished to, and if it were legal, at Mount Vernon I could only free the slaves I own outright."

"What's wrong with that?"

"Well, regardless of ownership, all the slaves have intermarried. If I free the Washington slaves but the Custis dower slaves remain in service—"

"In bondage!"

"—what happens to all those families, half slave and half free? Where do they live or work?"

It was Matt's turn to be silent. He hadn't been aware of this complication.

"Also, frankly, the divergent opinions of my family present another problem. My respect for Africans has increased markedly since the beginning of the Revolution. Many Black freedmen and slaves have enlisted in the Continental Army and served with conspicuous bravery.

"But my family is of the opposite opinion. My brothers and sister, my wife and most of her family, are firm believers in the slave system and would never agree to free the Custis slaves without full compensation. I fear they would sell them posthaste, were I to be absent from the discussion.

"I did oppose enlistments by slaves early in the war, but I have changed my mind. We desperately need soldiers, and some colonies have offered freedom to slaves who enlist in their militias. If they fight for our nation's freedom from England, I am beginning to believe they should be allowed to earn their own freedom from bondage.

"When Rhode Island provided this opportunity, thousands of Black men enlisted in the 1st Rhode Island Regiment to fight the British. In recent months, they acquitted themselves with great heroism at the Battle of Rhode Island. But not all colonies, including my home Virginia, will grant freedom to slaves who enlist."

"So in your army, there are slaves who fight for the freedom of the colonies, yet remain enslaved? Don't you see the massive moral contradiction in that, sir?"

Silence. Then a slow response. "More and more I do, especially for men of African descent with whom I am personally acquainted. Billy Lee, for one."

"Who's that?"

"My manservant, who has accompanied me through all the travails of the Revolution thus far. Until my diversion into your century, that is. His service to me has been exemplary."

"Your manservant is a slave? And you brought him north to New England, New York, and Pennsylvania to serve you during the War for Independence?"

"Yes."

"Isn't that immoral, or at least illegal? Isn't he fighting for his freedom alongside you? Why is he not a free man, if he has left the South and resides in the North, even if it is in a war zone?"

"Please remember that, in my time, slavery is legal in all the colonies."

"But immoral everywhere."

George pressed his lips together and knotted up the ridge between his eyebrows. He looked composed, but troubled. Finally he answered.

"Yes, LaMatthew, I am beginning to understand."

Chapter Fifteen
EXPERT

Berkeley, September 1, 2014

It took a while to get an appointment with Matt's professor, who was busily preparing for the start of fall classes. We took George on trips to Big Sur and the Napa Valley, and we watched a lot of baseball. The Giants won their last six games in August, two of the victories going to their ace pitcher Madison Bumgarner. They were starting to look like a contending team again, though they remained mired in second place behind the surging Dodgers.

When the prof was finally available, we drove up into the Berkeley hills above the Cal campus. My old Corolla emitted a throaty, macho growl as we climbed steep Marin Avenue, then turned right along the ridgeline, onto Grizzly Peak Boulevard.

We pulled over to check out the sunset. The skies were clear, the view spectacular. The lights of the East Bay sprawled below us in a dazzling display, San Francisco and the Golden Gate in the distance. George was impressed.

"So many people. How many live in this vicinity?"

"Over seven million in the Bay Area."

That left him thoughtful, contemplating the massive growth of this nation he was nursing through its infancy.

The professor lived on a side street off Grizzly Peak that twisted and turned uphill, then down. His front yard was steep and landscaped like a park. We walked on stepping-stones, winding through a small grove of trees and past a park bench. A few small, strategically placed lights illuminated precarious corners.

Professor Albert Kronos met with us in his study. A small, balding man with gold-rimmed glasses, he impressed me with his easy air of learned expertise. Matt had told him about our visitor. Kronos greeted Matt warmly, then turned to George and extended a hand.

"General, it's a pleasure to meet you."

George shook the professor's hand and bowed gravely, impressed by this gesture of respect. And belief. I wondered if Prof. Kronos believed this was George Washington, or if he was playing along.

I told Kronos about the scene at the park the day I found the General, then George told his side of it. To Matt and me, it did seem more and more plausible that General Washington had skipped through time and ended up on a train across the country. Crazy, yes, but somehow plausible.

"How momentous," Kronos said with a smile, "that General Washington has traveled forward through time over two hundred years. What an amazing tale."

So did this expert, the Cal professor, believe George's story? I began to feel less gullible, more sure of myself and my judgment. The tall guy with the ponytail was not a phony.

"If we examine the literature," the prof continued, "we

see many examples of travel forward and backward through time, some of which also involve a change of physical location. In Twain's *Connecticut Yankee*, for example, the main character, an engineer from New England, experiences a bump on the head and wakes up centuries earlier in Old England. In Dickens' *A Christmas Carol*, Scrooge is able to travel forward and backward in time to see himself as a hopeful youth and as a friendless, unmourned miser, in various locales around metropolitan London."

He sounded scholarly and learned, and I wanted to believe him. Matt nodded slowly, enraptured by his mentor's wisdom. George looked nonplussed. Twain and Dickens meant nothing to him.

"H. G. Wells' *Time Machine* was capable of moving his time traveler to new times and places, as was Doc Brown's DeLorean in the *Back to the Future* movies," Kronos continued. "In *The Time Traveler's Wife*, the main character is suddenly transported through time and space without warning—and without his clothes. But in Woody Allen's *Midnight in Paris*, Gil, the Owen Wilson character, needed only to show up at a given corner in Paris as the clock struck twelve, and he'd be transported to an earlier era, in the same location."

Why was everyone talking to me about movies and books?

"But Professor Kronos, there's one problem."

"What's that?"

"These are all examples from fiction."

"Well, naturally. The concept of time travel is impossible and violates the laws of physics."

"Impossible?"

"Well, theoretically possible, I suppose. But physically impossible. I'm not a physicist. Time travel does have a long and checkered career in fiction, of course. And yours is a compelling narrative."

Is that why we were here? To impress him with our story?

"What department do you teach in, sir?" I asked.

"Comparative Literature, of course. I was LaMatthew's adviser after he declared his major."

I shot Matt a dirty look. I thought we were going to see a scientist, some whiz-bang, string-theory egghead who would drone on about molecular regrouping and expedited temporal shifting. Not a guy who taught novels, movies, and story arcs. Examining the literature. Literally.

"Hasn't there been scientific discussion of time travel?" I asked.

"Great minds have been brought to bear on the subject, including that of Stephen Hawking, and there have been some physical experiments."

"You mean, scientists have tried to send people through time? For reals?"

"No, but some physicists have attempted to transmit photons through a tube of cesium gas in a way that suggests they exited the tube nanoseconds before they entered."

"But only nanoseconds? And no people?"

"No real objects of any kind, actually. Have you ever seen a photon?"

"No."

"Exactly."

I was deflated, but still curious. Matt took up the inquiry.

"Professor, I know it's hard to accept, but let's suppose this really is George Washington."

George stirred. "Of course I am."

"I know, I know. Professor, if this is George Washington, and he really has been separated from his men at Valley Forge, what happens if we can't get him back to them?"

"LaMatthew, I'm no historian, but as I recall, Washington's inspirational leadership was key in getting the Revolutionary Army through the privations of the winter at Valley Forge. My guess is that, without him there, they could lose heart and fail to rally against the British in the spring."

I knew what was supposed to happen that spring and summer. Pressure from the Continental Army would force the British to retreat after evacuating Philadelphia and losing at Monmouth, the battle depicted in the painting in the Doe Library.

Critical battles. A turning point.

The feeling of dread returned, the same knot in the stomach I had felt when we viewed the painting.

Chapter Sixteen
EXCELLENCY

Valley Forge

His Excellency approaches!"

"General Washington! Greetings!"

The General rode through the camp on an inspection tour, accompanied by General Lafayette and a small group of soldiers. The Valley Forge winter had turned rainy, the roads churned up in an unholy mud stew. But the spirits of the men were good, those who still remained in camp. Of the 11,000 soldiers under his command at the beginning of the encampment, thousands were sick and had been transferred to remote field hospitals. Many others had died of disease, particularly typhus. Quite a few had gone home, some deserting, some at the ends of their short enlistment periods.

The remaining soldiers had clear-cut a nearby forest and built nearly a thousand crude huts, each housing about a dozen men. *Supplies of food are still erratic*, thought Washington, *but with constant foraging and use of the many bread ovens we have built, I believe we are going to get through this.*

High atop Blueskin, he was clearly a man born to sit a horse. Jefferson had called him the "best horseman of his age," and he sat tall in the saddle, with the easy, athletic grace of a lifelong rider.

He gazed at his companion with fatherly affection. Marquis de Lafayette was only twenty, yet Washington had made him a general and part of his personal staff. The soldiers, many of them crusty farmers, had failed to take the young French nobleman seriously at first, amused by the foppishness of his silver wig and bejeweled saber. But Lafayette had gained the men's respect at the Battle of the Brandywine, where he had acted with conspicuous bravery, despite being wounded in the leg. He had grown close to Washington, who treated him like the son he never had.

Despite the fact that the troops under their command endured marginal sanitation and uncertain hygiene, the General demanded that his officers maintain their uniforms meticulously.

To command respect from his men, an officer must present himself as worthy of their devotion.

The men gathered around them at each stop. All wanted to see the great Washington, referred to universally as His Excellency.

On one stop, the General realized that Blueskin was high-stepping silently in a slow, floating prance, his hooves hovering a few inches above the road. No one seemed to notice.

The men cheered him wherever he rode. Conditions had improved since Washington first sent General Greene out to find food. The irony of thousands of freedom fighters suffering from malnutrition and starvation amidst the lush countryside and prosperous farms of eastern Pennsylvania had been cruel and unjust. But the Continental Congress refused to tax their member states for funds to help feed the army.

Despite a lack of hard currency, Washington had been forced to appropriate food from the surrounding area. Local farmers often refused to sell supplies in exchange for colonial paper money. Some were Loyalists who sided with the Redcoats. Many preferred the shilling and pound coins of the English forces. British-occupied Philadelphia was only thirty miles away from Valley Forge, and the two armies often competed for supplies.

The soldiers continued to call out "General!" and "His Excellency!" He looked back at Lafayette, who watched with amazement as Blueskin continued to float above the mud. Washington shrugged. Some things could not be explained.

The horse suddenly soared high in the air. In the distance, still miles removed, a small group of riders approached Valley Forge. The General squinted as he gazed upon them from a great height, barely able to make out unfamiliar uniforms. He looked far toward the east and saw ships on the ocean, flying a foreign flag.

His eyes burned. He squeezed the lids together tightly then blinked.

Chapter Seventeen
TURNING POINT

Berkeley, September 5, 2014

A car honked, and he opened his eyes. The room was dark, except for a pink nightlight on one wall. He groaned, yawned, and turned over, looking chagrined.

I watched from a chair in the corner of the room, where I lay under a pile of clothing, then whispered, "George?"

"Yes, Timothy. I am still in Berkeley?"

"Are you all right?"

"I am comfortable at this moment, thank you, but I have had another odd dream. I fear I am missing the most important events of my life. Awareness of that fact makes it difficult for me to sleep."

"Yes."

"This damnable war has not gone well. Yet, in my heart, I feel we are at a significant turning point. Several things have occurred that brighten my spirits and those of my men, this very month."

"Which month?"

69

"Now. Well, *my* now, at the time I left Valley Forge, February of seventeen and seventy-eight. We have now been there for two months. The men are finally housed well, or well enough anyway. They have food, though that is a constant struggle. My wife, and the wives of several other general officers, have come to join the effort. They are an enormous help with the sick and wounded soldiers, and their presence brightens our souls.

"Lafayette provides an uplifting boost to my military family, an infusion of passion and steel. Young Hamilton brings genius and diligence. I have great fondness for both. But as a fighting force, my army, we are a rabble. I have failed to create a professional army."

He stopped suddenly, a perplexed look on his face. He was not a man accustomed to revealing much of his inner life, especially feelings of inadequacy.

"Please continue, George."

He sat quietly for a long time. In the distance, I heard the low, mournful sound of a train whistle.

"We began as a force of Yankee militiamen who snuck through the woods and shot from behind trees, and we have progressed little. The troops have an iron will, but no discipline. Many are farmers who know how to shoot because they grew up hunting. Few have uniforms, and none have had military training.

"My scouts have told me of the imminent arrival of von Steuben, that Prussian general you mentioned, a confidant of Frederick the Great. He has met recently with the Congress, at their new home in York, Pennsylvania, and I know he is on his way to meet with me. I am hoping he can help bring order to the chaos of my army."

"What's the problem?"

"The camps are carelessly laid out in meandering patterns, with neither rhyme nor reason. The latrines and kitchens are often near each other. It is impossible to find the command tents without considerable inquiry. Sanitary conditions are deplorable. But mostly, the men are individual fighters. They have never trained in group battle techniques, and they suffer from vastly differing levels of support from their various colonial legislatures."

I changed position, my chair creaking in the quiet night. "What can von Steuben do?"

"He is much heralded as a leader of armies in the European style. I am hoping he can teach my men how to fight together as a unit, rather than a herd of individuals."

He brightened up. "Another source of encouragement just this month is the imminent support of our cause by the government of France. Ben Franklin has been there for more than one year, attempting to win King Louis to our side, and Lafayette has much influence among the nobility. I hope and pray for an announcement soon that the French will send ships, and possibly also troops, to help us win our independence."

I smiled in the dark as George continued.

"One memory in particular keeps hope alive for me. You mentioned our crossing of the Delaware. I gather there is a painting of that momentous event. On Christmas night, in the year 1776—a bit over a year before I was spirited away from Valley Forge—we loaded our entire army onto boats, horses and all, and braved the icy Delaware River. Once assembled on the far bank, we surprised the British forces, particularly their hateful Hessian mercenaries, and dealt them a terrible blow. But we have neither the forces nor the supplies to hold territory once gained.

"This continues to be a war of attrition. I fear we will never have the capability to defeat the Redcoats entirely and drive them out, furlong by furlong, mile by mile. Instead, we must be as insects to them—pesky, deadly, and annoying, too peripatetic to defeat. If we obtain the assistance of the French, and if we can become a more cohesive fighting force, then we will indeed be impossible to ignore, and eventually they will go home. That is my dream."

Chapter Eighteen
CHALLENGE

Berkeley, September 6, 2014

The Giants played an afternoon game in Detroit. In the second inning, the Tigers batter tapped a lazy ground ball to the left side. The Giants third baseman charged the ball, fielded it cleanly on two hops, and whipped it sidearm to first. The first baseman stretched toward the throw and swiped his mitt to catch the ball. At virtually the same moment, the runner touched the base.

"Out!" I yelled at the TV.

"Out!" called the first-base ump, in perfect position, using a vigorous, twisting, downward punch to sell a very close call and ward off doubters. His team already down two runs, the Tigers manager popped out of the dugout and consulted with the umpires. The out call left the Tigers with two outs and a man on second, but they thought the runner was safe at first.

"They're gonna challenge that call," Matt said.

George leaned forward curiously. "It appears they will

indeed repeat it. Is this also right now?"

Much activity on the field. A young man in a dark hat and a blue jacket brought out a black duffle bag. Two of the umpires joined him and donned heavy-duty headphones wired to the equipment in the bag.

George was puzzled. "What is happening?"

"Haven't you seen a manager challenge a call before?" Matt asked.

George stopped. "I have observed the phenomenon so common in these looking-glass programs, where they seem to repeat a ball scene, diverting from right now to the very recent past."

"But no replay challenges?"

He looked blank.

We all watched intently as the broadcasters showed and discussed a half dozen different camera angles for the play at first base.

"These replays are not right now, George, but they are from just a few moments ago."

From some camera positions, it appeared that the ball had, indeed, beaten the runner to first.

"What's happening here," Matt said, "is something new this year. For years, they have shown replays on these TV games, sometimes over and over, often in slow motion. But this year they've added a new rule, so that a manager can challenge the outcome of a play. If he does, the officials can change the call, modifying an umpire's original decision."

George thought about that for a while. We all watched intently as they continued to replay the hit, the throw, the catch, the runner's foot hitting the bag, the two umps with the headsets. The viewpoint changed from low to high, from left to right, from profile to straight-toward-the-lens. Normal speed, slo-mo, super slo-mo. My parents' 42" Panasonic immersed us in the action.

"Why do they wear these odd things? Are their ears cold?"

"Those headsets let them hear and talk to other umpires who are deciding whether the call was correct."

"Those other men are not on the field?"

"No, they're not even in the stadium. They're in New York, watching the game on their own looking glasses."

"New York! This is wondrous indeed! So very far away. How is that possible? How much time is required to send a message from here to New York?"

"Just seconds," Matt said.

George looked amazed, then amused. I'm sure he thought we were playing him. In his world, sending a message meant dispatching someone on horseback with a written note. It could take weeks to move a physical message as far as my Toyota could drive in a day. But now, instantaneous telecommunications trumped all that.

He looked at me with a stolid expression. "Is this not, then, a form of time travel? In the mode described by your aunt?"

Aunt Rachel had dropped by a couple of days earlier, fascinated to meet George. Clearly they had liked each other, and she seemed to accept his story instantly. "You know, Tim," she had said excitedly, "your time travel story is very different than most."

"How's that?"

"Well, in many stories, the hero travels back in time to change the past, and that's where logistical difficulties, split universes, and impossible paradoxes develop. How can anyone go back in time? If you go back to a date during your lifetime, would there be two of you? How can that be? And if you go back to a date before you were born, well, that's just plain crazy. How can you possibly exist before you were born?"

"What's your point?"

"My point is that this is different. Your hero has come *forward* in time, where he's a bit of a fish out of water."

I had told Rachel about the Stephen King book I was reading, *11/22/63*. The hero goes back in time to try to stop the Kennedy assassination, with cataclysmic results.

"But Rachel, please abide with me here in the world of reality for a while. This isn't a time-travel story we're talking about. This is my life."

George recounted what she had said about traveling into the past in order to change what happened. "Are these men in blue not deciding to alter the past?"

"Well, yes, in a way, the Tigers are trying to change the past. The Giants don't want it to change, and the umpires are the enforcers, the judges. The replay umps in New York will watch the same angles we see, and they will confirm or overturn the call that was made on the field."

"Extraordinary."

"Yeah, we think it's pretty amazing, too," I said. "Since this is the first year, no one was too sure what to expect. Many cynical people thought that replay reviews wouldn't work for baseball, even though other sports have long since adopted them successfully. Some feared the umpires would resent having the machines show them up, embarrass them for making bad calls, but that hasn't been the case. The umps are highly skilled. Of course, they make mistakes, but they do want to get it right. Especially when the replays are being shown anyway, and all the spectators in the park and at home know when they've blown a call."

"Timothy, for several minutes now, we three and many others staring at this game have left the 'right now' with our eyes and our brains and our thoughts. Certainly, as everyone awaits the decision, we have all, collectively and meditatively, journeyed into the past together. And they might decide to change the past."

"If you will."

In one freeze-frame from the right side, the runner's foot had clearly touched the base while the ball was still an inch or two from the glove. The umpire crew chief spoke a few words into his microphone, removed the headset, brought his hands together, palms down, then vigorously swept them to the sides.

Safe! The Tigers' challenge succeeded. As Yogi Berra said, "It ain't over till it's over."

"What is the consequence of this decision?" George asked.

"Dude, the runner is safe at first," I answered, "so the Tigers have two men on base and only one out."

"So, Timothy, even though I have witnessed a runner signaled out at first base and he has left the field, all that has changed?"

"Well, yes. He's coming back out now."

"We have all journeyed together to fixate on a recent moment in the past—and then changed it."

"Sure."

"Time travel."

"Uh ..." I didn't know what else to say.

Matt smiled at me. "You'd better start believing in time travel stories, Timmy. You're in one."

Chapter Nineteen
MONEY

Berkeley, September 9, 2014

George was full of questions.

"Timothy, you said that I was elected president of the colonies—"

"The United States."

"The United States. By whom was I elected?"

"By an institution called the Electoral College, supposedly advised by a vote of the people."

"By which people?" George asked. "Who participated in this election? Certainly not the poor, who own no land."

"Well no, not in your day. For many years, only land-owners could vote."

"Did Catholics vote?"

"No. Not at first."

"Jews? Indians?"

"No."

"Or the slaves?" he asked, with a glance at Matty, who glared back at him. Matt had felt the impact of the General's charisma, but hanging out with a tall, commanding, muscular slave-owner still gave him the willies.

"No, not until much later, after the Civil War."

George paused in shock. "Or women?"

"Much, much later. After a worldwide war."

He considered these developments.

"So who voted in the election when I was selected as the president?"

"Mostly white men, landowners."

This satisfied him. The Father of Our Country seemed unable to conceive of a world of universal suffrage. But we are all products of our time.

I had stopped at the bank to pick up some currency and handed him a few bills. He blinked without recognition at the face on the five, a bit shocked at the beard.

"That's Abraham Lincoln, who freed the slaves," Matty said.

"Why?"

"Because no one should own another person. It's immoral. We talked about that!"

George nodded, then turned back to the bills.

He didn't recognize Jackson on the twenty, of course, or Grant on the fifty, but he was startled to see Hamilton on the ten and Franklin on the hundred.

"Alexander and old Ben? They were presidents as well?"

"Well, no. You appointed Hamilton the first Secretary of the Treasury. He might have become president someday. But he was, or will be, killed in a duel by Aaron Burr."

I immediately regretted telling him.

"Burr? He always was a scoundrel! But why?"

"Never mind. Franklin was an elder statesman and guiding light for the early United States, but never president.

He died before you finished serving your two terms."

"And Tom Jefferson? Brilliant writer, but a headstrong bugger. Never liked him! Why is the denomination of his note twice as large as mine? In fact, they are all larger."

"That's true, but Jefferson's two is actually quite rare. Your one-dollar bill is the most common bill by far!"

He turned, stone-faced, and glared at me in silence for a while.

"So? Why would I celebrate being common? Explain yourself, young man."

I muttered that future rulers would embrace and champion the common man, but he didn't hear. He kept staring at Franklin's C-note and his own single dollar, comparing the two, shocked that one Ben was worth 100 Georges.

"Where is the justice?" he muttered. "Is he the one stuck in a miserable hellhole in his beloved Pennsylvania, enduring the winter with a ragtag army? No, he's off in Paris, that den of iniquity, with his paramours, his damnable chessboards, and that outlandish fur hat."

His voice trailed off. It was difficult enough for him to accept that he had stumbled forward into the future, to deal with our ridiculous new world. But seeing himself twenty years older on the dollar bill depressed him, and his long-dead peers on the other currency creeped us all out.

I couldn't stop my brain: if he couldn't get back to Valley Forge to rally the troops during their greatest trial, how would that affect two-plus centuries of human history since then? And what, if anything, could we do about it?

Chapter Twenty
WEEDS

Berkeley, September 9, 2014

My Aunt Rachel was ten years younger than Uncle Chuck. Despite her sadness about his death a few months earlier, she bubbled with a youthful exuberance. She used to teach American history and now worked as a reference librarian.

Rachel came over to watch the game with us. She shared George's developing passion for baseball. He grew to love the Giants—the name, the players, the orange and black colors.

"Baseball is the quintessential American game," she told him, "steeped in history. Team loyalties can go back a century or more. Our local Giants team, for example, was originally founded in New York in 1883."

"I have spent much time in and around New York during this accursed war."

"The founding of the Giants is actually closer in time to the Revolution than it is to our present, 2014. Baseball gives us an easy connection with our past."

She knew a lot, my aunt. What she didn't know, she knew how to find out.

That night, the Giants handled the Diamondbacks with ease. Fresh-faced rookie Joe Panik, despite his name, stayed calm and stroked five singles in five at-bats.

George enjoyed watching the games with us on TV. I taught him baseball lingo and explained that behind the leisurely pace of the game lay a cerebral chess match, a head game of guesswork.

"The catcher is the sergeant on the field. He uses finger signals to suggest the next pitch—fastball, curveball, changeup, slider. The pitcher nods or shakes him off until they agree. They try to create a pattern of pitches so the batter will guess what's coming next. If the pitcher starts with two fastballs waist-high and inside (close to the batter), he's trained the batter to expect the same a third time. The pitcher might then throw a curveball low and outside, to trick the batter into swinging and missing."

The Giants announcers were particularly skillful at describing the pitchers' choices and the batters' guesses. "Right now, I think the Panda is layin' in the weeds," Mike Krukow told us and the rest of his TV audience.

"There is a panda? Is that not a type of bear?" George asked.

Matt tried to explain. "Sandoval of the Giants is called the Panda, because of his resemblance to a cartoon character called Kung Fu Panda."

"Kung Fu?"

"Never mind. It's a nickname, like Patsy for your wife. By 'laying in the weeds,' Krukow means this: the other team thinks they are setting up Sandoval to anticipate a particular pitch, but he is actually looking for a different one. The pitcher sets up the batter to expect a fastball, then throws a slider instead. The batter correctly guesses slider, adjusts his swing accordingly, and hits it!"

George got that right away.

"Ah. So 'laying in the weeds' means making surprising choices?"

"Yes. Outthinking an opponent who thinks he has you outsmarted."

Later, between innings, I beckoned Rachel into the kitchen and showed her images of George I had found on the web.

"They're remarkably different! Some don't even look like the same man."

"I see differences between the youthful Washington and the older," she said.

"Of course. But look at the shape of his jaw. His face seems to get shorter as he gets older."

"He lost most of his teeth and that led to loss of jawbone. He does look old and unhappy on the dollar bill, especially now that we've met him as a young, vigorous man. What a specimen!"

"You think he's a hunk, Rachel?"

"I do. I always liked men with long hair." She laughed. "Here, Tim, look at this."

She pulled out her change purse and dumped out some quarters. We stared at the familiar bas-relief of George: middle-aged and vigorous, strong jawline, determined profile.

"The design of the coin is based on a bust done by the French sculptor Houdon, who spent weeks with Washington at Mount Vernon, after the Revolution and before his presidency. In addition to detailed measurements and drawings, Houdon made a life mask of Washington, placing wet clay over his face for an hour to mold the shape exactly. Mrs. Washington considered it the best likeness of George."

"It is powerful. Why isn't this on the dollar?"

"I don't know. It's a dramatic portrait. George sat for Houdon during the height of his vigor, when he was extolled as both a victorious general and a revered civilian, before he became president and the cares and difficulties of birthing the new nation had taken their toll. Gilbert Stuart painted the portrait that appears on the dollar ten years after the Houdon bust, toward the end of George's presidency, about two years before his death."

We knew that George had died in 1799. And yet, oddly, George was there with us in Berkeley, in the here and now, in 2014. We could hear him in the next room, talking to Matt about baseball. We looked at each other in wonder.

Chapter Twenty-One
BALLPARK

San Francisco, September 24, 2014

Baseball season was almost over. After losing to the Dodgers the night before, the second-place Giants were on the brink of elimination in the race for the Western Division.

George was curious to see a baseball game live. We invited Rachel to come along, and the four of us piled into the Corolla and headed for the Bay Bridge. San Francisco glistened and twinkled across the water.

"I must say, from the bits of your baseball I have viewed through the looking glass, it reminds me of wicket."

"You mean cricket," Matt smirked at him.

"No, wicket. I believe it to be an old form of cricket, which is, as yet, not terribly popular. But wicket is played in various locales in the Colonies, and your baseball seems similar. One player throws a ball towards a player with a bat, who endeavors to hit it. In cricket, he bowls, or hurls the ball on one bounce. In baseball your pitcher has the advantage of bowling down from a small knoll."

"The mound. The hill. The bump."

"Quite so. In wicket, he skims the ball along the ground. If the batsman succeeds in striking the ball, he runs between the bases. The more bases he touches, the greater the score. Like cricket, wicket has only two bases. My soldiers enjoy this game. Playing boosts morale. But tell me how your teams can work and support their families, if they play games every day?"

"Baseball is their job, man," I told him. "They're professionals."

"Many players make millions of dollars a year," Matt said.

George was shocked.

"Millions? Millions? How is that possible? Has your money become so worthless? Is everyone in your world—in your era—so handsomely remunerated?"

"No. Only the very best professional athletes make salaries like that, plus some actors, entertainers, and businesspeople," I said.

Rachel added, "Most people, including teachers, for example, earn only a tiny fraction of ballplayers' salaries."

George shook his head.

We rolled through the carpool lane at the toll plaza and started across the bridge. The day was clear, the Bay full of sailboats running before the wind. George poked his head out the window and looked up at the bridge, then out toward the water.

"What a grand structure and a magnificent view! This is indeed a land of great beauty! I must confess, Timothy, I am beginning to like it here."

Uh oh, I thought. *Dude, that's not good. Who's gonna lead the Revolution?*

86

As we approached the city, he marveled at the heights of the buildings.

"Are these homes or businesses?"

"Both," I said.

"How do the residents, or leaseholders, climb up so many steps to their own premises?"

"These tall buildings all have elevators."

"So that they might ... elevate?"

"Exactly. The elevator is a small room. You and your companions step in, and a machine lifts you up to the desired level or brings you down to the ground."

George seemed dubious. "Truly? That does sound precarious indeed."

"They're really quite safe," Matt said. "Unless you get trapped in an elevator that won't open. My mom is scared of elevators, but there are actually very few mishaps."

We parked near the bridge and walked a few blocks on the Embarcadero, along the waterfront to the Giants ballpark. George was still favoring one leg.

It was a glorious, sun-drenched day. On one side of the road, a whole neighborhood had sprung up in the fourteen years since the ballpark had opened, what appeared to be block after block of upscale apartments, probably with fantastic views. Rents in the City were among the highest in the country.

We turned a corner and the Giants ballpark came into view, surrounded by tall palm trees. On the bay side of the Embarcadero, tidy marinas provided mooring for hundreds of fancy-looking sailboats, cruisers, and yachts. George looked up at the impressive brick edifice.

"It's a baseball palace," I said. "One of the most beautiful in the league."

"Impressive indeed. Do all teams have ornate palaces such as this one?"

"Mostly," said Rachel. "Tonight we are playing against the hated Dodgers, rivals of our Giants, from Los Angeles, California, almost four hundred miles south of us."

"This is, indeed, a large state, this California."

We pushed through the crowd, past huge posters of star players, then joined the throngs pouring in through the Willie Mays Gate.

"I see many of the other fanatics are wearing special clothing with the Gigantics' name in the colors of the tiger, as are we," George said.

"Fans. And they're the Giants."

George wore my orange-and-black panda hat, his long hair tucked into a Giants player jersey that said "Pence 8" on the back. George liked the shirt but maintained with a straight face that he was sure he was worth more than eight pence.

"After all, my silver coin is twenty-five pence, and my bank note is 100. Why must I wear an eight-pence tunic?"

"'Pence' is the name of the Giants right fielder. 'Eight' is the number on his jersey."

"Hmm. And why have you put me in this odd bear hat?"

"That's a panda, man. I told you. It's Sandoval's nickname."

"Which one is he?"

I pointed.

"The round, brown one?"

Matt, also round and brown, cringed at the description.

"Yes, the one with the big smile and the bubble gum," I said. "He's always joking and having fun with his teammates.

Everyone loves the Panda. A lot of them have nicknames. They call Gregor Blanco 'the White Shark.' And Ángel Pagán was known as 'Crazy Horse' earlier in his career."

We shuffled slowly forward through the crowd.

"My goodness, Timothy, how many people attend these games?"

"Usually 40,000 or more for the Giants, and the tickets are expensive. That's how they get millions to pay their players."

Though our seats were on the lower level, I led us onto the long escalator to the upper concourse. After careful examination, George hopped on nimbly and grinned. I knew he would enjoy it.

"You said the elevator was a small room, Timothy, but this structure consists of fantastical steps whisking us skyward."

Matt grinned at me. "Did he just call this a stairway to heaven?"

"No, George, this is an escalator, a moving staircase. The elevator's over here."

We pushed through a knot of fans.

"Now check this out." I pushed the button. The doors slid open, a few people got out, and George led us gamely into the shiny aluminum box, examining it carefully.

He loved the ride down, which lasted less than a minute. Kid in a candy store.

We walked the promenade around the park, marveling at glorious views of the water, the boats, the bridge, the hills of the East Bay. George asked about the giant Coke bottle behind the left-field bleachers and the enormous billboards. He was familiar with the concept of advertising from ads in Colonial newspapers, but he found huge public displays like this to be startling.

We passed the fifty-foot-tall glove that loomed above the bleachers.

"Notice it has only three fingers, plus a thumb, an homage to the gloves of the old-timers," I told George. "Baseball honors its history. This glove is a shrine to yesteryear."

Chapter Twenty-Two
DOGS

George loved the traditions, the throngs, the excitement in the air. We stopped at the concession stands.

"Food and baseball go together," I said. "And beer."

"Everybody has their favorites," Matt said. "I remember ballpark foods in Philly that they don't have out here. My fave here is the Giants Dog at the Doggie Diner stands."

"Of course, you do not eat dog!" George grimaced.

"It's just an expression. Hot dogs are just sausages, with beef, veal, or pork meat. No dog."

We stopped to sniff at each food stand and admire the gustatory offerings. George inhaled the happy aromas with a sigh.

"The brats are best," I advised.

"What are brats?"

"Bratwurst. Veal sausage. Tasty!"

My intonation reminded me of the enthusiastic bass voice in Candy Crush. "Tasty!"

Aunt Rachel piped up. "For beer, try an Anchor Steam,

made right here in San Francisco."

An aggressive aroma assaulted our olfactories from a smoke-filled stand up ahead.

"Garlic fries," we chorused.

"Eh?" George was mystified.

"Potatoes fried with garlic. The Brits call them chips. So good!"

The Giants were warming up as we arrived at our seats, the Dodgers in their dugout. The sun set behind the stadium, and a warm glow filled the sky. The lights were starting to have an effect.

We all stood while a vocal trio sang a familiar tune.

"I know this song," said George. "But why is this crowd singing about 'rockets' red glare'? What is this?"

"'The Star-Spangled Banner.' It's our national anthem. It's based on a poem inspired by a battle in the War of—well, a future war. They sing it at every sporting event."

"I believe I have heard this melody sung by drunken English soldiers, with bawdy content. I can still recall a line or two: 'I'll instruct you like me to entwine, the myrtle of Venus with Bacchus' vine.' For sure, 'bombs bursting in air' has a more serious tone. But the tune lacks melodiousness and sits harshly upon the ear."

I laughed.

We sat close to the field and could hear the umpire yell "Play ball!" to start the game.

After a few innings, George looked approvingly at the diverse group of players on the field.

"Some are White, some Black. None are slaves, of course," he said carefully. "A few appear Oriental."

"Asian."

"Yes. Are they all Americans?"

"Most are, but many players come from the West Indies, or South and Central America. Spanish-speaking lands. A few from Asia. A number of the Giants come from the American South, including Buster Posey from Georgia."

"Ah, Mr. Posey. You have mentioned him before. Apparently you were not referring to flora. I do know a Captain Posey in Virginia, whose estate borders on Mount Vernon."

"Posey is the catcher, the man crouching down behind home plate, with the mask and chest protector. He's the Giants' biggest star," Matt said.

"Meaning?"

"Their most accomplished and most important player."

The Dodgers' batter fouled off a pitch. The ball glanced off the bat and hit Posey squarely in the head. His hockey-style helmet bounced.

George, like most of the spectators, jumped and oohed at the loud impact.

The plate umpire removed his own mask and touched Posey kindly on the shoulder. He then stepped around him, bent over, and, with a flourish, cleaned off the plate with a stiff brush from his pocket.

"The umpires make certain the rules are followed," Aunt Rachel said. "The plate ump has chosen to slow down the game, to give Posey a few extra moments to recover from getting hit in the head."

Buster stood up, removed the mask, took a couple of steps to the side, and spat into the dirt.

"Why do they spit or adjust their breeches so frequently?" George asked.

No one had a good answer.

Posey and the ump put their masks back on and stepped behind the plate. Buster squatted. The batter stepped in, smiled, and respectfully tapped Posey's shin guard lightly with his bat.

"Play ball!"

Chapter Twenty-Three
KISS

George assessed the athletes on the field.

"They are mostly fine, strapping lads who would make good soldiers. Tall, muscular, confident. At first, I doubted that anyone could throw as accurately as your fantastical head game presupposes, aiming with great precision for one side of the platter or the other."

"The plate."

"Yes. Seeing these bowlers and batsmen in action, in person, from so close, I can see that they are quite skilled and practiced at what they do. Your Gigantics are quite good."

"Giants."

He regarded me with a stony face, a hint of a twinkle in his blue eyes. I looked over at Rachel, who silently mouthed, "He's messing with you."

It was a warm evening. George got overheated and removed the fuzzy panda hat. The Monterey Bay Aquarium logo appeared on the massive scoreboard looming over center field, with the words "Kiss Cam" and "Share-the-Love."

The disembodied voice of Frank Sinatra began to sing "Strangers in the Night." Animated octopus tentacles on the screen threatened to engulf the live video images.

I had once kissed my old girlfriend Marnie on the Kiss Cam, a few months after we started dating, when things were still going well between us. I didn't miss her, exactly. She had treated me badly. But the memory brought on pangs of loneliness. The camera focused on a young couple in the stands, who watched as their image came up on screen, then dove into a passionate smooch.

The crowd cheered. Though he still wasn't sure what was happening, George was shocked by these indecorous public displays of affection. The camera cut to an older couple, who responded with a much more dignified buss. Light booing and laughter from the masses.

Sinatra continued to croon to "Strangers in the Night." George was mortified.

"Timothy, this song and these people seem to be celebrating romantic liaisons of the most crude and casual type. How offensive!"

The screen cut to a pimply young guy, who practically leaped onto his cute girlfriend, attacking with a scary abundance of tongue.

"Ewww," a girl behind us called out. Our whole section laughed.

The image on screen switched to George, with Rachel beside him. In that strong left profile shot, with his pale skin, high forehead, prominent apple cheeks, graying russet hair tied in back, and aquiline nose, he looked just like the guy on the quarter.

The camera seemed to stay on them forever. Finally, with a good-natured grin Rachel gave him a prim peck on the lips, then lingered an extra second or two. The fans screamed their appreciation.

I was speechless, overcome with dread, though not sure why. How had this happened? We had brought the Father of Our Country out in public to a baseball game in San Francisco. And his iconic face was up on a giant screen, being kissed by a woman not his wife, as Sinatra sang about getting lucky.

I shared the moment with 40,000 of my closest friends at the ballpark. I hoped all their intentions were friendly.

The Dodgers won, 9-1. Each team had eight hits, but the Giants just couldn't move runners over or score. With the win, the Dodgers won the Western Division championship and advanced to the playoffs, though there were still a few games left in the schedule. The Giants, despite being relegated to second place by their loss, could still make it to the playoffs with a win in the upcoming Wild Card Game.

Chapter Twenty-Four
FOG

A chill wind greeted us as we left the ballpark, swirling San Francisco's famous fog around us as we hurried toward the car. The temperature had dropped ten degrees as night fell.

Carl Sandburg was wrong. The fog didn't come in on "little cat feet," stealthily tiptoeing across the hills. It was only picturesque from afar. When the fog engulfed you, it was like getting hit in the face with a cold, wet mop. Maybe Mark Twain never actually said that "the coldest winter I ever spent was a summer in San Francisco," but summer days often turned cold and foggy, and changes in temperature could be dramatic and sudden.

The Giants always played Tony Bennett's "I Left My Heart in San Francisco" as a victory anthem after home games. Despite tonight's loss, I sang a few comforting lines to myself as we walked out into the howling wind.

Ironic words for a gloomy night. The mood of the exiting Giants fans matched the angry weather. A few drunks in the crowd started to chant, "Gi-ants suck! Gi-ants suck!"

Other fans booed the drunks halfheartedly, but too many were silent, annoyed that the Giants had tanked all week, losing five out of six.

Rachel took George's hand as we followed the crowd. I heard someone up ahead of us baiting L.A. fans who had come to the game in full Dodgers regalia. Baiting in a nasty, personal way, beyond the bounds of good-natured sports rivalry. Someone began to chant, "Fuck-the-Dodg-ers!" and a minute later I heard yelling, the smash of a glass bottle, and running feet. I shuddered. Just wanted to get back to Berkeley.

We walked along the foggy Embarcadero, and the disappointed crowd boiled off the sidewalk and into the driving lanes. Traffic slowed and cars swerved as angry fans jaywalked against a DON'T WALK light.

A black sedan careened out of a side street at great speed—headlights off, despite the thickening fog—rattled across the tracks onto the Embarcadero, and raced toward a small gap in the swarming crowd just ahead of us. I realized that the sedan was aiming directly for a couple of Dodger fans up ahead, along with George and Rachel.

He never saw it, but Rachel spotted the imminent danger, lowered her shoulder, and smashed her diminutive body into George's midsection, just below the word "Giants" on his jersey. Caught unawares, he toppled over backward out of harm's way, but she somehow stayed on her feet in the path of the car.

BAM! The car sideswiped Rachel and spun her like a top. She crumpled to the ground.

BAM! The car hit a guy in a Dodger jersey, then sped away. I tried to read the license plate, but it was too dark in the gloomy night.

Someone yelled, "Call 911!" I feared the worst. George and Matt were by Rachel's side. She lay facedown on the pavement, the other victim about ten feet away. My heart was in my throat.

Oh my god, I thought. *She's dead.*

George bent over her, talking quietly into her ear. She opened one eye and lifted her head. She looked wildly at him.

"I'm fine, let me up."

"You need to stay down."

"No, I don't. Just because I kissed you, that doesn't mean you're the boss of me."

Her remark embarrassed him, but he shut up and helped her get to her feet.

"Rachel, are you sure you're all right?" I asked.

"Sure." She nodded vigorously, then groaned, clutching her side in pain, as one knee buckled beneath her. "No, I guess not."

An ambulance took her to the emergency room at San Francisco General. I rode along with her, and George and Matt followed in the Corolla. Hours later, a nurse rolled her out in a wheelchair.

"I've got two cracked ribs and a messed-up knee," Rachel told us.

"That's all?" I said, with a laugh. "I thought you were dead."

"Sorry to disappoint you. Just so you know, it hurts like hell."

George gazed upon her fondly.

Matt looked on with concern. "Why would anyone want to hurt you? What was with that goddamn car?"

Rachel squinted at him. "What happened to the other guy who got hit? The Dodger fan?"

"He's upstairs in surgery," Matt said. "With a broken leg."

George smiled. "I feared we had lost you, kind lady. Thank you for your efforts to keep me safe."

"You bet. They taped up the ribs and put this big ugly brace on my knee. Nothing is broken. Now take me home."

"Home?" I couldn't believe it. "Have you been released?"

"There's nothing else they can do for me. No bones to set, no concussion to observe. Just some strained and torn ligaments in my knee and sore ribs that will probably ache for months as they slowly heal. I'll be black and blue for quite a while. On the plus side—"

"On the plus side," I said, "you're still alive."

"Right. And, they've given me some kick-ass pain pills. Verrrry relaxing."

We rolled her to the curb, and I brought the car up. George relinquished the shotgun position and helped Rachel into the front passenger seat. It was now after three in the morning. The fog hung low over the freeway as we approached the Bay Bridge. In the distance, the ghostly outline of the ballpark loomed against the sky, lights off.

What had just happened? Was that some crazy driver who had imbibed too many beers at the game or some pissed-off, psychotic fan aiming for people in Dodger blue? Or maybe, just maybe, it was someone deliberately trying to harm the General. But who? And why?

We drove across the Bridge, silent and lost in thought. Our fun evening had ended badly. Very badly, indeed.

Chapter Twenty-Five
FBI

Berkeley, September 26, 2014

Aunt Rachel had been getting in my face.

"We all want to get George back to Valley Forge and to his own time," she said. "But we don't have a clue as to how to proceed. And we're trying to do it all alone."

"What should we do?"

"Contact the government. They have a stake in getting him back and making sure that the Revolution unfolds the way it did. Don't you think Obama would want to meet Washington?"

I'd been having this conversation with her for a while now. I was wary of trying to "take George to Obama," but she kept pushing me to try to get government help. She was now walking with a cane, hobbling around carefully, still nursing her injured knee and sore ribs.

"Of course Obama would like to meet him. But why would they believe us, and how do you introduce someone to a sitting president, anyway? They frown on storming the

White House."

"Try taking him to the Secret Service."

"Too scary. They're the president's bodyguards, not his schedulers. They'd probably sic the dogs on George. Plus, we have to face the question: do we wholeheartedly believe that he is the real thing? If he's not, taking him in could be foolhardy, embarrassing—even dangerous."

"Then take him to the FBI," Rachel said. "They investigate. If anyone can get to the bottom of this, they can."

"I dunno …"

"Listen, I know a guy who works for the FBI. He went to school with Uncle Chuck. In fact, we used to date at one time. I met Chuck through him. Let me call him. Think of it. You could be the one who presents George Washington, our first president, to our first Black president. You could make history!"

I never would have agreed if I'd had my wits about me, but my aunt knew how to play to my sense of posterity. I'd seen plenty of TV news interviews with FBI agents in San Francisco, and I could imagine how it would play out.

First Matt and I would introduce George to the wonders of BART, the Bay Area Rapid Transit system. We would jump on a train in North Berkeley and ride it *under* the Bay and into the heart of the City in just thirty minutes. George would love it. The speed, the sleekness of the trains, the sliding doors that whooshed open and closed. Fast, quiet, efficient, public transportation.

As Nevada provided a proud canine honor guard, we would emerge from the bowels of BART. George, in full uniform with cloak and sword, would strut purposefully through the sun-splashed streets of San Francisco, followed by Matt and me. Perhaps the Feds would provide an escort. Passersby would ooh and aah as we strode past the government temples of Civic Center, in front of the beaux arts facade of City Hall, near the gray eminence of the California Superior Court, around the Earl Warren State of California Building, and up to the thirteenth floor of the Philip Burton Federal Building. The FBI office would be an impressive high-tech fortress, with armed guards, security monitors, detectors for explosives, and bulletproof glass.

We would effect a diplomatic handover, transferring the Father of Our Country to the care of the government that had descended from his finest efforts, receiving in return, at least, the thanks of a grateful nation. The exchange would be public, and surely there would be a press conference. We would stand in front of microphones and cameras with the Special Agent in Charge, then hand the General over to the Feds, so they could send him back to save the Revolution. Maybe the mayor would come, or maybe even President Obama himself.

At least send Michelle or Joe Biden. I mean, this is kind of a big deal!

Or so I thought.

It didn't go down that way at all.

Rachel's friend worked at the FBI's Oakland office, not in San Francisco. We made an appointment for the next day, which turned cold and foggy. George's uniform seemed a bit theatrical for a trip to Oakland, so he wore street clothes. Since they only allow service dogs on BART, I thought of digging out Nevada's old blind-service harness from the trunk of my car, but ultimately decided she would be a distraction.

Dressed in jeans, a black hoodie, and a yellow rain slicker, George walked with us to the BART station and up to the platform. But when the train arrived, he didn't want to board.

"I'm sorry, gentlemen, but I am loath to enter any of your rail conveyances. The last time, I was forced to board the car quite inadvertently, and egress was difficult to effect. Being trapped in a moving tube is a less-than-satisfying mode of transportation."

The doors of the train slid closed, and it left the station—without us.

The moist fog had turned into a steady, cold drizzle, and the wind came up. Even in times of drought, we still had bits of rain.

"George," Matt said, after an awkward silence, "this is how we are going to the FBI office. We've gotta take the next train."

"Must we? Can we not take Timothy's toy crawler?"

"Toyota Corolla."

"Indeed. With the hundred horses he has yet to show me. And a door I can open."

"Yes," Matt added, "but finding a place to park can be an issue, and we want to be responsible citizens."

"How so?"

"By not driving everywhere. By reducing our carbon emissions."

That lost him completely. He had grown up with privilege and was quite used to being exceptional and having things his own way. "Everyman" was not on his agenda. "Carbon emissions" meant nothing.

We were getting wet. The cold wind howled around us, the Bay Area's natural air-conditioning.

"Listen, George," I pleaded. "We're here. This train is nothing like the one you were trapped in. It's well lit, carpeted, quiet, and smooth."

"You say."

"Besides, if we don't take the next train, if we bail out and walk home through this wind and rain to get the car, we'll be late for the appointment. You don't want to be late, do you?"

He looked at me, expressionless, and stopped objecting. His face grew grave and solemn, as he contemplated the horror of tardiness. I had to chuckle. *Father of His Country, late for his meeting. That just wouldn't do, would it?*

The next train arrived.

"See?" I said. "Smooth and easy, and it has windows. You won't get trapped in there."

He faced the door, paused for a moment, and, without a word, stepped into the car.

I smiled at him. "Make sure to hold on."

The doors whooshed, the car lurched, and we were off.

Chapter Twenty-Six
ORECK

The Oakland FBI office was in a downtown building that also housed a pediatrician, a builder, a bank, a dry cleaner, some finance companies, and the offices of Pandora Media. Special Agent Angus Oreck met us at the door and waved us casually through security.

Oreck was in his fifties, of less-than-medium height, chubby and red-faced, with Brylcreemed hair the dirty beige of wholewheat pasta. He acted friendly, but I couldn't fathom him friends with Uncle Chuck or dating Aunt Rachel. I tried to imagine what bad guys he could take down, if granted the opportunity. He led us into a small office.

"This is Mr. Chow," he said, introducing us to a lanky, athletic-looking Asian man with long legs carelessly wrapped around a chair. "He's our consultant." Chow nodded without expression.

Oreck began. "I know why you're here, Mr. Morrison, and I want you to know that I am only meeting with you as a favor to your aunt. I don't anticipate this will lead to any action by the FBI."

"How can you know that? We haven't even talked yet."

"Of course. My apologies." He turned to George and smiled with condescension. "And you are General Washington, I presume?"

"Yes sir, my pleasure to meet you both." A courtly bow.

Oreck laughed. Chow looked worried. Neither seemed convinced that they were in the presence of a guy who really needed to get back to the Revolution.

"Please tell us how you got here, General," Oreck said.

George described the wintry night during the party in Valley Forge, the aurora, the shaky ground, hitting his head, losing consciousness.

"The northern lights in Pennsylvania? Ridiculous," said Oreck. "And there are never earthquakes in that part of the country."

"I know what I saw and felt, gentlemen," George said.

"Can't you investigate whether those natural phenomena actually occurred when he said?" I asked. "Wouldn't they be recorded somewhere? I mean, if the aurora was actually visible that far south, surely someone would have noticed and reported it."

"I noticed," George said.

"Of course, General," Oreck smirked. "I believe we're discussing corroboration from another source."

George stiffened. He was not used to having people mistrust his word.

"Please go on with your story."

"I believe I lapsed in and out of consciousness for several days. Eventually I woke up in a large moving box, which I now know is called a boxcar."

"On a train?"

"Indeed, sir. The door was locked at first, but later I found it ajar."

"How did you survive for days without food and water?"

"There were other men in the boxcar, locked in as I was. They tended to my comfort and gave me sustenance."

"Hobos helped you?"

"I know not this term, sir."

"Bums? Itinerant tramps?"

"You doubt me, sir?"

"I'm afraid I do." He looked at George's clothes. "You just don't look much like our first president."

"That's in his future, Agent Oreck," Matt piped up. "He's still years shy of becoming president, and nearly twenty years younger than that awful picture on the dollar bill. But look at his face. He's George Washington. He's gone missing from Valley Forge. And we need to get him back there."

Mr. Chow stirred in his chair. "Why?" he asked.

Maybe this guy would believe us! I stood up too fast and began to get woozy. Dizzy. Head spinning. The room started rotating around me. Around and around and around … I couldn't stay on my feet, sank down into the chair, and began to hyperventilate, my breath harsh and gasping.

Do I believe George? Isn't it a bit late to be asking myself this question? Am I willing to go to bat with the FBI on his behalf?

I think I was having an anxiety attack. Matt thumped me on the back as if I'd ingested a chicken bone.

"Why?" Chow repeated.

"Breathe deeply, Timothy," George said. "And slowly." He held my shoulders and murmured comforting, calming words, as I imagined he would to a nervous horse.

After a few moments contemplating my respiration, I

109

turned to Mr. Chow.

"I think we're in for disaster if we can't get the General back to Valley Forge. I think the Revolution will founder without him. The Brits will squash all opposition and continue to rule."

George listened closely. He had a rough idea of what was going to happen. He knew that, at some time in his future, the Colonial forces would win the revolution, create a nation, and elect him president. His name and image and presence were too ubiquitous in our modern culture to keep him in the dark about those momentous events. There was even a Washington Avenue a block from my house.

But he didn't know details or timing. Since the incident with the Battle of Monmouth painting, Matt and I, with Aunt Rachel's urging, had tried not to tell him too much, and he didn't ask too much. He respected that he had to live his life and let events surprise him.

Chow scowled. "So?"

"I don't know what would happen from there. But I'm sure that the crumbling of the American Revolution—an inspiration to democratic movements around the globe—can't be a good thing for our world."

"We're hoping you'll help him get back to Valley Forge. And back to his own time," Matt said.

Oreck broke in. "Mr. Morrison, Mr. Johnson, General, thank you for coming in."

"You don't believe us? Doesn't it all make sense?"

"Yes, Mr. Morrison, it all makes sense if you believe in time travel. Otherwise, it all seems a bit preposterous. Especially because, here we are, in the twenty-first century, and the United States is still a democracy, Washington still a hero. Have you checked the dollar bill lately? It hasn't changed."

"Can't you even find out if the aurora and the earthquake occurred in Pennsylvania that year? Wouldn't that help prove something?"

"Sorry, sir, that's not on my radar. We are not the Smithsonian. We don't do historical investigations. We pursue serious violations in the present: terrorism, cybercrime, corruption, violent crimes, major thefts, civil rights. Subjects that have a deeply negative influence upon other Americans' pursuit of happiness. Impersonating historical figures—"

"Impersonating?" George was taken aback by this impertinence.

"—is an age-old, time-honored tradition in many cultures, often in service to the gods of satire. It requires a novelist's imagination and a charlatan's chutzpah. In a way, I respect that. But this is the FBI, gentlemen. We don't do history, and we don't do time travel. Mr. Morrison, please pass along my kind regards and condolences to your Aunt Rachel. I have fond memories of her, and your uncle was a brilliant and engaging man. Thanks again for coming in, gentlemen. We're done here."

In moments, we were back on the street. So much for our glory-tinged diplomatic handover. We trudged back to the BART station, the cold summer drizzle blowing in our faces.

Now what?

Chapter Twenty-Seven
DENTURES

Berkeley, September 27, 2014

The encounter with the FBI frustrated us all.

I was annoyed that they were so stupid and closed-minded, pissed off that we couldn't prove George's identity, anguished that I still wasn't sure myself.

"Listen, George, it's time to come clean about your teeth."

"My teeth? I assure you that I clean them regularly. Not that such practice is any concern of yours, I am sure."

We were talking over coffee at Aunt Rachel's house, subdued after our rejection by the FBI. We had told her about our encounter with Agent Oreck.

"I was afraid he and those lunkheads at the FBI wouldn't believe you. He always was a bit of a nerd," she said.

"You actually dated him?"

"Well, when I was young and foolish. Not my finest hour."

My own feelings oscillate wildly on a pendulum of uncertainty,

I brooded, *from trust to doubt, from total belief to utter skepticism. How can this ridiculous story be true?*

I turned to George. "General, I feel that you are who you say you are, and you come from where and when you claim to. I feel that in my heart, even as a deep cynicism in my intellectual being tells me I'm crazy."

"I agree with you," Rachel said, "which makes us both crazy."

George regarded us with a benign expression and a tight, dignified smile. The man did have charisma.

I studied him carefully. "But before we can continue to advocate for you, you must prove your identity to us, once and for all. Which brings us back to your teeth."

"This is not a subject I wish to discuss, Timothy."

"I know, and I understand. But perhaps your dental work can help prove your identity."

"With all due respect, General," Rachel said soothingly, "please understand that, many years in your future, it will be a matter of historical record that you had problems with your teeth and used some ingeniously designed dentures."

"Ingenious? They are ludicrous, crude, painful appliances."

I realized then that, though his teeth still clicked quietly, I had grown used to the sound and rarely noticed it anymore.

He began to get flushed. "They stick and poke and pinch and bulge. They are only marginally successful in assisting me to masticate my food. And their use does nothing to relieve the constant pain in my jaws. In fact, quite the opposite."

He paused, suddenly aware that he had, by his standards, revealed too much about himself. George Washington was not used to admitting to pain, discussing personal intimacies, or showing any weakness. He had just stepped over a line, one he rarely even approached.

But he needed us, and he knew it.

A long silence. We waited. Finally he continued.

"I have long had dental problems, inherited from members of my father's family. I cracked walnuts with my teeth from a young age, and perhaps that loosened them in their moorings and caused them to decay prematurely. To date, a number of my teeth have had to be extracted, because they have … rotted beyond recovery. I do clean them regularly with various costly toothbrushes and scrapers. Eventually I may lose all my teeth."

He paused and looked at us, wondering if this admitted vulnerability would taint our opinion of him. Rachel beamed warmly at him. Matt looked interested but was still wary of George since their discussion of slavery. I stared openly, awestruck by his sudden frankness.

"In the past two years, I have engaged the services of a dentist, a Dr. John Baker, who has constructed this new set of dentures for me to wear. I am very self-conscious about the poor natural teeth in my mouth, but frankly, I have needed help chewing my meat."

"Can we see them?"

He looked horrified. "What possible end would that serve?"

"If your false teeth look authentic, like something from the eighteenth century, that might help establish when you are from. We should also have a careful look at your clothes. And your sword."

He stood up and drained his coffee, which he took with cream and three sugar cubes. He leaned over me.

"You wish me to hand you my clothing and my teeth,

so that you can inspect them?"

I was suddenly aware of his physical power. He gave me a commanding glare.

But he wasn't my commander. I looked up, met his gaze.

"We would like to be able to prove, to ourselves and others, that you are who you say. We want so much to believe you, but your story borders on fantasy. Yet I feel an urgency to get you back to Valley Forge."

"Yes."

"We can't do that alone. We need help from someone, perhaps not from Agent Oreck or the FBI, but we need help. We need proof. I have no other agenda here. I have no particular desire to look at your dentures or your clothing for any other reason, though I would love to see your sword."

He saw the logic and made a quick decision.

We returned to my house. George went into my sister's room and soon returned with a pile of his Revolutionary War clothing. He stepped over to the sink, turned his back, removed his false teeth and rinsed them, then brought them to Rachel on a small white plate.

"Here is Dr. Baker's finest work. Such as it is."

His voice sounded funny without the teeth, and he wouldn't look me in the eye. That was fine. I had no desire to embarrass him more than we already had.

We crowded around. On the plate was a crude denture which immediately reminded me of a wind-up chattering teeth toy. Most of one side, probably the upper, consisted of teeth carved from a solid block of something that had once been white.

"What's this part made of?" Matt asked.

"It is ivory."

"From an elephant?"

"No, from a hippopotamus—a large animal from Africa, I believe, but not so large as an elephant."

"And these teeth here, on the lower? Where did they come from?"

"Cows. Other farm animals."

"Not from slaves?" Matt asked.

"These dentures have no human teeth, though I have heard that affluent people do sometimes buy teeth from slaves, and from others."

The carved plate on one side and the teeth on the other were connected by lead and gold plates, augmented by squeaky springs. Clearly this was not a modern contraption, but an item from another century. I couldn't imagine putting it in my mouth, especially knowing it was partly made of lead!

What will Oreck say when he sees this? I wondered. *Will he be convinced? Should we even go back to him, or is he too blinded by his own preconceptions?*

"Thank you, General," Rachel said. "I can see how wearing this must be very uncomfortable for you. I believe we've finished with your dentures now."

She took them to the sink, rinsed them again, and returned them to him on the white plate. His face relaxed in a closed-mouth smile, pleased by her efforts at courtesy.

Chapter Twenty-Eight
NATURAL

Now let's look at the clothes," Aunt Rachel said.

Matt asked, "What are we looking for?"

"Well, they should look completely handmade. I make period costumes for our community theatre. With a sewing machine, of course. With the General's clothes, we're looking for small variations that could only be done by a needle pulling thread and would not occur in a machine-sewn or manufactured seam. They must all contain natural fibers, of course, and no modern labels."

The buttons on his jacket were brass, the buckles on his breeches silver. No plastic anywhere. Rachel turned the trousers inside out to examine the inseam. Here the double stitching was tight and straight, but not machine-perfect. Quality hand tailoring. A monogrammed "GW" in the lining, along with the hand-sewn mark of Charles Lawrence, a London tailor. No "Made in China" or "Polyester Blend" labels. No care instructions, sizes, or product numbers. The cape was scratchy wool, the pants something more cottony, the shirt silk.

"No synthetics," Rachel said. His three-cornered hat had clearly been shaped by hand from black beaver felt, the sides and back carefully trained up against the crown. The soles of his boots were not perfectly symmetrical, as if cut out separately by hand.

"Wait," Matt said. "May I ask a question?"

George looked at him and nodded slightly.

"Don't you wear a wig?"

George allowed himself a small smile. "Many men of my station do wear wigs. Yes, LaMatthew, that is true."

"But you don't?"

"I do not. I have always kept my hair natural. I do not consider myself a fancy gentleman, like so many of the be-wigged aristocracy, even in our young country, who emulate the hair and wig styles of the French and English kings. I am a farmer and a soldier. To be precise, at the moment, I am a soldier who pines to return once again to the farm."

Matt was persistent. "But why does your hair usually appear white in the paintings that have come down to us?"

"Ah. As you can see, my hair is brown—"

"I would call it russet," said Rachel.

"And it is ever more flecked with gray, particularly as this war drags on from year to year. My manservant does, from time to time, powder my hair. With white powder. However, it would be quite unusual for me to lead troops into battle with powdered white hair."

"Despite the battle paintings of you looking that way," Matt said.

"Usually painted years or even decades later," I put in. George nodded grimly.

Rachel turned toward us and added, "Men's wigs were

starting to go out of fashion in his era. Younger men like him considered lightly powdering their natural hair to be more stylish."

Then she turned back to him. "Now your sword, please, General."

He looked at her and nodded, left the room again, and returned with the sword, which I had not seen since our last visit to Point Isabel. I wasn't even sure where he kept it. It was tied up in a burlap bag he had found in the garage. As he unwrapped it, the handle gleamed like an emerald.

"I have several swords, mostly ceremonial. This is my battle sword, actually a hunting weapon crafted for me about a year ago. The grip is of green-dyed ivory, with a decorative silver strip."

He pulled the sword from its silver-trimmed, leather scabbard with care.

"It was forged of steel with a slightly curved, grooved blade, by an immigrant cutler from Sheffield, England. At the hilt it has only a simple silver-mounted cross guard and pommel, no shell or knuckle guard, as none is needed for hunting."

"Unless you're hunting Redcoats," I said.

It was clearly a handcrafted work of artistic weaponry, created in a different era, neither modern nor manufactured.

"Have you used this sword in combat?" I asked. "I mean, do you actually fight with the sword in hand-to-hand combat, or do you mostly wave it around while leading your troops?"

"I have sometimes been forced to use this sword against other soldiers, Timothy, yes," he said in a quiet voice.

Rachel whispered to me. "I think it's on exhibit at the Smithsonian."

I thought about that for a while.

How can George's sword be in two places at once? How can it be in Berkeley with us and also in a museum in Washington? How can George be here in California, while his remains are in Virginia?

How does all that work, anyway?

I searched on my phone for images of Washington during the War of Independence. In most paintings, he was dressed as I had first seen him at the dog park: breeches, shirt, jacket with brass buttons and gold epaulets, boots, hat, cape. The same clothes we saw today. In the Battle of Monmouth painting we had seen at Cal, he brandished a sword with a curved blade similar to this one. Though it's difficult to see the grip in the painting, the sword appears to have no guard at the hilt, only a small cross piece, like the one he had just shown us. But in Leutze's other famous painting, *Washington Crossing the Delaware*, he stands in the boat, one leg raised up on the gunwale in a heroic pose. Hanging saucily from his belt: the green-gripped sword from the burlap bag.

It all fit.

Of course there was no photographic evidence from that era, and I knew that Leutze had painted his Revolutionary War scenes more than half a century later. But now we knew that George's garments and sword looked authentic.

But wait. Despite being born in 1732, the George Washington standing in my kitchen was clearly only 46 years old. If we could do forensic testing, would it show that the sword in the bag was 260 years old, like the one at the Smithsonian? Or would the tests show it was still relatively new, after traveling through time with its owner?

The conundrum deepened!

Chapter Twenty-Nine
PIERRE

Berkeley, September 29, 2014

Baseball season ended, the Giants mired in second place. Their only road to the playoffs led through the Wild Card Game later in the week.

I slept late, then staggered to the front door to pick up the *San Francisco Chronicle* before I made coffee.

One of the stories on the front page, an account of a shooting in San Jose, was written in Spanish. Very odd. No acknowledgment of this unusual choice, no explanation of this deviation from the norm, just in Spanish. The rest of the front-page stories were in English. Of course they were. This was an English-language newspaper in a primarily English-speaking country.

I looked through the paper. About a fifth of all the stories were in Spanish. Also, a few ads in the back pages appeared to be in Russian.

My phone rang.

"Hello?"

"Mr. Morrison? This is Chow."

"Who?"

"Pierre Chow. I met you recently with Agent Oreck."

"Oh, the FBI guy."

"I'm a consultant."

"Whatever. What's up?"

"I need to meet with you."

"Why?"

"It's very important, trust me."

"Trust you? Why should I trust you when you guys laughed us out of the office at our last meeting?"

"Oreck laughed at you and sent you on your way. I was and remain very concerned about your discovery."

"Discovery?"

"You know what I mean." He paused, then added in a hissing whisper: "The General."

"Oh." *Does he believe us?*

"I need to meet with you."

"When?"

"Now, if possible. I'm nearby. On Solano Avenue, near the BART tracks."

"You're here in Berkeley, around the corner from my house? Are you stalking me?"

"No, of course not. But I am in your area. Please meet with me. It's of vital importance."

I was intensely curious, of course, but wary. The memory of my anxiety attack at the FBI office rippled through me. I needed to reduce my stress level, to get someone else to take responsibility for George.

Approach with caution alarms clanged in my head.

"Okay, I'll meet you, but only if I can name the place."

"Anywhere."

"Walk down Solano, away from the hills. One block before you get to San Pablo Avenue, on the left side, you'll find a place called the Burger Depot. Opposite the Albany Theatre. I'll meet you there in fifteen minutes."

"Okay. Please come alone."

"Why?"

"I don't think the General should be seen in public anymore."

What the hell does that mean?

I hurried off to the rendezvous, through the familiar neighborhood where I had grown up. At first, everything seemed much the same on Solano Avenue. The copy store and the sandwich shop were still there, the post office across the street, the movie theatre on the next block. Then I noticed that what had been a Thai restaurant now advertised *¡Empanadas! ¡Tamales!* from a large, crudely handprinted sign. Next door was a small shop selling piroshkis. Oddly, though I didn't remember either place, these shops looked run-down, as if they had been there for a long time.

I arrived at the meeting place I had described to Chow. The building I remembered from my childhood was still there, but the sign said *La Estación de Hamburguesas.*

When had this happened? I had frequented the Burger Depot since I was a wee tot. Actually, since I was *in utero.* It had always been run by a kindly couple from Hong Kong named David and Daisy. I entered and walked up to the counter.

"Where is David?" I asked the stranger at the cash register.

"*¿Cómo?*"

"*¿Dónde está David?*"

"*¡Yo soy David!*" He emphasized the second syllable and

looked nothing like the Chinese guy I was asking about.

"How long have you owned this place?"

"*¿Cómo? Margarita, ven aquí!*"

Margarita? This David's wife was named Margarita, not Daisy.

The menu was similar to the one I remembered, except that some items were missing—gardenburgers, frankfurters, and egg salad. And some items were new: *chili relleno* burgers, *chorizo* on a bun, Cordoba steaks, and Madrid sandwiches. I ordered a plain hamburger.

"*¿Salsa?*" asked *el nuevo David*.

"Uh, no thanks."

I looked around. The paint job felt unfamiliar, the place shabby, run-down. In one corner, as always, an interior door led into the next storefront, the ice cream counter for what had been the Burger Depot. For as long as I could remember, the sign over this walkthrough had said Ice Cream Avenue. Now it said *Avenida de Helado*.

Pierre Chow waited at a corner table, watching me closely.

I approached him. "Mr. Chow. What's up?"

"Mr. Morrison."

"Everyone calls me Tim."

He offered me a fist bump, then signaled me to sit, his long legs entwined among the wire legs of the chair. I took the seat opposite him.

"Why did you call me? You and Agent Oreck didn't believe us. He practically threw us out of the office."

"Oreck is a fool. The FBI is still caught up in its Hooverian, gangster-fighting image. Their favorite wet dream is pursuing Al Capone or Ma Barker."

"They're both dead."

"So is J. Edgar. The Bureau lives in the past."

"Did you bring me here just to trash your employer, Mr. Chow?"

"They're not my employer. And call me Pierre."

"Okay. Pierre."

"I did fact-check some of your story. There were indeed two earthquakes in the Philadelphia/Valley Forge area the year Washington encamped there. Highly unusual, but a historical fact. And the aurora *was* visible from that region, during a spectacular display one or two nights that same winter. Both events scared superstitious soldiers."

He paused and looked out the window at the alley in back. "As Agent Oreck mentioned at our meeting, I am a consultant to the FBI. But my employer is a different federal agency."

I listened attentively.

He flipped open a leather badge case.

"Department of Homeland Security?"

He nodded. "I need your trust, Tim. I work for the POA."

"What does that stand for?"

"The Positive Outcomes Authority. It's a branch of DHS."

"Isn't Homeland Security just a bunch of baggage sniffers?"

"No, our department has a quarter million employees in many areas. Besides TSA and airline security and divisions that plan against nuclear, biological, and cyber-based threats, DHS's responsibilities include FEMA and disaster management, citizenship and immigration, customs and borders, the Coast Guard, and the Secret Service."

"So?"

"The POA has been a small part of DHS since the founding of the Department after 9/11. Before that, we were in the Department of Defense. We are consulted whenever a case like yours comes up."

"What does that mean?"

"We attempt to influence developments in a positive way, to create outcomes in line with the results we seek."

"Like a lobbying group?"

"Well, yes, a bit like that, though we aren't charged with influencing the votes of legislators or the decisions of administrators."

"An advertising agency?"

"It's a bit more direct than that."

I thought of *Independence*, my video game. "Are you assassins?"

He laughed, the first time he had broken his poker face, then, with a sigh, unwrapped his lanky legs from the chair and straightened them out. He seemed to come to a decision.

"We always attempt to influence events peacefully, to stimulate a positive outcome. Hence, the name."

"I'm lost. You influence events, but you don't lobby and aren't assassins."

"Rarely."

"Please explain. And what does this have to do with me? And George?"

"As I said, we are often called in to consult on cases like this."

"Like what? What do you want from me?"

I'm getting annoyed. Where is this conversation leading?

He hesitated. We sat quietly, staring at each other.

"What do you want?" I repeated.

"Situations like that of your friend, where someone has

apparently ... undergone an inadvertent displacement of his temporal vector."

"A TVD?"

"What?"

"A temporal vector displacement? Isn't everything a TLA with you guys?"

"What's a TLA?"

"A three-letter acronym."

"Of course." He smiled tightly.

"Displacement of the temporal vector occurs, Mr. Morrison, when a person becomes relocated, so to speak, in the chronological sense."

"Oh. Time travel."

"Now do you understand why I have contacted you?"

"You believe me."

"Yes. We believe you, and we believe it is essential to get General Washington back to Valley Forge."

Chapter Thirty
EINSTEIN

I froze for a minute. I could feel my heart pounding in my chest as I tried to get a deep breath.

"Let's, let's get out of here," I croaked.

"You haven't eaten your burger."

"Not hungry. Let's go."

We stepped onto the street, strolled up one side of the block, then down the other. Chow looked at me with concern. I took a few deep breaths and began to feel better.

"Coffee?"

"Sure."

We entered the café on the corner, ordered lattes, and took a table in the back, away from people. Chow was carrying a black laptop bag. In the background I could hear Charlie Parker playing "I Didn't Know What Time It Was," and I tuned right in. Uncle Chuck had taught me a lot about jazz.

We'd been close. I missed him every day. The heartache ebbed a bit when Aunt Rachel gave Nevada to me, and I kept her service harness and his white-tipped cane in my trunk to honor his memory. He also left me twenty thousand dollars, which would help with grad school.

The soft music in the café calmed me down.

"Does this happen often? Where someone's temporal vector has become displaced?"

"More often than you would guess, I expect. Displacements can occur either deliberately or accidentally. We strongly suspect that General Washington's displacement was accidental. An error, really."

That was a lot for me to chew on.

"So, George is here by accident? Tell me, what could cause a deliberate displacement?"

"We could."

"The POA?"

"Yes. To create positive outcomes. As I said earlier."

Do I want to know more?

"How do you do that?"

"We … have a device."

"A time machine? Oh sure!"

"We don't call it that. H.G. Wells co-opted that term. But yes, that's what it is. Surely you believe in time travel, after your weeks with the General?"

I thought about that for a while. I did think that the man I had left at home in my "Tokyo Sushi. That's How We Roll" T-shirt was the real George Washington. But I had no idea how he had been transported to the twenty-first century. Until recently, I had never considered whether time travel could be real, much less deliberate or accidental. I gulped down my latte.

"I am starting to," I said finally. "Tell me more."

Again, he hesitated.

"Dude, you can't just leave me hanging."

"How much do you know about the American Revolution?" he asked.

"A bit. And I've learned a lot more since meeting George."

"Do you remember much about the foreign officers who joined Washington's staff during the war?"

"Like Lafayette?"

"Yes. Lafayette was a French nobleman, certainly the best known, and personally close to Washington. There were others, including a Polish cavalry officer named Pulaski, and, quite prominently, a Prussian general named Baron von Steuben."

"What about them?"

"We sent them back to help Washington win the war."

"What? When?"

"Over a long period of time. Analysts at our agency, and its predecessors, decided decades ago that the Revolution was not a sure thing."

"Decades ago?"

"That's all classified, of course, but suffice it to say that, during World War II and the Cold War, the U.S. military conducted scientific research in time travel, spurred by Albert Einstein. He had it all figured out early in the twentieth century. He foresaw time travel as early as 1905 with his Special Theory of Relativity and his Theory of General Relativity. He explained that space-time exists in four dimensions, and that both time and space can warp as speed or mass increase to massive, near-infinite levels. At least theoretically. So the Allies had to co-opt him, bring him over to our side."

"How?"

"It wasn't difficult. Germany in the '30s became a dangerous place for Jewish intellectuals. Einstein moved to Belgium, then Britain for a while. Eventually we induced him to settle far from the Nazis' devastation of Europe, in Princeton, where he spent the rest of his days thinking, researching, and interacting with the most brilliant minds on the planet. Much of his time was spent working on the device."

"Einstein invented it? During World War II?"

"During his lifetime, he was deeply involved with creating a crude prototype, until his death in 1955."

"Wait. You're telling me that the government has had a working time machine—"

"Device."

"A working time displacement device, since the 1950s?"

"Well, the final version wasn't perfected till about the mid '60s, but yes."

"Final version? That's the latest technology? From the '60s?"

"There have been some upgrades. Originally, our technicians had to perform many calculations and auto-location protocols manually. Now we've added a plug-in GPS module, some portable structural elements, and a PC interface."

"You can control it from a computer?"

"Or a smart phone!" He beamed with pride. "There's an app for that."

Did he wink?

Somehow, in the context of the past few weeks, this all seemed perfectly plausible. Hanging around with a 200-years-dead ex-president had begun to feel normal. You believed it because you believed it, because there was no other explanation that seemed any less cray cray. Occam's razor postulated that the simplest explanation, the one with the fewest assumptions, was most often likely to be true. This all made sense, as long as you believed in time travel. If you didn't, it was all gibberish.

"Okay, so you have this device, and you've had it for a long time."

"Yes."

"And you've sent people back? To the Revolution?"

"Yes. Most of those foreign officers who appeared at Washington's side were sent back by us. Did you really think they just magically materialized?"

"Yes. That's what I learned in school."

"Well, I suppose that's not hopelessly naive. Most Americans bought it."

"Lafayette wasn't a French nobleman? He came from our time?"

"Lafayette *was* a French nobleman from Washington's time, but he was apolitical. We plucked him out of France in his teens, took him to a training center in another century, schooled him in military technique and leadership, and re-educated him to support the American cause. Then we sent him back, provided a convincing backstory about how he got there, and dropped him on Washington's doorstep."

"Why would Lafayette agree to that?"

"We promised him fame, adventure, women. And once he had embraced our political education, he realized he could have a huge influence on the revolutionary movements in both the U.S. and France. The man was a true patriot, on both sides of the Atlantic."

It makes sense, I thought. *I always wondered how Lafayette got involved in our revolution.*

"Pulaski was the real deal. He came over from Europe under his own steam, truly wishing to assist the American drive to independence. But Baron von Steuben was a completely different kettle of fish. That's where the anomaly arose."

"The Prussian? How so?"

Chow glanced around the café furtively, satisfying himself that no one was paying attention to us.

"Well, he isn't really a baron, and he isn't really a general. He's an actor, a stuntman really. We recruited him from a Hollywood studio backlot in the 1930s. He's a tough guy, homely, unattached, a German immigrant with poor English skills, but a strong personality. We took him to the same re-education center as Lafayette. Got him indoctrinated and drilled in military procedure, discipline, and tactics. Then, a few weeks ago, when he was ready, we sent him back in time to meet General Washington."

"Where? And when?"

"Our plan was to send him from Valley Forge, after the park was closed for the night. We had a spot picked out north of Farmer Potts' house, Washington's headquarters. An old boarding platform next to the railroad track, near the trees and overlooking the river. It was easy to find and secluded, and only an occasional freight train comes through there these days. We sent von Steuben back to an evening in February 1778, on Washington's birthday, a week or two after the General's wife arrived in camp. We hoped that would be a crucial month for the Colonial forces. We felt that Washington sorely needed von Steuben's assistance, and we knew that the French would soon be announcing their alliance with the fledgling United States. That was largely Lafayette's doing. He needed no prodding to proffer his influence with Louis XVI, the French king. Ben Franklin, who was posted to Paris for many years, also had a lot to do with that."

"This is a lot to take in," I said, getting up from the table.

I went to the counter and carefully selected a chocolate chip cookie. Something by Coltrane was playing, something mellow that I couldn't name.

I looked around. The other patrons chatted casually or seemed absorbed in their newspapers, phones, and laptops. Here in this chill, uber-normal setting, no one had any idea that a lanky, Asian-American Homeland Security agent—no, a POA agent!—was telling me the most preposterous tale about the workings of vast historical forces.

I sat back down with Chow.

"What was the anomaly?"

He looked uncomfortable and started twisting his long legs.

"You can't hold out on me, man. What was it?"

"The bounce."

"The bounce?"

"Occasional anomalies can occur with our device. When we send an individual back in time, we sometimes inadvertently bounce another person out of the past, someone who is fairly close to the arrival of a deliberate temporal displacement. We think that's what happened with General Washington. Oddly, when we sent the baron back, Washington was in almost the same location, back in his own time, probably right about where the train track is now. He got sucked into the future."

"This has happened before? This bounce effect?"

"Yes. Einstein couldn't solve it, but it hasn't been a terrible problem before this."

"Why not?"

"Most of the time, the person who gets bounced is easy to find. But just as von Steuben was sent back, the freight train came along, in 2014. We were surprised. No one had checked the schedule. 110 cars. It took the train six minutes to pass that point. Washington apparently ended up in one of the cars, but we didn't figure that out for quite a while. Weeks ago, we had a report that he was seen at a Giants game. Then we lost touch with him. Until you brought him in to Oreck's office."

"Why didn't you contact me sooner?"

"We were glad to know where Washington was, but we didn't realize, until recently, how much danger you faced."

Chapter Thirty-One
PARANOIA

Chow stopped and glanced at his watch. He looked stricken. "I have to go."

"Go? How can you go now? I have a million questions! Where is the time machine? Can I see it?"

"In time, Tim, I have no doubt that you'll see it."

"You can't show it to me now?"

"I don't have it with me," he said, with careful sarcasm. "It's not something that fits in your pocket."

"What's in the bag? Did you bring a laptop?"

"Yes, but it's not for that. There's something else I was going to show you, but I've spent far too much time explaining and not enough time planning. You'd be surprised to learn how little you really need to know."

"Really? How could I possibly know how little I need to know, when, as it stands, I don't know a damn thing?"

Chow shrugged. "You speak in riddles, grasshopper. The point is, for today I've run out of time."

"What do we do with the General? How much danger

is he in? And how about the rest of us?"

I had told Chow about Aunt Rachel's hit-and-run "accident" and wondered aloud if it had been intended as an attack on George. I was desperate to resolve something, afraid that after this incredible tale Chow would slip away, and I'd never see him again.

"We still need to figure out what to do, Tim. The consequences of his not returning to Valley Forge are huge, as you can guess. We must get him back there. And soon."

"Frankly, Mr. Chow, I fail to see why this is my problem. Why don't you take him with you now?"

He smiled. "That does seem like it would be simple, doesn't it? But there are dark forces at work, and we must sit tight for right now. Not everyone has the same goals here. The next time I see you, I'll tell you more about that, and we can hatch a plan together. Meanwhile, keep the General under wraps. Indoors. And keep your eyes and ears open. Washington has now been gone from Valley Forge for a while, and changes have begun to occur. Have you noticed anything?"

I thought about the *Chronicle*, the empanada place, the Burger Depot.

"Things are becoming much more Mexican around here."

"Not more Mexican, Tim. Much more Spanish. And more Russian."

The piroshki shop.

"Without Washington leading the American Revolution, colonialism might flourish for another millennium, around the world. We'll talk about that next time. Be alert. And be careful."

He slipped out the door, laptop bag in hand.

I sat there, stunned, and closed my eyes.

"Bitches Brew" washed over me, Miles Davis' discordant trumpet solos, clanging chords, and oddly compelling percussion rhythms jangling my nerves. A shudder of uncertainty overtook me. I sat for a minute, then opened my eyes. Not much had changed. I was still sitting in a suburban coffee house, still nursing the last slurps of a latte gone cold. But now I was suspicious of everyone.

Who are all these people, sitting in this cafe in the middle of the day? Why aren't they at work or in school?

Dark forces? What did he mean by "not everyone has the same goals here"?

I stared out the window at a sign for *Banco de España*. Hadn't that place always been a Wells Fargo?

I walked back to my house. The neighborhood was placid, but I felt utterly paranoid. I scanned every shadow, peeped around every corner. I recalled one time in high school, when Matt and I dropped Ecstasy and went to a 10 a.m. show of *Carrie*, the Stephen King horror flick. After watching Cissy Spacek degenerate through that ghastly and immersive tale of teleportation, hellfire, and revenge, we emerged—blasted out of our minds—into a noontime crowd in sunny, downtown Berkeley, afraid Carrie could be lurking in any doorway. But whereas she had sought vengeance, the folks around us merely sought lunch.

I shared most of what I had learned with George and Matt, though I decided not to tell George yet that Chow's people were sending him foreign officers to assist the Revolution.

"What is this DHS?" he asked.

"Department of Homeland Security," Rachel said. "Among other things, they spy on people."

George brightened. "They spy? On whom do they

spy?"

"Well, lately, it seems, on all of us," she said. "Americans spying on Americans, and on foreigners, too."

"Why should we trust those guys?" Matt said. "I don't trust anything about Homeland Security!"

"For one thing," I explained, "they believe us—or at least this guy Chow does. They are responsible for George being here in the first place, and they want to return him to Valley Forge."

"Indeed," George nodded, "that is a compelling argument. I am intrigued to hear more about their spying. It is of vital importance to know your allies—and your enemies too, of course."

He leaned in and lowered his voice.

"My army needs better intelligence. I need a network of spies to provide information. Yes, Americans spying on Americans—and on the English, of course—all to benefit our fight for freedom." He looked wistful. "I would dearly love to know about enemy fortifications, size of military units, troop movements, ships arriving or departing, soldiers bragging about their exploits, or sailors gossiping about their service orders.

"I wish to understand more about the 'head game' of spying. Strategy is best decided based on accurate intelligence, combined with a deep-seated desire to outlast your opponent. Attack when fortifications or troop strengths are weakened, stand pat when they are strong."

"But, George," Matt said cautiously, "the very nature of spying is living a lie. Isn't that all a bit dishonest?"

"Yes, LaMatthew, I suppose it is. But all in a good cause, eh, lads?"

"Doesn't that work against your reputation for honesty?" Matt challenged. "You know, the cherry tree thing."

"What cherry tree thing?"

"When you chopped down the cherry tree, then admitted to your father that you had done it."

George scowled. "My father died when I was eleven years old."

"Yes, but we learned in school that you chopped down a cherry tree when you were a young boy. When asked about it by your father, you confessed, saying 'I cannot tell a lie.'"

"I chopped down no cherry tree! And I shall willingly lie, steal, or cheat to free our people from tyranny!"

"Matty," I said. "I think it's a myth."

"I'm sure," offered Rachel, "that George never threw a dollar across the Potomac River, either. It's over a mile wide."

Despite George's tribute to espionage, we were all befuddled, uncertain how to proceed. Clearly we had to get him back to his army. It was difficult to sit tight and wait to hear from Pierre again.

Meanwhile, odd things continued to happen. Within a week, nearly half the *Chronicle* was in Spanish, as were some of the network TV stations. A Russian-language newspaper appeared in the beat-up news racks on Solano. Another restaurant or two popped up serving dishes with names like *pollo de ajo* and *judías con jamón*. A Chinese joint on the corner disappeared, and a run-down lunch counter selling borscht and beef stroganoff took its place, looking as if it had been in that location for years.

Perhaps it was my imagination or my foul mood, but the traffic seemed slower, the energy and creative juices of the people appeared to ebb. The sparkling cultural community I had grown up in began to feel stale and uninspired. For the first time in memory, a few vacant storefronts appeared in the neighborhood.

The changes were sporadic and incremental. Many eating places remained the same, and baseball season continued uninterrupted. Cal continued to function as a university, and other schools were open and teaching. At times, it felt as though the world were devolving into something else. Yet much of it remained intact.

Small comfort. My paranoia continued. Several times I was convinced that someone was following me on the street, so I ducked into a doorway. I spotted a nondescript fellow in a Raiders cap checking out store windows, staying about a half block behind me. Another time, I was sure a green van was following me in the Corolla, but it continued past me when I pulled over.

Chapter Thirty-Two
EXTRAS

The Giants' first challenge of the postseason was a single-game playoff against the Pirates, the Wild Card Game. I watched with Matt and George and Rachel, who seemed to be on the mend.

The Giants won handily, 8-0. Bumgarner pitched the whole game, a four-hit shutout. A big, powerful country boy with a dark beard, long hair, and arms like tree trunks, he looked unhittable and unbeatable.

The next opponent was the Nationals, in a best-of-five series. Game two was an epic battle. The Nats scored in the third, then led 1-0 the rest of the way. Until the ninth. Down to their last out, the Giants rallied to tie it. Both teams bore down. The tenth inning came and went, then the eleventh, with no further runs for a long time. The game dragged out over six hours.

Finally, in the eighteenth inning, the Giants' Brandon Belt ripped a home run to deep right field to win it. Amazing! The longest postseason game in the 130-year history of Major League Baseball. We jumped up and down with excitement and exhaustion.

I tried to show George *Independence*, the Revolutionary War game I was playing on my laptop, but it didn't go well. The Washington character didn't look or sound much like George did IRL (gamer talk for In Real Life). And he had trouble understanding if the game was something real from the past, a live event, or a movie.

Those were the limits of his understanding of looking glasses. I explained that the game was like a movie, except that we could control where the characters went and what they did. This interactivity puzzled him, especially since he was the main character.

Chapter Thirty-Three
FORESIGHT

Berkeley, October 7, 2014

I had no way to reach Chow, so he had to initiate the next contact. It took more than a week.

"Where have you been?" I asked, nearly in a panic.

"Trying to make some arrangements. I've got stuff to show you. Where can you meet me? Someplace with Wi-Fi."

"Come to my house."

"No, I don't think that's a good idea."

We met at the Starbucks at the top of Solano Avenue. A nice, airy place, easy online access, good sight lines. Again, he brought the laptop bag. We grabbed a corner table, out of the flow of traffic.

"How are you, Tim?"

"Awful!" I snapped, in a hoarse whisper. "Why did you tell me that ludicrous story, then run out? If what you say is true, then why aren't *you* taking the General back to where and when he belongs? How could you leave me hanging like that?"

"Okay, I'll explain everything, all in good time. Everything I told you is true, and we need your help to move General Washington to Valley Forge."

"That's ridiculous. Why would Homeland Security need my help? And how do you expect me to believe that you send people back in time?"

"It's true."

"If you could do that, why wouldn't you guys take other actions to change history? What about World War II?"

"What about it?"

"How could you allow that to happen?"

"Something had to be done to stop Hitler."

"Yeah, but that's my point—how could you allow Hitler to happen?"

Chow opened his mouth, as if to speak. Then he closed it. He wouldn't meet my eyes.

"Oh my god, your agency is responsible for Hitler?"

"I didn't say that."

"Will you deny it?"

Silence. Then, "Tim, there were some elements in the Authority who thought Hitler would be ... useful ... to help Europe shake off the economic devastation of the 1920s and 30s and oppose the spread of Bolshevism. Obviously, he got a bit ... out of control."

Still wouldn't look me in the eye.

"So you played God and unleashed that malevolent force upon the world! That immoral decision cost millions of lives!"

"I'm not proud of the agency's history there. But we did give FDR the atomic bomb."

It was my turn to be silent. How could all this have happened? Furthermore, if Hitler came to power as a result of the POA's meddling, it was suddenly much easier to imagine the colonists losing the Revolution and the resultant catastrophic effects on our culture and history.

"Back to the business at hand. Please!" Chow insisted. "Have you noticed any changes going on around you?"

"Hell, yes!" I told him about the dereliction and degeneration I'd seen in the community.

"Right. Very similar to what we expected."

He pulled out the laptop, logged in to the wireless, and launched an application. Soon we were looking at a satellite map of our section of Berkeley.

"Mr. Chow," I began.

"Pierre."

I wasn't used to that yet.

"Okay. Pierre. What program is this? It looks like Google Earth."

"The engine is quite similar, as is the reliance on satellite maps. But this is Foresight, a proprietary computer modeling program the POA developed."

"Did Einstein invent this, too?" I was feeling snarky.

"No," he laughed. "This is much newer. It allows us to visualize any part of the world, then model the effect on the future—or even the present—of a change in historical events or circumstances."

"Explain." Despite my sarcasm, I was interested.

"If we zero out everything, applying no changes to our world, then we can view neighborhoods, cities, even larger areas as they appear today. That's when it works just like Google Earth. But even small changes in our time can cause enormous changes down the road. Have you heard of the butterfly effect?"

"Isn't that just sci-fi mumbo-jumbo?"

"Only if you choose to see it that way."

"How can the beating of a butterfly's wings change the course of a faraway storm?"

"Perhaps it can't. But the American colonists losing their Revolution could certainly change world history."

That shut me up.

"Without the inspiration of the American War of Independence, the European colonialists could thrive and dominate the globe for centuries. Check this out."

He typed in the address of the block where I lived. The bird's-eye view was familiar and crisp.

"I've preloaded a new model, where the Brits defeat the United States. The thirteen colonies remain just that."

He clicked through some screens, then hit a green button. The bird's-eye view changed. As we zoomed in, I could see that the cars looked old, the brands unfamiliar, the foliage overgrown everywhere. He clicked on Street View, and we "drove" down my block. My house looked awful. Run-down, filthy, a sickly green color, the front porch askew from a sinking foundation or perhaps earthquake damage.

"Hey, Timmy, how ya doing? What's that? Some kinda map?"

A guy I'd gone to school with was sitting at a nearby table. I chatted distractedly with him till he lost interest, then turned back to Pierre. He had closed the laptop.

"What a nightmare!" I whispered tensely. "Is it like this everywhere?"

"I've looked this over pretty carefully. Most of western North America is still a colony of Spain, and Russia has a significant presence in the Northwest."

"Russia?"

"Remember, they had colonies in Alaska and down the

California coast as far as Fort Ross, less than 100 miles from San Francisco. The eastern half of the continent is still English in this model. The mother countries all exploit their colonies, impose high taxes, control production and agriculture, bleed the colonists dry, and provide few services for their long-suffering populations. Except for a handful of local exploiters, most North Americans are powerless, poor, and defeated. Now do you understand why we need to get the General back?"

"Of course I do. But why are we wasting time? Why don't you and your POA just fly him to Valley Forge and send him back to his own time?"

Chapter Thirty-Four
COMPLICATED

Pierre looked sheepish.

"Well, it's complicated."

"Why, because there are 'dark forces'?"

"Exactly. Not everyone believes we should send him back."

"Really? How could anyone want this bleak future?"

"Evildoers believe they could subjugate and pillage the population more effectively if North America remained under the thumb of the imperialist powers."

"Evildoers?"

"Powerful people who dominate others through illegal drugs. Some want to keep this continent colonized, so they can sell addictive drugs to a beaten-down population."

"Cartels?"

"The drug cartels sell their narcotic poisons to down-trodden slum dwellers. They willingly destroy the fabric of society for profit."

"How do the drug cartels know about this awful alternate reality?"

He looked embarrassed. "They also have computers."

"But only Foresight can give them this projection, right?"

"Exactly. They are criminals. And they use deadly force." He left the rest unsaid.

"They stole Foresight?"

"Essentially. We believe they have compromised someone in the POA and stolen the software. When we found out, we changed our log-in procedures and other security protocols, but now I'm not sure who I can trust. So, I'm trying to run this operation without involving too many other people in the Authority. Apparently the bad guys know from their mole that General Washington disappeared from Valley Forge. They have modeled the future and come to the same conclusions that we did. But they probably didn't know where the General was until the day you took him to the ballpark and his image was splashed across a huge screen."

"Oh no! The Kiss Cam!"

"Yes. His face was seen by thousands in the ballpark and millions watching on TV. Their spies are everywhere. They probably still don't know exactly where he is, or they would have closed in by now. I don't want to worry you, but have you seen or felt anyone following you?"

"Spanish guys? Russians?"

"Thugs of any description. They're an equal opportunity employer."

I told him about the guy in the Raiders cap, the green van.

"Hmm. Sounds like they're not watching you too closely. Probably not sure if you're the guy they want. Try to move evasively. Lead them in circles till they get tired of following, but don't reveal that you know you're being followed. Most of all, continue to keep General Washington inside, under wraps. Do not show his face in public again. And soon—very soon—we'll get him out of town and back where he belongs."

"What are you waiting for?"

"I have to move slowly, since we're a bit stymied by the mole at the POA. I'll be in touch in the next week or so. No longer, I promise."

Despite my ambivalence, my path was colliding with vast forces that were shaping world history. I remembered Frodo moaning, "I wish none of this had happened" in *The Lord of the Rings*. And Gandalf's response, "It is not for you to decide."

But I wasn't a hobbit in a fantasy saga. I was just a regular guy, a former teacher and future grad student, stuck in a bureaucratic limbo till my fellowship started in January.

"Please give me your phone number, or some other way to contact you."

Chow—or Pierre—thought for a moment, hating to break his own cover, then said, "I'll send you a text. Reply to that text only if you must contact me urgently."

"Okay."

"Trust that I'll get back to you as soon as I can. Do not place a voice call to that number."

"One more thing. How can I see more of Foresight and show it to George? He's getting to like it in the present. Life is much easier here and now, but I don't want him to get too comfortable. He's got to go back and front the War of Independence. I think it would be helpful for us to poke around with your computer model. Maybe we can discover something about our future world that will help us in the present. And the past."

"I wondered about that. It's strictly against the rules, of course. But frankly, I'm already breaking a lot of POA rules. Because of the mole, I have to act independently."

"You're going rogue?" I thought of Sarah Palin and smiled with ironic pain.

"I am willing to go out on a limb here. I could get you a copy of the software, but ..." He hesitated.

"What?"

"Well, the software is for Windows only, and you seem like a Mac guy."

Unbelievable. The future of our world was at stake, and the application that could save us was platform-specific!

"I am a Mac guy, mostly, but I also have a Windows laptop for gaming. I'm playing *Independence* on it, which has a storyline involving George Washington. It's got good processor speed and a killer graphics card."

Pierre glazed over. "Okay, okay, I'll get you a thumb drive. Installation is easy and setting up the computer model should be pretty straightforward. It's an online app, so you need Internet access. The drive will just give you the interface; the data and future-simulation processing all come from the cloud."

"How will you get it to me?"

"I will get it to you."

He stood up.

"Don't follow me out too quickly, and take a circuitous route home. You're just out for a stroll. No goal or schedule. The more purposeful you look, the more they'll assume you're involved in something serious."

"I am."

"Yes, but now you have to show off your acting skills.

I'll be in touch very soon, and we'll get you guys on the road."

"Get *us* on the road?"

"Don't worry, I'll be with you. Or someone will, anyway. Talk soon!"

He slipped out the door. I waited a while, then headed out in the opposite direction and meandered home.

Matt, Rachel, and George were watching the Giants win their playoff series against the Nationals. Washington (the team, not our General) had won only one game. The Giants won each of their three victories by just one run.

Matt turned to me as the game ended.

"No homers again."

"What is the significance of that statement, LaMatthew?" George asked.

"Each team had only one home run in the entire series. Belt's blast in the eighteenth inning was the Giants' only homer."

"This dearth of home runs is typical of a huge change of direction in baseball," I added. "In the early days of the twenty-first century, the now-notorious steroid era, performance-enhancing drugs allowed ball players to bulk up their biceps and pump up their pectorals so they could hit the long ball with ease."

George's eyes narrowed. "Drugs? Does such behavior constitute a form of cheating?"

"Yes. Organized baseball ignored it for a while, because the players' chemically enhanced hitting power was exciting to the fans," I said. "Then they began to clean up their own nest, but by that time the cheating had gone on for years. Now, in many cases, professional baseball is returning to the basics.

"Timely hitting, stifling pitching, sharp fielding, and

radical defensive alignments based on player hitting data have led to a reborn small-ball style. Teams can manufacture runs by getting men on base and advancing them relentlessly with walks, singles, and sacrifices, often without hitting the ball into the stands."

"Adapting their strategy to make the most of their talents," said George, impressed. "The clever triumph over the mighty."

So far, it had worked for the Giants.

Chapter Thirty-Five
DEAD DROP

Berkeley, October 14, 2014

I chewed my nails for a week, waiting for something to happen. Eventually I got a text from a blocked phone number. A text message with no text, just a photo. It seemed to be a driveway or an alley, empty and bleak, but I was at a loss to identify the location.

"Maybe it's from Chow, about the software for Foresight," Matt said.

"But what does it mean? What is he trying to tell me?"

George examined the picture carefully.

"Perhaps Agent Chow has hidden the item he is giving you here. Perhaps he wishes to avoid direct contact, so he has left this thing, this thumb driver—"

"Thumb drive."

"Quite so. Perhaps this thumb driver is in this location, and he is attempting to communicate the location to you."

"In a cryptic way."

"Yes, quite surreptitious, Timothy."

"George is right. It's a dead drop!" Matt said.

"Eh? What is the meaning of this term?"

"A dead drop, George. It's a spy term. Chow has something for Tim, so he leaves it in a tree stump or under a bush, Tim retrieves it, and *voilà!* The item has been passed without the danger of Tim and Chow having another face-to-face meeting."

"That makes sense, but where is this place?" I asked. "And what took him so long?"

"He told you that his organization's internal security has been jeopardized," Matt said. "He's trying to keep this on the down low, as secret as possible."

"Okay, I can buy that. But where on earth is this?" I wondered, looking at the picture again.

That evening, we settled in to watch the first game of the National League Championship Series. The Giants shut out the Cardinals 3-0 in St. Louis. Round, brown Pablo Sandoval had three hits and a walk. Our boys would go on to win three of the first four games, all relying on small ball, without the benefit of a home run.

I went for a walk and strolled idly down Solano, lost in thought. George hated being confined to my house. I felt I had to trust Chow, despite the fact that I couldn't figure out his picture riddle.

I stopped at *La Estación de Hamburguesas*, greeted *el nuevo David*, eschewed the Spanish food, and ordered my favorite avocado-mushroom-turkey cheeseburger. I waited at the same table where I'd sat with Chow, staring out the window. Behind the place I still thought of as the Burger Depot, I could see the alley where the owners parked their cars.

After a few minutes waiting for my burger, I blinked, pulled out my phone, and compared my view through the window to the mysterious photo from Pierre.

Same place.

I stepped out back. Studying the picture, I zoomed in on the touch screen and scrolled around with finger swipes, puzzling over the meaning.

The picture looked much the same as the alley, except that, on the right side, some of the trash cans had been moved. Of course that happened every week when the garbage was collected. That alone meant nothing. But when I moved the can in front, then a second one, I spotted a black drainpipe that protruded about a foot from the wall then turned straight down and disappeared into the ground. Under the horizontal segment of the pipe, in the wall I found a gap a couple of inches high.

I reached inside. I could feel something—something plastic. I couldn't quite grasp it, so I pulled out a pen and stuck it into the hole, careful not to push the object in deeper. I wiggled and pried with the pen until the corner of a plastic bag emerged.

I pulled carefully. A snack-size ziplock bag. Inside I found a small, rectangular item made of red plastic. One end had a rounded cap, which covered a USB connector.

A thumb drive.

Chapter Thirty-Six
SPYCRAFT

Berkeley, October 16, 2014

George loved that he had been right about the dead drop. Matt and I offered to show him books and movies with more spycraft techniques.

"I wrestle constantly with the quandary of transporting information about the enemy," he explained. "Usually the information acquired is more complex than can or should be committed to the memory of one mere mortal. So we have the dilemma of moving written documents from behind enemy lines, without their discovery and confiscation by the English. These messages are often passed along by several people before their eventual delivery to me or my staff."

"Surely you know about invisible ink?" Matt asked.

George perked up, blue eyes glittering. "I have heard tell that such a thing exists, but know little else about it."

I jumped up. "There are several ways to do it."

I ran out to the lemon tree in our front yard and picked several bright-yellow fruits, ripe and bursting. Dashing back inside, I halved them, palmed them into a hand juicer, and released the tangy citrus juice into a bowl.

"You can also do this with milk or the juice of an onion," I added.

I then grabbed a sheet of paper and whipped out a black ballpoint pen. Leaving extra space between the lines, I proceeded to write, "Hi George. I have been wanting to tell you about the wonderful burrito I ate the other day. Lamb and vegetables, beans, rice, and hot sauce. Delicious!"

He watched over my shoulder with a puzzled frown.

"Timothy, you know I have become partial to the food of Mexico so prevalent in this area. And I recognize that you are using a French word, I believe, to indicate tastiness."

Matt laughed and told him, "That's not the point. Timmy and I used to do this in Boy Scouts."

"But how is this helpful to me?" George continued. "Your writing is plainly visible to the human eye. Will the juice of the lemons cause the writing from your stick pen to disappear?"

I dipped a toothpick into the lemon juice and asked George to sit across from me, so that he could watch me writing but not see the paper.

"I'm pretty sure you can do this with a writing quill, but I don't have one to test out."

I showed him the paper after it dried. It looked just as it had before I wrote in lemon juice. Then I held the paper over the floor lamp, close enough for it to heat up.

Between the banal burrito lines in black ballpoint, my secret message appeared in ominous brown letters: "General Washington, we must return you to your army in Valley Forge. Our world is falling apart!"

"Ah," George said. "I see now. And point taken. I

wholeheartedly agree with the sentiment expressed therein."

"There's another element of spycraft you should know about," Matt said. "Codes and ciphers." He looked at me. "Let's take him to see that movie on Solano. It's about breaking codes and ciphers in, uh, a recent war in England."

We took a chance and slipped George out of the house after dark and over to the Albany Theatre. I couldn't figure out how to give George any historical context for the film, so I advised him to keep an open mind and focus on the code techniques, not the world events depicted.

The Imitation Game was a biopic about Alan Turing and the breaking of the German Enigma Code by the British military in World War II. Even in that pre-electronic world, the Brits met the challenge with technology that would be impossible to transport to the late eighteenth century. At first I was disappointed that the story and the effort to beat the Enigma seemed irrelevant to the technology of the Revolutionary War. But George came away with a smile.

"I find the alliances a bit confusing, I must say. These people appear to be English, and yet the story convinces us to like them. Nevertheless, I am inspired by this great work."

"But obviously, you can't build a machine like the Enigma in Valley Forge."

"That does not matter, Timothy. The Enigma Code uses substitution, letter by letter. I agree that this would be too challenging for my own era. However, think about this: I would wager that we can make up a code where we substitute *words* for other *words*, assigning special meanings to significant words, so that we know, perhaps, that 'I ate a tasty apple' means 'the English attack Brooklyn on Monday.' Or some such thing."

"You would have to write a code book, detailing the

meanings of the substituted words," I pointed out. "And everyone participating would need a copy of the code book."

Matt warmed to the idea.

"A series of words, perhaps names of animals, could mean different cities. Names of various items of clothing could designate particular actions. You could list men's first names for days of the week and use women's names for months."

"There are indeed many possibilities," George agreed. "Perhaps numbers could substitute for words."

Dead drops, disappearing ink, codes and ciphers. The basic tools of spycraft. We mulled them over constantly. It helped to pass the time during George's confinement.

Chapter Thirty-Seven
CORRIDA

Installing Foresight from the thumb drive was easy. I plugged my laptop into the big flat screen in the family room, and we all settled in to watch. George draped his long legs gracefully across the leather recliner, fascinated that we could tie one looking glass to another. Aunt Rachel, who was still on the mend from her injuries, sat next to Matt and me on the couch, Nevada on the rug at our feet.

Foresight's first screen featured a slowly spinning Earth. A Current/Future onscreen toggle defaulted to Current. I typed in my address, and the globe spun to North America. Then it zoomed in on the West Coast, followed by California, the Bay Area, Berkeley, and, finally, a bird's-eye view of my neighborhood. I clicked on Street View, and we saw our block.

"Is this right now?" George asked. "It appears similar to that Gargle Earth you demonstrated to me recently, Timothy."

"Google Earth. These pictures were probably shot

in the past year or two from satellites orbiting miles above. For Street View, they send cameras mounted on cars up and down all the streets in America."

George scoffed. He didn't laugh often, but clearly both of these ideas were absurd to him.

"How could anyone ride a horseless carriage up and down all the streets in the nation? Ridiculous, even if one had 100 horses-power."

Foresight had a huge database organized into several drop-down menus, including Wars, People, Inventions, Movements, and Culture. Menu options in the People category included: Change Birth Date, Change Death Date, Change Education, Change Family, Change Accomplishments, and Change Acquaintances. For Inventions, some of the options included: Schedule Earlier, Schedule Later, Share Credit, and Cancel Invention.

I chose Wars, then American Revolution, and was presented with these options: Change Outcome, Change Start Date, and Change End Date.

I clicked Change Outcome. New choices appeared: Americans Win (default), British Win, Stalemate. I selected British Win. A green button appeared: Apply Changes. I clicked. Foresight reverted to its start screen, with a new view of the globe spinning.

Another window then came up alongside the main one: Select View Date. Its options were: As of Last Changed Event, As of Today, and Set View Date.

I clicked on As of Today, then a Render Model button. The globe continued to spin and tilted on its axis. Foresight slowly zoomed in on my neighborhood.

On the big-screen TV, the degradation of the neighborhood looked worse than it had on Pierre's laptop. The careful landscaping in our yard was gone, replaced by dingy packed clay. The neighbors' lawns were either brown or overgrown fire traps. Many houses had sagging porches or rooflines. And the cars! Instead of the sleek automobiles of our era, the cars in the simulation looked decrepit, boxy and non-aerodynamic, like a cartoon or an eight-year-old's drawings.

We cruised to the end of my virtual street and turned right on Solano. The laundry on the corner looked half the size I remembered and now offered only hand-wash services. No more machines. The school across the street was abandoned. The shops on Solano looked tired and worn. An empty lot on the corner was piled with garbage and debris, and about half the storefronts were vacant. The few eating places offered cheap grub, crude signs promoting caviar and fish, *tortilla española*, and greasy paella. Seen in this light, Berkeley felt old, neglected, and stuck in its past. A colonial backwater.

"Dude, this is awful," I moaned.

"Your immediate neighborhood certainly appears to have deteriorated," George agreed.

"But Timmy," Matt chimed in, "you know neighborhoods can change. Good neighborhoods sometimes become slums, and slums can get gentrified. Let's check some other areas."

We went back to the bird's-eye view. The roads were much less developed than the sophisticated, high-speed freeway system of our era. A few miles north, downtown Richmond was still run-down, but even worse than how we knew it. Most of the hilly areas held large, upper-middle-class homes perched above the Bay. But in Foresight's simulation, the hills were barely built up, forested and undeveloped or bald and scorched by fire. There were just a few rural-looking

164

houses with scraggly yards on dirt roads. Occasional ruins sat forlorn and neglected. Further to the east, however, we found a few hilly areas with magnificent mansions behind high walls.

"Let's check San Francisco," Rachel suggested. "Is there still a bridge across the Bay?"

There was, but it was nothing like the elegant steel-and-concrete structure we knew. In the present day, our version of 2014, proceeding west from Oakland to San Francisco, you drove several miles on a futuristic, five-lane causeway that linked the East Bay to Yerba Buena Island. West of the island, a traditional, double-decker suspension bridge carried traffic the rest of the way to the City.

But in this Foresight projection of 2014, the bridge was vastly different, much closer to the water, much older, in much worse repair. It had rusty iron construction that looked like an Erector Set gone bad, weathered wooden signs, and a dusty blacktop surface. Many potholes. Slow, sparse traffic. Garbage and abandoned cars in the marshlands.

As we flew toward San Francisco, most of the magnificent, modern skyline was gone, replaced by smaller buildings clustered in the valleys among the hills. Skyscrapers, former signs of a prosperous culture, were scarcer in the model. We did see a few expensive dwellings on the hills. Even in this exploited colonial culture, someone was making money.

"What about the ballpark?" Matt asked.

Continuing the simulation, we flew off the bridge and along the waterfront. The lovely, tree-lined Embarcadero boulevard that we knew was now a bleak, four-lane road crammed with cars. On one side, the Bay was jammed with hundreds of small, dilapidated boats, many inhabited, haphazardly tied up along the banks. The other side of the street was a wreck of vacant lots and tumbledown warehouses, interspersed with occasional gated compounds with walls topped by razor wire and glass shards. Poverty and wealth lived side by side, reminding me of photos I had seen of India. Did all colonies have a small, wealthy ruling class?

We turned the corner, the point where we usually caught our first glimpse of the slick, old-new red-brick Giants ballpark. Instead, we were surprised to see a dingy, concrete stadium. Circular and colonnaded, it was awkwardly plunked down at the edge of the water.

"Damn," Matt said. "What is that?"

"I don't know," said Rachel. "But it looks old, and it needs work. Is it a football stadium?"

"No," I replied. "Football fields are 100 yards long, and fifty-something wide. A rectangle. Wouldn't fit well into a circle."

"No," Rachel said. "I meant soccer."

"Same idea. Rectangular field. Why would anyone put soccer in a round stadium?"

We got closer, then flew down to street level. The detail in the simulation was amazing. We could read posters on the side of the stadium:

Plaza de Toros Monumental de San Francisco
Gran Corrida de los Gigantes
6 Magníficos y Bravos Toros

"It's a bull ring!" I couldn't believe it.

"Eh?" George asked. "What does that mean?"

"They hold bullfights here!"

The posters featured individual events and bullfighters:

Pablo Sandoval "La Panda"
Ángel Pagán "El Caballo Loco"
Gregor Blanco "El Tiburón Blanco"

"Panda, Crazy Horse, and the White Shark. Familiar nicknames!"

"Bulls fight?" George asked. "Where's the sport in that?"

"Men fight the bulls," Rachel said.

"Oh. Does it involve strength, agility, or skill?"

"In a way. The bullfighters tease the bulls and tire them out by enticing them to charge a bright-red cape. The fighters wear tight, shiny pants as they posture and prance around the ring. It's part of the traditional cultures of Spain and Mexico."

"Ah."

"Then they stick spikes into the shoulders of the bulls, to weaken the muscles and lower the bulls' heads when they charge."

"Good gracious, they deliberately maim the bulls? That does not sound like a sporting endeavor."

"The chief bullfighter, the matador, takes a sword and plunges it into the bull's back, trying to pierce the heart and kill the animal with one thrust. It's a blood sport, ultraviolent, with ceremony and attitude."

We were all silent for a while.

Finally George turned to Rachel.

"What is the usual outcome of these proceedings?"

"The bull dies. The bull always dies."

What an odd consequence of the colonies losing the Revolution. In our own era, bullfighting in Mexico and Spain was in steep decline, a target of animal rights activists. Attendance was way down, and the region of Catalonia in Spain recently banned it. But if Foresight was accurate—if the Brits defeated the colonists—California would remain Spanish, with an overlay of Russian culture, and the primary sports palace in San Francisco would be a Plaza de Toros.

"I think I prefer baseball," George said. "Definitely more sporting."

We tired of the simulation after a while.

Over the next few days I showed George some pictures of bullfighting on the Web, but he had lost interest. Despite Foresight's dire predictions, In Real Life the ballpark in San Francisco remained intact. And the Giants defeated the Cardinals, four games to one, in the National League Championship Series.

In the final game, Travis Ishikawa, the Giants back-up left fielder, came to bat with two men aboard in the bottom of the ninth and the score tied. Ishikawa lined the third pitch deep into the stands in right for a three-run walk-off homer.

Pandemonium! When Ishikawa's ball reached the seats, we all went crazy and cheered. Matt gave me double high-fives, and Rachel hobbled over to hug George, who looked startled for a moment, then gave in and hugged her gently and properly.

Another close series. Three of the five games decided by a single run. My Giants had started the season as the best team in baseball, degenerated into one of the worst for a quarter of the season (because my parents left for Italy, I maintained stubbornly), and only finished second in their division. But they had won championships in 2010 and 2012, and now, in an another even-numbered year, they were going to the World Series again!

Chapter Thirty-Eight
IMPATIENT

Berkeley, October 20, 2014

The next week was excruciating. I couldn't sit tight. And George was going stir crazy, having to stay in the house and out of sight all the time, often with me and Nevada as his only company.

I tried running Foresight again. This time I chose George Washington and changed the date of his death to his forty-sixth birthday, February 22, 1778, the day he had disappeared from Valley Forge. I then clicked Render Model.

The software's new default became Americans Lose. The results were similar to the model we had scrutinized earlier. The Brits put down the Revolution, and colonialism reigned worldwide.

When Matt and Rachel came over later, I blurted to them, "Why can't we just take George on a plane today? We could be in Valley Forge tonight."

Matt looked at me. "I thought Chow told you to cool it till you hear from him."

"He did. I'm just too antsy. Why do we need Chow anyway? We can fly George back there right now. We've had him for weeks. The future is bleak if we don't do this."

"I, for one, would welcome this idea," George said. "Or, frankly, any idea that would get me out of this house."

"Well, for one thing, George doesn't have any ID," Rachel said. "How would we get him on a commercial flight?"

"For another thing, he's got a big honkin' sword," Matt said. "They prohibit passengers from carrying weapons or anything sharp. My grandmother had her antique nail scissors confiscated by the TSA. How do you think they'd feel about George showing up with a three-foot sword?"

"Why would the authorities care if I carried a sword? I have no ill intent. What would be their basis for concern?"

"Well, in recent years, there have been many instances of terrorism, of hostile acts of piracy from passengers who have smuggled weapons onto airplanes."

George thought about that for a while. The idea of hurtling through the air in a tin can was still disconcerting to him. The thought of being trapped in that can with an armed aggressor made him want to have his sword with him even more.

"In any case," Matt said, "you have no identification. They will not let you board a plane. My dad lost his wallet while traveling in New Jersey last year. He lost his driver's license, money, credit cards, everything. Even though he had his ticket, they would not let him on the plane until we scanned his passport here at home and sent him the copy. No license, no passport, no ID? You won't be able to get on a plane. Not a commercial plane, anyway."

"Why doesn't Chow move him on a government plane?" Rachel asked.

"Maybe he will," I said. "But he's contending with a mole within the POA. I'm sure he's afraid that any plan he makes could be discovered and compromise his whole operation."

"Even assuming we can get George back to Valley Forge, then what?" Matt asked.

"At that point, we need Chow and his people. We need to use the Einstein device to displace George's temporal vector, to send him back to 1778. We're powerless on our own."

I knew we had to leave soon, one way or another. I gassed up the Corolla, stopped at the bank, and withdrew a few thousand dollars in cash from my inheritance. At least we'd be able to eat.

Nevertheless, we didn't leave. The days ticked slowly by, as we became more impatient. And things began to get worse. Each time I went out, I was certain I was being followed, sometimes by a slim blond guy in a green jacket, sometimes by a young Asian girl in tight black pants and a leather coat. There was always someone—or so it felt—even when I took Nevada for long, random walks on mostly empty residential streets.

Then the harassment began. One day I found one of my tires flat. Totally flat. Not cut, not visibly damaged, just very flat. Two days later, a rock found its way through our front window. Hard to imagine how that could have been an accident.

Soon after, Nevada was out in the backyard when I thought I heard a gunshot. Or was it a car backfiring? Then another. I brought her in and waited, but it didn't happen again. The next day, I found a couple of round holes in the back wall of the house. Small-caliber holes.

Chapter Thirty-Nine
PLAN

Berkeley, October 21, 2014

We had to get out of town, that was clear. I hadn't heard from Chow, but the dark forces—drug cartels, whatever— seemed to know where to find us. If we couldn't fly George to Valley Forge, shouldn't we drive him—and soon? Surely the Corolla would make it. It needed a new clutch, but it would have to wait. I wanted to get out of town quickly.

I could see now why George was my problem. The world was starting to go to hell.

After a sleepless night, I ran next door and woke Matt.

"Let's go, we're leaving now."

"Where are we going?"

"Not sure."

"Can I put on my pants first?"

"Okay, if you have to. But come over right away, man. We've gotta go."

George had been up for hours pacing. Rachel was at work and couldn't come over. Matt, complete with pants, slipped in my back door. He took one look at me.

"Man, you've really got a bee in your bonnet, don't you?"

"Yes, that's it exactly. A bee in my bonnet and two bullet holes in my house."

I took them out back and showed them.

"Oh my," Matt said. "That's not good."

"Who are these varlets?" George asked, his face red with anger. "I'll take them down a peg or two!"

"That's not a solution, George. We don't know who or where they are, and the only weapon we have is an old sword."

"It's a fine sword."

"Of course, but it's not much good against an unseen enemy with guns."

"A cowardly, dastardly enemy."

"That's true, but it doesn't change the situation."

"What do you suggest?" Matt asked.

"I think we should put George in the car right now and drive east. We can be in Pennsylvania in about three days, if we take turns driving. Then we'll hook up with Chow, somehow, and use his time machine."

There. I'd said it. Pierre called it a temporal vector displacement device, but to me, it was a time machine. H.G. Wells be damned.

My thoughts began to spin out of control. We needed the time machine to get George back to his own time, assuming I believed Pierre's cockamamie story about sending von Steuben back to assist the Revolution and the ensuing temporal bounce anomaly. And if I didn't believe it, then who was the tall guy with the grim visage sitting next to me?

"I've got to stop overthinking this," I ranted to Matt,

"or I get caught up in too many what-ifs and how-abouts. I think one side of the question is convincing, then I argue with myself and realize I now agree with the other side. It's my own personal, mental Möbius strip! I feel like I'm going crazy!"

"What do you think we should do, Morpheus?"

"Möbius. I'm not in *The Matrix*."

"Fair enough. But what should we do?"

"I already said, I think we should get in the car and drive east."

Matt was pensive. "But isn't that just what they'll expect us to do?"

"Hmm?"

"If they know Washington's AWOL from his army."

"What does *that* mean?" George asked.

"Away Without Official Leave."

"I am *not* AWOL!"

"Okay, Tim, you're the boss, aren't you? If the bad guys learn from the mole that the General is separated from his army," Matt glanced over at George, who nodded slightly, "and they know that he's with us, won't they *expect* us to take him back there?"

"I guess. So what?"

"What if you're driving into a trap?"

George piped up. "LaMatthew makes sense here. Perhaps you are not aware, but I have accumulated a great deal of knowledge about clandestine operations and evasive actions during my time as commander. Surely discretion here could prove the better part of valor."

I stared at him. "That's Shakespeare."

George looked embarrassed. "I may not be as well educated as my friends Mr. Adams and Mr. Jefferson, but I am familiar with the works of The Bard."

"*Richard III?*"

"*Henry IV. Part I*, I believe."

"Okay, okay, let's not geek out here," Matt said. "What do you suggest?"

George thought a moment.

"We could lie in the dirt."

"What?"

"That baseball term. Making a surprising choice, when another option seems much more likely."

"Oh. Laying in the weeds. A baseball solution seems appropriate, since the World Series starts tonight."

"Yes. Can we lay in the weeds together?"

We all laughed.

I thought a moment.

"Let's slip George out of town quickly to shake the bad guys, then see what Chow advises." I paused. "And I know just the place. Mendo. Matty, will you come too?"

"Sure."

"What about Taco Bell?"

"It's a lame-ass job for chump change."

"And school?"

"I'm working on my thesis. I'll tell them I'm going on the road to do research. I'm ready for a greater challenge than assembling Triple Steak Burritos."

"Like saving our way of life?"

"That'll work. Let's do this."

I left the room to make a call.

My dad's old pal Hank had moved to a small town near Mendocino, on a beautiful piece of land with redwood and pine forests—and no one else around. Off the grid.

I had known Hank for most of my life. He and my

dad used to work together, before Hank and his wife Maggie moved up north to begin a career in farming. When I was little, I thought he was the strongest guy in the world. Every time I saw him, with great entitlement, I would demand that he lift me up to touch the ceiling. I grew quickly, however, and was bitterly disappointed at age eight when Hank told me he couldn't get me up to the ceiling anymore.

He taught me a lot. He knew I was afraid of ladders and, one day when I was about twelve, he decided to teach me a valuable lesson. He scampered up a fifteen-foot extension ladder through a hatch into the attic. I was reluctant to follow. He came down and asked me kindly what I was scared of.

"I'm afraid the ladder will fall down. Or I'll fall off."

"Okay, go halfway up. Slowly. Take your time."

I complied.

"Now hold on tight." He grabbed the ladder with both hands and shook it violently.

"Whoa, Hank!" I squawked. "Dude, what the heck are you doing?"

"I'm showing you that the ladder is not going to fall down, even if someone shakes it or there's an earthquake. The ladder is not going anywhere. It's like a vertical sidewalk. You aren't dumb enough to fall off a sidewalk, are you?"

"Okay …"

"Now, you've made a deal with the ladder. It promises not to fall down, and you promise not to fall off. Always be aware of what you're doing, step carefully, and hold on tight. It's not difficult, once you learn that you can trust it."

Good lesson. I also knew I could always trust Hank.

Now I was calling him to say that Matt, Nevada, and I were coming to visit.

"That's cool, Tim. It will be great to see you all."

"We're bringing a friend, too."

"Sure. You know your friends are always welcome here."

"We're bringing George Washington."

He chuckled. "Of course you are."

"No, really, Hank. I know this sounds crazy, but ..."

I filled him in: Point Isabel, the FBI, the teeth, the clothes, the sword, and Chow. He grunted agreeably during my story, but it was difficult to tell how much he believed. All the same, he was a good friend, salt of the earth, and he told us to come ahead.

I stopped for a moment to contemplate my previous reluctance to get involved. Now I could see clearly that I had to help George.

I was committed.

I went back to the group.

"We're set."

For a change, everyone looked happy. My dad had always told me, "You've gotta have a plan. Doesn't have to be a great plan, or a final plan, but you've gotta start with a plan."

We had a plan.

PART TWO
Fleeing

"Since baseball time is measured only in outs, all you have to do is succeed utterly; keep hitting, keep the rally alive, and you have defeated time. You remain forever young."

—Roger Angell, *The Summer Game*

Chapter Forty
FLIGHT

Berkeley, October 21, 2014

I called Aunt Rachel to tell her of our scheme to take George to Mendocino. When I told her about the bullet holes, she became worried for our safety. Heading for the hills seemed like a good idea.

"I can't go," she told me. "I can still barely hobble around, though I'm back at work. But you should bring Nevada. She'll be good for protection, and she's fun to have along on a trip."

"More protection than George's sword?"

"You can't just whip out that sword at the drop of a hat, for any vague, perceived threat. That would startle people, attract attention. But, as a deterrent, you could bring out your large, black dog with the huge mouth."

"She wouldn't harm a flea."

"You might be surprised, though we both know she looks a lot fiercer than she acts. And when she barks ... "

"What?"

"Well, she's got that deep, bassy *WOOF* that gives people pause."

"She only barks about once a month," I said. "Nevada is a notoriously bad watchdog. She loves everyone and considers them all welcome in her world. And she won't be any help against guns."

"Of course not," Rachel responded. "But perhaps she can lick the bad guys to death."

"The cartel thugs? Sure!"

"Make sure to take dog food. Now go! Call me when you can." She hung up.

George gathered up his sword and scabbard, still wrapped in burlap, and stuffed his uniform into a kit bag, along with some civilian clothes I provided.

"It is a good thing we are almost the same height," he mused, as he donned scruffy jeans, dirty open sandals, and a UC Santa Cruz banana slug T-shirt. He stuffed his long, reddish-brown hair into a black knit cap and walked into the garage.

"I do long to be out in the sunshine. I have hated being confined for so long."

He reached for the door of the Toy Crawler.

I called out, "George, you ride shotgun, with those long legs of yours!"

He knew shotgun meant he should sit next to the driver, but I'm sure he didn't know why it was called that. Nevertheless, he was grateful and felt talkative.

Matt and Nevada sat in the back.

"I shall miss your aunt, Timothy," George said. "I respect her knowledge, her advice, and her graciousness."

"And that kiss?" I teased.

He blushed. "Yes, the Kissing Camera embarrassed

me. I have always enjoyed the company of ladies, but that gesture of friendship from such an attractive widow warmed my heart and made me appreciate how much I miss my Patsy. You and LaMatthew are both companionable, eager, and bright, but also young, inexperienced in matters of the world, and, well, male." He fell silent and thoughtful.

"On the other hand, Hamilton and Lafayette are considerably younger than both of you. Or they were. Both have been dead nearly 200 years, by your current reckoning. Whatever 'current' means anymore. The thought depresses me."

Just before we left, I texted Agent Chow: *Bolting.*

Matt opened the garage door and looked in both directions. I backed the car out, piloted it down the street, and, just that quickly, George's exile in Berkeley was over.

We drove west across San Francisco Bay, then north on U.S. 101 for about an hour to Cloverdale. George was excited to get out of the house, enthralled by the miles of cultivated fields, curious about everything.

"What do they grow here? Are those grape vines on the other side of the road?"

"Yes. There are lots of wineries here on the West Coast."

"Fascinating," said George. "I long for this horrific war to end, so that I might return to farming. Oh, to be at Mount Vernon!"

He fell silent and contemplated his surroundings.

"Is there much rainfall here? The hills appear brown, but the fields are green. Do they irrigate? Where does the water come from?"

"Yes, they irrigate, mostly with water they pump out of the ground. In this climate, the way our seasons usually work, it doesn't rain for half the year, most years. But the past couple years, we've had severe drought. Water has become much scarcer."

I punched some buttons and music began to play. A soulful ballad.

"What is that?" George asked.

"It's Lady Gaga," said Matt. "Tim's a closet Gaga-head."

"This is a torch song from her new album," I said. "It's called 'Ev'ry Time We Say Goodbye.'"

"Torch song?"

"A slow, sultry love song. About lovers who are forced by circumstance to spend long periods of time apart."

George took the song to heart. He told us that he and his dear Patsy said goodbye often, enduring long separations, though she'd been able to come stay with him during winter encampments. He had missed her often since leaving Valley Forge. He sat back to listen as we drove along, his face grimaced in the dull ache of longing.

Chapter Forty-One
MENDO

Farnsworth, Mendocino County, October 21, 2014

Starved, late in the afternoon we pulled over at Hamburger Ranch in Cloverdale and sated ourselves with barbecue. No one noticed George. We had to leave Nevada in the car, but we brought her water and the bones from our short ribs.

"Now the curvy part," I said. We headed west from Cloverdale on Route 128 and, for the next thirty miles, we careened and tacked our way through fabulous hilly woodlands, as the sun peeked through in splashes of dappled light. Eventually the road straightened and flattened out. We emerged in Boonville and pulled over near the fairgrounds to call Hank and let him know we were nearly there.

Had there always been so many Mexican restaurants in Boonville?

Another few miles to Farnsworth (sneeze and you miss it!), past a few wineries, then we left the pavement to turn onto Monk Hill Road.

Chow called—much to my amazement—and I filled

him in on our escape. When he heard about the bullet holes, he said he was relieved that we had left Berkeley. He promised to get back to us with an updated plan but cautioned again that his operations were compromised. The bad guys seemed to know his every move.

The rest of our journey to Hank's house was on dirt.

We wound our way up the hill, passing only a few houses and a vineyard, then climbing the ridgeline up and out of the trees, as the golden land fell away to the south.

George seemed unfazed by the bumpy dirt roads. By the warm light of early evening, we stopped to let Nevada out and enjoy the view of the Anderson Valley laid out below us.

"They call it the Golden State," Matt said. "I mean, it looks pretty brown to me. But 'golden' does bring in more tourists."

We turned past a wooden sign that said "Heaven's Hollow" and pointed down a rutted, winding, potholed road deep into the woods. A couple of times I felt the clutch slip. At the bottom of the hollow, we passed through the gate into Hank's half-mile driveway, a slippery, dirt-and-gravel, uphill slalom course through the redwoods.

I guided and gunned the Corolla around the turns and up to the house, high on the hill. As we rounded the last sharp turn before a particularly steep and slippery section, the light waning a little more each second, I called out, "This is the worst part of the road, from the vegetable garden up past the yurt."

"Yurt?"

"You'll see," I chirped. "It's there on the right beyond that fence, where the road bends left and uphill. This is really off the grid, George."

"What does that mean?"

"They're too far from the cities to get power."

"They have no electricity?"

"Well, they have solar power collectors, large panels that soak up the energy of the sun and turn it into electricity."

I paused to let that sink in. George's eyes gleamed in the warm evening light, as he contemplated harnessing the power of the sun.

"And they have generators," I continued, "Engines like the ones in cars, that make their own electricity. This is the most isolated place I know of, and we thought we could hang out here for a while."

At the top of the hill we pulled up to a flat spot near a small, single-story house. A sign read "Hippies use backdoor. No exceptions."

Hank came around the corner, wiry and grizzled in jeans, a Hot Tuna T-shirt, work boots, and his usual brown fedora.

"Hey, big guy!" he yelled, wrapping me in a bear hug, then greeting Matt and Nevada warmly. Next he sized up our companion, awaiting an introduction. Hank was about five inches shorter than George, about ten years older.

I did the honors.

"Hank Goldsmith, this is General Washington."

"Of course it is," Hank said, extending his hand. George drew himself up to his full 6'2", then bowed.

"The pleasure is mine," George answered. Even in modern garb, he managed to look stately.

Hank graciously lowered his hand and bowed back.

"Welcome, General. We are honored to have you here as our guest."

"I am very grateful for your hospitality, sir."

A smiling woman with long brown hair walked up, hugged Matt and me, and scratched Nevada behind the ears. Hank grinned and presented her to George.

"General Washington, this is Maggie. My better half. Far better."

"My pleasure, madam." He bowed.

"Well, boys," Hank said, turning to Matt and me, "how about those Giants?"

He brought us up to date: our Gigantics had won Game 1 of the World Series in Kansas City, pounding the Royals 7-1. Bumgarner again was the pitching hero for the Giants. Sandoval had three hits, and Hunter Pence two, including a homer. It was a good start.

Chapter Forty-Two
GANJA

Farnsworth, October 22, 2014

The next day Hank took us on a tour. After weeks of confinement in Berkeley, George marveled at the spectacular setting. Trees in every direction: redwoods, pines, and California live oaks. Not another house in sight. Every now and then, the sound of birds or a car far off in the distance. Otherwise, silence, except for the gentle susurration of leaves in the breeze. Who could find us here?

Near the edge of the flat hilltop Hank showed off the kitchen garden, which poured forth a bounty of corn, sunflowers, lettuce, tomatoes, squash, peppers, and berries. He also showed us the chicken coop around the side. Then we traipsed down a short, steep slope behind the house to a large, fenced patch near a creek.

"Behold the cash crop. Ganja!" said Hank.

"Hemp!" said George. "We grow hemp at Mount Vernon. Though I fear most of the farming operations there are foundering lately, since my absence of nearly three years."

189

"We grow two major types of hemp here, General. One strain which is high in CBD, for medical use. It doesn't get you stoned."

"CBD?"

"Yes, half these plants have a component that is used now to treat cancer patients and others, yet it's not intoxicating. We grind up the leaves and make a liquid extract, a juice that can help relieve pain, shrink tumors, suppress epileptic fits, and soothe symptoms of numerous diseases."

"Truly?" Matt piped in. "Has that really been proven?"

"Well, it's mostly anecdotal so far. The government won't allow any controlled research, because marijuana is illegal."

"What is marijuana?" George asked.

"Another name for the hemp plant," Hank answered. "We also call it cannabis, pot, weed, grass, dope, lotsa names. It's been illegal since the 1930s, a remnant of the Prohibition Era, when alcoholic beverages were also banned."

"Alcohol was illegal?"

"Yes, from about 1920 until 1933, then legalized again. But national laws against marijuana cultivation, sale, and possession were never repealed. Now many places around the country ignore the pot laws with a wink, and some states have started to legalize it."

"Including California?"

"It's still technically against the law here, though it's easy to obtain legal permission for medical use. Most of the other pot laws are very puritanical. I think they want to avoid letting people have too much fun." He grinned.

"In what way is it fun?"

"Well, that's what the other part of our crop is for. Removing the male plants causes the females to develop with a much higher level of THC, a different chemical that enhances psychoactive properties. It gets you high. Stoned. The CBD stuff doesn't."

"I do not believe that I catch your meaning, sir."

"Please call me Hank. THC mildly alters your consciousness. It enhances your sense of time, taste, and the absurd. It's intoxicating—relaxing and stimulating, like a glass of wine or beer or other spirits."

"Oh. It gets you high. I see." A short pause. "An apt turn of phrase, eh?"

"Let me show you."

Hank pulled a small, metal pipe out of his belt and lit it. His butane lighter impressed George as much as the pipe or the pot. Hank took a long toke of the weed, while maintaining eye contact with the General.

My jaw dropped. Was Hank going to get Washington baked?

He passed the pipe to George, who recoiled as if Hank were handing him a snake.

"Very kind of you," George said, "but if it is, as you say, illegal, I am not certain I feel comfortable flouting the law of the land."

"Smoking together can be kind of a ceremonial or communal thing for us, General, but please do as you wish. If you like, I can take you to a doctor tomorrow who will certify that you need medical marijuana to help relieve your knee pain."

"I beg your pardon?"

"I've seen you limp a little."

"Perhaps from jumping out of trains," I put in.

"Or you could tell the doctor you need relief from stress," Hank said reassuringly. "Surely leading the Continental Army must be stressful."

George thought for a moment, then accepted the pipe and gingerly took a puff.

"At Mount Vernon, we primarily raise hemp for use of its fiber, especially in making rope."

Hank showed us how he and his helpers had built bamboo-stick cages around each plant. They bent back the vertical branches of the plants in gentle arcs and tied them to the bamboo, exposing more cannabis buds to the sun. As the plants grew taller and wider, the workers added new tiers to the cages. Under each plant, black tubing delivered water, drop by drop, to the thirsty roots.

"My friend, I have many questions for you about farming and irrigation!" George said.

"Sure. The drip irrigation soaks in deeply, with little surface evaporation." Hank smiled. "Hemp fibers, as you know, are long, strong, and durable, particularly good for making paper. If only it wasn't illegal. Growing hemp on farms could save millions of acres of woodland from being destroyed each year to make paper that's often used once, then discarded."

I had heard this lecture from Hank before.

"The women of Mount Vernon must be aware of hemp's medicinal qualities as well," said George. "I have difficulty understanding why its cultivation should be against the law."

"Me too," Hank said. He passed the pipe. "As I mentioned, General, using only female plants leads to the most potent buds."

"Quite so. How does one determine the difference?"

They chatted for a while about marijuana cultivation.

The sun's rays filtered through the trees as we climbed

back up to Hank's house. Near the house was a diamond-shaped ditch in the ground, lined with railroad ties. Nevada sniffed the spot, then marked it for future reference.

"And here," Hank said proudly, "is where *Dark Star* will go. I'm excited that you guys will be here to see her arrive!"

"*Dark Star?*"

"My boat! They're delivering my sailboat tomorrow!"

Chapter Forty-Three
SAILBOAT

Why, sir, do you need a sailboat?" George asked later that evening. "I cannot imagine there is a river in this hilly terrain large enough to sail on."

We had just finished watching the Giants lose Game 2 of the Series in Kansas City. It was their turn to get pounded by the Royals, this time by 7-2. The series shifted next to San Francisco.

"Is there a lake nearby?"

"No, no," Hank chuckled. "The boat belongs to my son Caleb in Berkeley. He bought it a few years ago, doesn't sail it, and hasn't been able to sell it. So, he offered it to me to use as a cabin up here on the land. It's beautiful, thirty-nine feet long, wooden, seventy-five years old. Lovely interior— oak, mahogany, brass. We often need extra beds for guests, so the boat's two bunks could prove useful, especially when the grandkids come up to visit. We can run power down to it and might even hook up the toilet. *Dark Star* is the title of a Dead song."

"A dead song? How can a song die?"

"The Grateful Dead. It's a musical group, a band. They

all come from Northern California."

George took all that in as he looked around at the yurt, a round, permanent tent on a wooden platform, twenty feet in diameter. A few minutes' walk downhill from Hank's house. The rest of us sat sprawled on couches. Nevada snoozed on the floor.

"Hank," I asked, "what makes you think you can get a forty-foot boat up that road?"

"Thirty-nine-foot."

"A thirty-nine-foot boat. It's not going to levitate up here, is it?"

"Perhaps you could put it on an escalator," George quipped, with a sly glance at me.

Hank looked puzzled. "It's definitely doable," he said. "My neighbor has a forty-foot house that he trailered down Heaven's Hollow, so I figure it can be done. Caleb came up here a while ago and shot a fifteen-minute video of the drive up the dirt, knowing that was the tricky part of the whole thing. Just under four miles. We found a guy to do the hauling through an Internet shipping site. Caleb set it all up. He put on the post that whoever bid on it had to watch the video— to make sure they understood what they were getting into.

"So, some L.A. fellow won the bid, a young guy named Ross. Once we had a contract, I had to prepare the site. I mean you can't lay a thirty-nine-foot sailboat with a four-foot keel on the ground. So we dug a ditch for the keel and lined it with railroad ties. That's what you saw up the hill near the house.

"But every time I talk to Ross, I get more concerned. He's a city guy from Los Angeles. He seems to be unaware of what he's facing once he gets up here from Berkeley Marina, completely inexperienced on curvy, steep country roads like these. Even before he gets to the dirt."

"Is there any way we can assist you?" George asked, always keen to make a difference.

"Maybe. I've been talking with friends of mine up here who own heavy equipment and have moved large things in tight places before."

"What kind of equipment?"

"Trucks and dozers. Workhorse vehicles, General. Tough and strong."

"Workhorses?"

"Well, not real horses. Machines. My friends like challenges and are quite enthusiastic. One of them repairs and restores old boats, and we've spent a lot of time discussing what it will take to get it up here. We're going to have to help the trailer and the boat around tight corners and up and down steep hills."

"Like *Fitzcarraldo*?" I ventured.

"What is that?" George asked.

Hank grinned. "Sure, like *Fitzcarraldo*."

"It's a movie." I explained the story. "A crazy Irish guy in Peru, in the Amazon River basin—and a lot of Indians working for him—struggle to drag a big steamship up and over a mountain to another river. In South America."

"Why?"

"So he can use the ship to transport rubber and make a fortune."

"Does he?"

"He does get the ship over the mountain, but he doesn't make a fortune. Oops, spoiler alert."

"So his effort is unsuccessful?"

"It's complicated. His trip was financially unsuccessful, yet he has met his challenge, and he's happy."

Chapter Forty-Four
DARK STAR

Farnsworth, October 23, 2014

The next morning we woke up slowly, the yurt bright and cheery.

Four clear-plastic windows allowed sunlight to penetrate inside. The knotty-pine floor reflected warm light onto canvas walls, girdled by an expandable wooden lattice. Radial wood beams supported a canvas roof.

I let Nevada out to do her business. It was warm and placid outside.

Hank and Maggie had satellite Internet and Wi-Fi, and I downloaded a couple of movies to show George later.

The calm shattered when Hank sped down the hill in his white Toyota pickup and screeched to a stop.

"I just talked to Ross. He's on his way with the boat, and I'm worried he won't make it, so I'm heading to Cloverdale to help him out. He's pulling nearly ten tons, and he's driving a goddamn Cowboy Cadillac—a fancy pickup truck with no real power! It might be okay on paved roads, but I don't know how he expects to drag that boat up the dirt!"

George stepped up. "How can we help?"

"I think I'm covered. Enjoy the show."

"Sir. May I please have the honor of accompanying you to greet the cowboy? Perhaps I can render some assistance."

Hank looked at him sideways, decided he might be helpful in a pinch, and agreed.

George looked over at me. I made a head-covering motion. He nodded, retrieved the knit cap from a pocket, and pulled it down over his hair and ponytail. He then called "Shotgun!" and hopped in Hank's pickup.

"I'll keep you posted," called Hank. "Meet us at the bottom of the hill in a couple of hours."

They sped off in a cloud of dust and gravel.

A while later, Matt and I drove back to the highway. About twenty local folks—and nearly as many dogs—had gathered at the bottom of the road. Where the dirt met the pavement, they visited and picnicked. There was food, drink, folding chairs, and cameras. Word spread that Hank would soon arrive with the boat. One guy had a huge boom box blasting Grateful Dead songs from the back of an ATV. We parked and snacked and listened to Jerry Garcia's complex guitar licks echoing through the woods. Nevada wandered around, sniffing dog butts and making friends, hoping for handouts.

Eventually we saw a little caravan coming down the road. First came Ross, who appeared to be about thirty, driving the Cowboy Cadillac, a Dodge RAM pickup much too glitzy for the bumpy dirt thoroughfare that was Monk Hill Road. Hitched to it was a forty-foot, blue boat trailer low to the ground. It carried a sweet old vessel with a white-and-sea-foam-colored hull and a golden-brown wood cabin. The mast, as long as the boat, rode next to the hull, lashed to the trailer. The boat traveled stern first, up on its keel on the trailer, the words *Dark Star* in gold across the aft transom. Hank, looking steamed, followed in his Toyota pickup, with George at shotgun.

We all applauded as Ross turned off the pavement, only to groan when his rig immediately lost traction on the dirt. He was barely able to get his payload off the blacktop.

Hank called a halt. He and George came over to us.

"His transmission overheated on the first hill," Hank said. "The very first hill! He pulled over on a curve, and the General and I had to direct cars around him until the transmission cooled down. Then, on the next couple of tight turns, his brakes started to overheat and fail. That's when the General had a great idea, to use my truck to help Ross brake."

George looked solemn. Hank went on.

"I pulled my pickup behind the trailer, we got a thick nylon strap that Ross had, and we connected the front of my truck to the back of his trailer. I kept my truck in first gear and used my brakes and engine compression to help ease him to the bottom of the hill."

He laughed and looked at George. "People were amazed as they passed. We got a lot of funny looks!"

I worried that George Washington in a Toyota pickup tied to a boat trailer on a winding, California mountain road might have attracted lots of attention. But he still wore the knit cap, and there was no Kiss Cam in sight. Hopefully no one had recognized him.

Hank looked wistfully at *Dark Star's* next challenge, sailing up the dirt-and-gravel river.

"The contract calls for him to bring the boat all the way up to our land. I have a crane coming out shortly to place the boat in the hole and re-erect the mast. But I'm afraid Ross is never gonna make it."

The crane operator arrived. A local guy, he knew how to drive roads like these, though his rig was nearly thirty-five feet long. Hank told him how to find the house and sent him on his way up the hill.

Hank huddled with his friends who had come to help, one of whom had brought a large dump truck filled with rocks for added traction. They decided that the best plan was to pull the boat trailer with the dump truck. But its tow hitch didn't match the one on the boat trailer. So they connected the dump truck to the front of the Cowboy Cadillac, still hitched to the forty-foot trailer with the thirty-nine-foot boat.

Because of its length, the trailer was difficult to maneuver over and around the many dips and curves in the road; so Hank had a backhoe follow along to help.

The caravan started dragging up the hill, very slowly. The guy with the boom box started to play the boat's namesake song, one of the Dead's long jam-band tunes, running over twenty minutes on their *Live Dead* album.

It took about forty-five minutes to move the first couple of miles. The turn from Monk Hill Road to Oak Bluff Road was tight and narrow, and Hank used the backhoe to scoop up the trailer and slide it around the corner. The dump truck labored up Oak Bluff hill, which was quite steep.

All this time, the crowd of neighbors and locals, now dozens strong, was having a grand old time, following and leading this tortoise-speed procession on foot and on ATVs. Many took photos and videos. Nevada romped around, playing tag with other dogs.

"For my grandkids," Hank told us, "this has everything that appeals to a four- or five-year-old: a dump truck, a backhoe, a crane, a boat, ATVs, trucks. I told them the boat was for them to play in, and boy, did their eyes light up! Grandpa's a hero today."

Chapter Forty-Five
DOZER

At the top of Oak Bluff, the scenic overlook where we had stopped with George the evening before, we reached the turnoff to Heaven's Hollow Road. Another summit meeting.

"There's no way that dump truck can pull the boat trailer down into the hollow and up to the house," Hank told us. "It's too goddamn long for all the twists and turns, and it'll never make it up the hill. The tires will spin. Not enough traction for a ten-ton load!

"But," he grinned, a twinkle in his eye, "General, wait till you see the bulldozer we're bringing!"

"Does it have the power of 100 horses?" George asked.

One of Hank's friends arrived in a yellow John Deere bulldozer with impressive, sturdy steel tracks like those on a tank.

They unhooked the dump truck and Ross's truck. Then, with its huge blade lifted up and out of the way, they attached the dozer directly to the front of the boat trailer. The backhoe would continue to trail behind.

The ATV with the boom box kept playing "Dark Star" as the caravan prepared to enter the trees and head down into Heaven's Hollow. The spacy guitar licks echoed around the hills and the redwoods.

I shuddered to think what would happen if *Dark Star* tore loose from its axis, while sailing hilly dirt roads stern-first through the forest.

The dozer and trailer inched their way down Heaven's Hollow, the worst road yet. Tight turns, slippery gravel and dirt, jarring potholes, tree roots, and deep ruts. The trailer had five wheels on each side, but on some corners several wheels hung over the edge.

Hank's buddies drove the bulldozer and the backhoe. Hank and George walked alongside for the length of the road, down into the hollow, and then up the other side toward the top of the hill. Matt and I followed. It was a hot day, the air in the woods still and muggy. George removed the knit cap, and Hank stripped to the waist. The final verse of "Dark Star" filled the forest, echoing through the hills like Caruso in the Peruvian jungle in *Fitzcarraldo*.

"Hank," Matt laughed, "seeing this boat come through the trees, on this narrow mountain road—it looks so weird."

George drank in the whole scene, perhaps thinking that a dozer or two would come in handy for hauling artillery.

Hank couldn't stop smiling.

"There's a deep water channel that goes all the way up the Sacramento River through the farmland of the Central Valley. Sometimes if you stand in the fields, you can see boats going upriver, even large ships, and it looks like they're sailing between the rows of corn. That's what this reminds me of, like a ship sailing up through the mountains. Backwards. Like something out of space and time."

Below the yurt they reached the hairpin turn where the road suddenly dipped, twisted sharply, then climbed steeply uphill. The dozer started to lose traction on the slippery roadbed, as the rear trailer wheels spun freely in space. I knew it would be hellishly awkward to inch it all down the hill to a flatter spot to get it going again. The backhoe, unfortunately, lumbered slowly about thirty yards behind and would arrive too late to keep the trailer-dozer rig moving. Matt and I realized at the same moment that the boat was starting to lose its momentum, and we were too far away to help.

Hank and George were close by. Both shouted and sprang forward at the same moment to put their shoulders behind the boat trailer, adding just enough force to maintain its uphill inertia. Matt and I and several others arrived moments later, and our combined efforts encouraged the trailer in its Sisyphean progress. The dozer's treads found traction in the soft, dusty road surface, and it continued its relentless plod uphill.

I knew Hank was a whatever-it-takes kind of guy, but I hadn't seen George act so hands-on before. This wasn't war, of course, but the incident gave me a glimpse of his physical power and agility. I could also see that he was a leader. It was easy to imagine him at the head of a charge, mounted on Blueskin, the green-handled Smithsonian battle sword high over his head. I daydreamed again of the painting of the Battle of Monmouth. "This way, you stout-hearted lads! Follow me!"

Dark Star made it to the top. Twenty voices erupted in cheers and applause as the crane operator lifted the boat off the trailer and lowered it keel-first into the diamond-shaped hole, the hull gently nestled against the railroad ties. Once he re-erected the mast, it was party time!

Hank and friends—all feeling quite proud of themselves—brought out beers and a bit of fine Mendocino herb. They made a fire in a barbecue pit near the boat and hung out, grilling burgers, popping beers, gabbing, laughing, and rehashing the day's events. Hank thanked everyone, then paid off Ross, who headed back to L.A. Relieved of its ten-ton payload, the Cowboy Cadillac could now easily pull his trailer back home.

"I gotta tell you, Timmy," Hank said, "when the dump truck was dragging the pickup *and* the boat up Monk Hill Road, Ross finally looked at me and said, 'You know, I really didn't know what I was getting into. You guys are saving my butt!'

"I said, 'I know!'" Hank laughed drily. "You know what they say. Old age and experience trump youthful exuberance every time."

"Dude, I thought it was old age and treachery," I ventured.

"Whatever. I was his age once. I was young and brash and knew better than anyone else, especially some older person telling me to be careful. So many times I got in over my head! You have to be able to foresee problems, to plan for and expect the worst.

"When I first spoke with him weeks ago, his question to me, on our first call, was 'Where is Mendocino, anyway? Isn't it right near Sacramento?' I thought, oh shit! He was off by 200 miles! He bid on the job with no idea where he was going. Never mind that he didn't have a powerful enough truck!"

"What now for *Dark Star*?" George asked.

"Well, I've gotta clean out the compartment where the engine used to be, set the stays on the mast, and paint the thing."

"What color?" I asked.

"I haven't decided. What color should I paint it?"

"How about a bright color," Matt asked, "like blue or green?"

I chimed in. "Or red, white, and blue?"

"Uh, no," said Hank, backpedaling quickly. "It'll be more of an earth tone. No neon greens. No flag colors. All due respect, General. But I might fly a flag from it on holidays."

"Is it worth all this effort and expense?" George asked.

"It's a thrill, General! My grandsons were wide-eyed, just the age where they'll remember this day."

Later we watched videos on Facebook of *Dark Star's* trek uphill, its song blasting through the trees. Eventually the party broke up, and Matt and I started the short stroll downhill to the yurt. I looked back and saw George and Hank, still sitting by the fire with Nevada at their feet. Hank, as usual, was talking intently.

They huddled together, intently discussing their common passion—farming.

Chapter Forty-Six
SHAKES

Mendocino village, October 24, 2014

We all slept late after the party, then Matt, George, Nevada, and I drove an hour to the Pacific coast to the village of Mendocino, the beautiful little town that gave the county its name.

Over 88,000 folks lived in Mendocino County, which included 3,800 square miles of some of Northern California's prettiest country. Lush pine forests, dramatic stands of old redwoods, hilly vineyards, and pot patches galore. Fewer than 1,000 people lived in the village, a picturesque coastal town with classic mid-nineteenth-century architecture and a laid-back attitude we jokingly called "Mendo Suavé."

In addition to tourists, the town was full of hippies, wine growers, pot farmers, and other locals, supporting a bevy of craft shops, art galleries, restaurants, cafés, and places to stay. We parked and took a quick stroll around "downtown" Mendo, an adventure in grassy paths, lovely gardens, hidden entrances, rustic house designs, and fanciful wooden towers, some with water tanks, some the former homes of windmills. All perched on a bluff above the Pacific.

George noticed a large sign that said Mendocino Shakesfest.

"Is this a festival? Do they indeed perform the plays of Shakespeare here?"

"Yes, but we can't go to a big public event. We need to cool it."

"No one here is aware of our presence, cool or otherwise," said George, a master of the vernacular. "I should like to attend a play. I shall wear a hat and keep my head down."

Once his mind was made up, he had a knack for getting his own way. That's often called leadership.

We entered the village and turned west onto Main Street, toward the ocean.

The slogan of the Mendocino Shakesfest was "Shakespeare at Land's End." It was easy to see why. The shows played to 800 audience members in a large white tent set on a cliff at the edge of town, overlooking the ocean and the Big River. We made a beeline for the box office and examined the program. They did have some plays by Shakespeare. But had they always had works by García Lorca, Cervantes, and Chekhov?

Most shows were sold out, but the young ticket seller told us gleefully, "I have three for *The Tempest*. The dog's gotta wait in the car."

Lucky for us, the play would start in an hour, so we had time to pick up some supplies Hank needed.

"Ahh! The magical tale of Prospero!" George exclaimed. The guy knew his Shakespeare. He smiled warmly and with great authority in my direction.

Shakespeare's tale carried us into a far-off land of magic and sorcery. A magnificent production on a bare stage with abstract stage elements, dramatic lighting, and sound effects. George loved it. He had seen plays before, both in daylight and inside on stages lit by candles and oil lamps. Modern theatrical lighting and sound effects during the storm and shipwreck scenes startled and thrilled him. At one point, midway through the first act, he turned to me and asked, "This is right now, is it not?"

"Are you asking if this is live?"

"Yes. These actors are actually here in the room with us? This is not some gigantic magical looking glass?"

"Nope, live and in person."

Shakespeare's theme of vengeance giving way to forgiveness impressed George.

"I am not a regular churchgoer, but I do believe in the Christian concept of compassion."

"That must be difficult to maintain," I said, "when you are fighting a war against an enemy who despises you and everything you stand for."

"Revenge only hardens the heart. Many Loyalist Americans in my own era oppose the Revolution. When we win this war, we will have to win the hearts and minds of all the people, not just the ones who have supported our quest. We will need to expunge our anger and focus on the future. Forgive our enemies."

"That's very high-minded of you."

"I believe it is very high-minded of Mr. Shakespeare to write of such acts of acceptance."

I drove us back to the yurt, then called Aunt Rachel with Hank's cell phone booster. As soon as she heard my voice, she said, "Well, it looks like you guys have been having quite a time."

"What do you mean?"

"Sailing Hank's boat uphill."

"How do you know about that?"

"There's a video on Facebook and Instagram that's gone viral. I even saw shots of George and Hank helping push the boat on its trailer."

"Oh no!" I said. Not good. So much for traveling incognito.

I was relieved to hear that she was healing well. I told her about our day in Mendocino and described George's reaction to *The Tempest*.

"In particular, he responded strongly to the themes of forgiveness and reconciliation. You know the play. Prospero forgives Caliban and Ariel, as well as his treacherous brother and the king, who plotted against him. George talked today about learning to forgive his enemies."

"Forgiveness, eh? That rings a bell. Let me do some poking around. I'll get back to you about that. Also, I was wondering if what you told George about home runs and performance-enhancing drugs was true. So I did a little research, and you're right. The total number of home runs in the majors this year was the lowest in nineteen years, dropping by over ten percent in just the last year. The overall total is down twenty-seven percent, compared to the highest year ever."

"When was that?"

"2000. The peak of the steroid era. This year, of the ten teams with the highest home run totals, only four made it to the playoffs at all, and none to the World Series. The Giants and the Royals have some of the smallest homer totals in the majors in the past two seasons. Bunches of homers don't necessarily lead to victories."

"So?"

"Well," She took a deep breath. "Reduced reliance on homers reminds me of what I've read about Washington's campaign. Pesky but relentless, making the most of limited power with cunning and guile."

"You don't think that's a little far-fetched, Rachel?"

"Hey, baseball is life."

I pulled out my laptop to check the scores. Playing in San Francisco now, the Royals had edged the Giants 3-2 in Game 3 of the Series and now led two games to one. Not good news.

I turned out the light. We were running for our lives from an unseen enemy, but reading about baseball kept me sane. More or less. Nevada circled a few times, then settled down on the rug, annoyed that she had missed going to the theatre.

Chapter Forty-Seven
WARNING

Farnsworth, October 24, 2014

But our day was not over yet. Just after lights out, Hank and Maggie came down to the yurt with disturbing news.

Maggie worked at the newspaper office in Farnsworth. On her way home that evening, she stopped at Orangina's Market. Doug, the owner, was relieved to see her and took her aside.

"Look, Maggie, some guys were in here earlier today, asking around, looking for three men traveling together, a big White guy and a short Black guy, both late twenties, plus an older White guy with a ponytail. Doesn't sound like anyone I know. I mean, it sounds like lots of people I know, just not in that combination."

"So?"

"Well, the first guy, who does the asking, acts all friend-ly at first, but the other guy with him is kinda creepy. Then the first guy gets, like, pushy when I say I don't know who he's talking about—but I don't. So he gets all kinda aggressive and oily at the same time. Anyway, Sal overhears us, and she jumps in." Sal was Doug's wife.

He looked away, as though he'd gotten to the part he didn't want to tell.

"What did Sal say?"

"Sal met your houseguests during that sailboat thing the other day, and she tells these guys about it."

"Oh dear."

"Yeah, they jump all over her trying to get more info, but I think she gets suspicious, starts to distrust them, acts kinda vague about where it all happened. She doesn't exactly tell them that you guys live off Monk Hill Road, but she does, uh, well, she implies that it was west of town."

"Huh, not too many people live on that side of town, Doug. This isn't exactly Gotham City."

"Yeah, but there are many miles of roads. And locked gates."

"Did they seem like locals? Growers? City people?"

"Not exactly. We get all kinds in here."

"What are you trying to tell me?"

"Well, Maggie, we know that we all grow weed around here. All the locals got a patch in their backyard. A dozen plants, maybe. But, you know, there are others, who come in here from somewhere else, and keep huge patches, deep in the woods."

"Cartels."

"Yeah. They slip into the Valley to tend their plants."

"Sometimes on government land."

"Yeah. And they bring their muscle."

"Were these guys Mexicans?"

"Nah. Mr. Oily had high cheekbones, a crew cut, and muscles. Maybe Russian?"

"How about Creepy?"

"I dunno. Just … creepy. Weird eyes, maybe different colors?"

Earlier Maggie had come to the yurt to tell us, but we hadn't returned from Mendo yet.

"They don't know where we live," she said, "but they could be driving up and down the roads west of town right now, hoping to stumble upon the General. Or asking around to find out if anyone in the hills owns a sailboat!"

"Oy," Matt said. Clearly, a lot of people knew about Hank's boat.

"Shit," I added. "Sal's got a big mouth!"

Hank and Maggie said good night and left. I felt strangely calm.

"Okay, let's pack up. We should leave first thing in the morning."

George wasn't so sure. "Because of their muscles?"

"Guys with guns."

"I am not afraid of their weapons." He said this in a convincing, matter-of-fact tone, without a trace of bravado. "In the French and Indian Wars, I had two mounts shot out from under me and later discovered four bullet holes in my clothing. None hit me."

Matt frowned. "Yes, but your forces were defeated and General Braddock died."

I laughed. "Oh, the king of Wikipedia speaks!"

"Where is Wikipedia?" George asked suspiciously. "Is it indeed a kingdom?"

"Look, General," Matt said. "Bravado aside, we're not an army, and we have no way to fight back. We are not going to stay here and make a glorious stand. Our task is to get you back to when and where you came from. Every day our modern world is devolving, and we suspect it's about to revert to a dreadful descendant of the colonialism you so despise. As Chow says, dark forces want to stop us. We're leaving."

I was so glad Matt stood up to him. I was tired of being the one to have to push George all the time.

"Pack up, guys. We leave at dawn," I said.

"Where to next?" Matt asked.

I turned to him. "Valley Forge?"

"ASAP."

We looked at George. He nodded.

We gathered up our things. George asked about our route.

"There's only one option at this point," I said. "We'll take the fastest route, driving east on Interstate 80 for a couple thousand miles. Eventually we'll veer off to another interstate, to eastern Pennsylvania."

"There are many of these highways," Matt added. "We could go further north and take a different route through the State of Washington. But that's too far out of our way."

"Ah. I was under the impression that the place named after me was the capital city, in Maryland."

"Yes, but one of the fifty states is also named after you."

George considered this for a minute. He didn't know what to say. This was astounding news.

"Are there other states named for leaders of the Revolution?"

"No. Some are named for royalty—the Carolinas, Maryland, Georgia, and Louisiana—and Pennsylvania for its founder William Penn," Matt said.

"And Nevada, of course, after our dog."

George smiled and bent down to pet the pooch. She

was comforting to have around.

We bedded down in our clothes so we could get an early start in the morning. Sleep did not come easily. I tossed and turned, trying to get comfortable, painfully aware of the restlessness of my companions. Eventually I dropped off and entered an altered state of consciousness.

Chapter Forty-Eight
DREAM

Farnsworth, October 25, 2014

I was a passenger on a massive yacht tacking against the wind as it traveled up a snowcapped mountain. Near the bow, a cowboy appeared, a lanky Asian guy on a white horse, dressed in shaggy, bright-green chaps and a lavender, ten-gallon hat, his saddlebags filled with potent-smelling ganja. He winked at me and galloped off toward the stern.

The yacht crested the hill and continued down the other side, slaloming left, then right, down snowy cliffs.

A loud whistle accompanied our descent: *Woooo! Woo-wooooooooo!*

Then a rhythmic *clackety-clack, clackety-clack.*

I was on a train, descending into a fertile, green valley, following a creek that meandered through a marshy flood plain. A village appeared in the distance, the weather morphing quickly from sunny to stormy. We pulled into town and rode the trackless train right down Main Street. Pedestrians scrambled to get out of our way. Lightning and thunder crackled around us. To my right, I saw five or six men with crowbars and huge axes breaking into a bank.

No one on the street noticed the robbery. What was happening here? The train began to slow down, and two shots rang out, followed by the sound of a speeding car. I wanted to shout something to the people on the street, but I was moaning loudly, my brain was foggy, my mouth was cottony, and I had to pee.

I opened my eyes. It took me a minute or two to remember where I was. The first light was coming through the trees outside the yurt. Nevada whimpered insistently near the door. She came over and put her front paws up on the bed next to me, bumped me twice with her snout, then ran back to the door. I got up and let her out.

She took off like a shot, up the hill toward Hank's house. Alarmed to see her do something so out of character, I woke the others and followed.

A gruesome scene awaited us. Hank lay unconscious on the floor. Maggie sat cross-legged next to him, stroking his hair. They were both covered with blood. She looked up wildly when we entered, tears streaming down her face.

"I called 911," she said. "They're sending an ambulance, but it'll take a while to get up the road."

"Shit!" I yelled. "What happened?"

"Didn't you hear the shots? I was out back tending the chickens—and someone came in here and shot him!"

Matt and I froze in fear. George dove right in, grabbed some towels, and applied pressure to Hank's chest to slow down the bleeding. Hank didn't move.

"I can feel his heartbeat," said George. "His pulse is very weak."

"I heard the shots," I said. "But I thought they were part of my dream. And I heard a car, too. Are you okay?"

"I'm terrified," Maggie said, "but I'm not hurt. I guess they figured out who had a sailboat on his land."

No one was sure what to do next.

Hank slowly opened his eyes. "Timmy," he said with great effort.

"I'm right here, Hank."

"Where's the General?"

"Here as well, my good friend."

"I think it was the guys who were nosing around in town, looking for you." He stopped and closed his eyes, wincing in pain. "One of them had strange eyes, kinda like Doug described. They didn't use the General's name, but they kept asking about a big guy in his forties with a ponytail. I didn't tell them anything. I guess they didn't notice the yurt on their way up here."

"That's okay, Hank, take it easy," I said. "No need to talk now. The ambulance will be here soon, and you'll be fine."

"Maybe," he said. "But you gotta get out of here. Now."

"No way are we leaving you."

"I told them I didn't know you guys, but I'm sure they didn't believe me." He winced in pain. "I pulled out my gun and ordered them off the property. They pretended to leave, then turned back and shot me, the bastards! They'll be back." Each word was labored, forced out between painful gasps. "General, you gotta go. You can't do anything here."

Hank closed his eyes again, exhausted by the effort of speaking. His head slumped onto his chest. Drops of blood appeared at his lips.

"He's right," Maggie said. "Go! I'll be here, and I'll keep applying pressure. You guys should get the General out of here."

"No! How can we just leave you here?"

"Because it's important for you to take care of George, and your staying here won't help Hank. I can handle this."

She stared me down with a stubborn expression. "Tim, please go." She was calmer now.

"It does kinda make sense, Timmy," Matt put in. "If we're going to send George back, we've got to get him out of here. As soon as possible. It's not safe here."

I turned to George, who nodded gravely.

I looked down at Hank. I had known him my whole life. He was like an uncle to me. Now he looked like hell. He had lost consciousness and appeared to be bleeding out on the tan maple floor of the little house he had built. How could I leave him?

On the other hand, George Washington. I had, in a way, assumed responsibility for his safety and eventual return.

They were right, there was nothing for us to do here, except help Maggie. And she was urging us to go. Adamantly. I was, indeed, all in. There was no turning back.

With tears in my eyes and a resigned, sighing sob, I turned away from Hank and headed out the door, desperately hoping the ambulance would arrive in time.

We ran to the yurt, snatched up our bags, hopped in the Corolla, and took off down the washboard road. I hated to bring Nevada. I'd considered leaving her there with Hank and Maggie. That was out of the question now, and Rachel had insisted the pup would prove useful. I had my doubts.

Still in full panic mode, we worried about blundering into the clutches of the bad guys. There was only one road out of the Hollow, and around every curve I kept expecting an ambush. I probably hit some of the potholes a little too hard and forced the balky clutch to overachieve while pulling us laboriously up and down the gravel and dirt hills. Once I pulled over to allow another car to go by, hoping it wasn't some thugs out looking for us. Finally, at the top of Heaven's Hollow Road, we were relieved to see the ambulance speed past us.

We raced east to connect with I-80. I couldn't stop looking in my rearview mirror.

Once we had put some miles behind us, we stopped at a Starbucks in Dixon, peed, washed, rested for a moment, and got thoroughly pastried and caffeinated. I texted Pierre: *Heading East.* Then back on the freeway.

About ten minutes later, I felt the clutch slipping badly. I revved the engine a couple of times—*vroom vroom*—with no effect and realized I'd better exit quickly, or we might get stuck on the freeway. I pulled off 80 at downtown Davis and barely made it up the offramp and through a green light. We lost our momentum and blocked the entrance of a supermarket parking lot, just as a huge semitruck was trying to exit.

The Corolla would take us no further. George and Matt hopped out to push the car into a space. The truck driver came over to help.

"Car trouble?" he asked, friendly but redundant.

"Yup," I said. "Bad clutch."

"And we've gotta get to Philly as soon as we can!" Matt blurted.

"Philly?"

"Yeah, it's super urgent!"

"Well, I'm goin' as far as Reno"—my brain filled with images of George Washington hitchhiking his way across the country—"but my cab isn't big enough for all y'all," the trucker went on. "You know, there's a train station near here."

"Oh?"

"Yeah, Amtrak. It's a sweet old building just north of here. You can almost see it from the freeway."

I thanked him, and he got back into his truck and drove away.

"Grab all your stuff," I told my friends. "We're going to the train station. Maybe we can take Amtrak."

"Uh, Timmy?" Matt said. "George still has no ID."

"I don't think they check."

"What about Vada? They don't let animals on Amtrak, do they?"

"Dude, they allow service dogs. I've been on the train with Nevada and my uncle as far as Tahoe. I can play blind on the train." I was improvising madly. "I have her harness in the trunk. Uncle Chuck used to let me play blind with Nevada at home. I would wear my dark shades and close my eyes. He laughed when he heard me crashing into things."

"Timmy, I don't know."

"It's the only way we'll get her on the train. We can't leave her here. I've got Chuck's cane too."

Before he could object more, I handed him a wad of bills. "You buy the tickets. I'm blind."

I slipped the service vest and harness on the pooch, opened the white-tipped cane, and put on my dark sunglasses. The change in Nevada was instantaneous. In a moment, she went from frisky puppy to cool professional, sat obediently, and waited for me to grab the harness and give her a voice command.

"Bring everything," I said. "We're not coming back here."

We shouldered our duffles and trudged off in the direction of the station. Under one arm, George carried the green-handled battle sword in its scabbard, wrapped in burlap.

222

Chapter Forty-Nine
DAVIS

Davis, October 25, 2014

We walked to the station in about ten minutes.

"Oh no! Timmy!" Matt gasped.

"What is it?"

"Looks like the station's changed, too. It's got a lot of arches. Terra-cotta stucco. It's become more Spanish."

I chuckled. "No, I've been here before. It was built just like this, a long time ago. The style's called Mission Revival."

Matt told the clerk at the ticket booth that we needed to get to Philadelphia.

"You're in luck. The Zephyr comes through here in half an hour. Goes all the way to Chicago, getting in Monday afternoon." It was Saturday morning. "Four-hour layover in the Windy City, then we can get you on the Capitol Limited to Washington."

I snuck a look at George, his face impassive at hearing his city name.

"That arrives in D.C. the next day," continued the

agent. "Then you hop a commuter train, and you're in Philly by dinnertime Tuesday."

"Sounds good. Do you have any sleepers?"

He looked at our group. "Big dog! Service animal, right? All of you in one room?"

"Yes to both," LaMatthew said.

"I can put you in a family bedroom in the last car. Got one left. Four bunks—two for adults, two for kids. Looks like you'll need that."

"Is it big enough for us?"

"It's the largest room on the train. It's also the only room available."

Matt looked at George and me, both over six feet, then shrugged and said, "Okay, I'll sleep in the kid's bunk. What choice do we have? Is there a bathroom?"

"Down the hall. Except for the dog."

The clerk issued the tickets, and Matt paid in cash.

"George, you'll like traveling this way much more than your last cross-country trip," he said.

George looked dubious.

"Really, it will be much more like BART than the box-car. Comfortable."

Soon the California Zephyr came around a curve, pulled by two massive blue locomotives, the number 199 emblazoned on the front of the first one.

The train's size and noise startled George as it chugged into Davis station.

I looked at him.

"You okay?"

"I would definitely feel more sanguine had we been able to continue our ride in your Toy Crawler. This appears to be a solid mass of steel with limited access. Nevertheless ..."

He squared his shoulders and began to march down the platform.

"Those are just the locomotives," I called. "Zephyr means 'gentle breeze from the west.' The passenger cars have comfy couches and lots of windows. Easy on, easy off. Trust me."

Chapter Fifty
ZEPHYR

Aboard the California Zephyr, October 25, 2014

I gave Matt my phone and had him take a photo of the Davis station to text to Chow. I was sure the viral video of George and Hank pushing the boat uphill had clued in the people pursuing us. I hoped desperately that a photo of Davis station would help Pierre figure out where we were and perhaps slow down whoever was after us.

We walked down the platform, past the locomotives and a dozen cars, and boarded at the end of the train. Michael, our sleeping car attendant, helped us to our accommodations. Then he took my arm and walked Nevada and me through the car together, showing us around. I swept the floor and walls with my white cane.

Our family bedroom ran the width of the lower level of the last sleeper car, about five by ten feet in all, with a window, recliner, and small pull-out table on each side, and a blue couch with padded headrests. At night, it converted to four fold-down bunks. Three shared toilet cubicles and a shower room were just down the hall.

Michael was a friendly, stocky, young Asian guy with spiky hair and blue-rimmed glasses. The tickets were in Matt's name, so Michael addressed him as "Mr. Matthew." He didn't ask the rest of our names. Our fares included all meals in the dining car, he explained, "except for the dog."

Comedians, all of them.

Nevada was sitting up, eagerly looking for attention, when the conductor came by to check our tickets. A beefy Irish guy, he pulled the door open and confronted an eager canine face looking for a hand to lick or a leg to lean against.

"Some big dog!" he said, noticing the vest. "Been on Amtrak with her before?"

"Briefly."

"As you know, sir, I am required to ask what function she performs for you."

"I'm blind," I said from behind the dark glasses, affecting an alert, listening attitude. *Duh!* "She guides me around, makes sure I don't walk into walls."

"A worthy goal for us all, I'm sure. Thank you, sir. As you may remember, she can go anywhere you can go, but not on the seats."

"She's too big for that, anyway."

"You'd be surprised, sir. Not all our passengers would agree with you. But she's a big one all right. We'll announce smoking stops all along the route, when you can take her out to do her business. Welcome aboard."

He hadn't asked for ID. So far, so good.

Besides the two locomotives, the California Zephyr consisted of a baggage car, three coach cars, an observation car with snack bar, a dining car, and three sleeper cars. Our family room was going to be great for viewing the scenery.

We sat down to watch as the Zephyr rolled us slowly out of Davis. We crossed California's Central Valley and headed toward Sacramento, Reno, Salt Lake, Denver, and points east. The train would make thirty-one stops in all, between here and Chicago.

We passed mile after mile of lush, green farmland against a backdrop of golden foothills and slowly started to relax after the crushing shock of Hank's shooting.

Rachel called, terribly upset about the attack. She had talked to Maggie and had a report for us. Hank was in the hospital, in critical condition. One bullet had just missed his heart, one lodged near his spine. He lost a lot of blood. The thugs pumped two rounds into his chest but failed to kill the tough old bird. So far.

"I hated leaving him, Rachel."

"I know, but you had to get out of there with George. Maggie told me. You did the right thing."

I told her about our panicky flight—the car, the breakdown, the train.

"Bummer," she said. "I'll try to go see Maggie and keep you informed about Hank and his condition."

"Thanks."

Long pause.

"Listen," she continued, "about forgiveness. I've done a little research and found a story from April 1778. That's just a couple of months after George bounced here from Valley Forge. While still encamped there, George pardoned a Loyalist traitor named Martin Widman, after an appeal from a local clergyman who called Widman his 'worst enemy,' but asked for mercy strictly as an act of Christian charity."

I laughed. "So perhaps *The Tempest* will have or has had some influence on him." I couldn't figure out what tense was appropriate. "Assuming we can get him back there."

"Hmm. Perhaps not. There's another thing. Years later, while in office George issued the *smallest* number of pardons of all forty-four presidents, all the way to the present. Just sixteen pardons in eight years. Apparently the quality of mercy *is* strained, after all."

"Is that from *The Tempest?*"

"*The Merchant of Venice.* Maybe you should have taken him to see that instead."

Despite our concern for Hank, we began to feel out of danger for the moment. From our room at the back of the last car of the train, we set out to find lunch.

George led, followed by Matt, then me—with collapsible white cane, glasses, and one hand on Vada's service harness. First we climbed ten steps up a narrow internal staircase in the middle of the car. Then we followed a corridor toward the front of the train—windows on our right, bedrooms on our left—pressed the button to open the automatic doors, and passed into the next car. And so on, before emerging at the dining car. The train had warm brown walls, cheery lighting, and abundant sunshine, though I had to pretend I couldn't see any of it.

Lunch was first come, first served, so we had to wait a few minutes to be seated. We occupied a booth, set with a tablecloth. A bit of a squeeze. George and I had long legs, so it was better that we not sit opposite each other; but Vada was too big to leave in the aisle, so inevitably she was on top of someone's feet under the table. She took advantage of the situation and placed her snout in my crotch. Homey, rude, and a bit too intimate for my taste.

The dining car servers tried to be friendly, but they were not too happy having a dog in there, much less a big one like Vada who attracted a lot of attention—which we didn't want. She was usually good at staying cool and professional in her service dog vest, but it had been several months since Uncle Chuck died. She was a bit out of practice.

We ordered off the menu. The food was cooked fresh, not the reheated airline-type food I had expected. Surprisingly decent.

George relished his burger and fries, followed by vanilla ice cream and execrable coffee. Then we strolled to the observation car. It was pretty full.

Booths with Formica tables lined a third of the upper level. In the rest of the car, swivel chairs faced large picture windows topped by bent glass that curved up to the ceiling. Downstairs we found a snack bar, a booze bar, and more tables for lounging. By now we had crossed California's fertile Central Valley, climbed slowly through golden foothills, snaked through the Sierra Nevada Mountains, and, finally, passed into Nevada's high country. After that, we traversed mile after mile of scrub vegetation to Reno.

I was playing blind as we passed the beautiful scenery, the wraparound sunglasses dark enough that no one could see my eyes. When I walked, I tapped and felt around with the cane, letting Nevada guide me. I took the time to count steps and trusted her to make sure the way was clear. The corridors were too narrow to walk abreast of my human companions, but just right for me and the puppy. When I didn't think anyone was watching, I sometimes got lazy and stopped pretending. I didn't take off the glasses, but I walked more confidently.

Mostly I walked with George or Matt, but late in the afternoon that first day, I got restless while they dozed. I needed to stretch my legs and prowl with Nevada. Walking through the three sleeper cars again, I tapped from side to side with the cane. Nevada led us through the automatic doors and back to the dining car, where the attendants were beginning to set up for dinner. I'd had enough and headed back.

At first it seemed there was no one else in the hallway of the first sleeper car, so I slacked off and began to walk like a sighted person. As I carelessly rounded a corner, I noticed a young woman in purple coming toward me down the narrow corridor. I pulled back to allow her to pass.

Too late I realized my mistake. The train was noisy. A real blind person wouldn't have heard her coming. I kept my head down, then looked up as the woman approached with a curious look on her face. She was pretty and brunette, about my age, sporting a flash of purple and a faint scent of lavender. I mumbled something apologetic, tapped a couple of times with my stick, fussed a bit with Vada's harness, and went on my way. Before she passed, though, I noticed that the woman stopped for a moment, looked carefully at me, and smiled.

A very lovely smile.

Chapter Fifty-One
WINNEMUCCA

Winnemucca, Nevada, October 25, 2014

The stop after Reno was Winnemucca, halfway across the state of Nevada. Michael advised us it would be one of the last stops for a while. We fed the pooch and decided to take her for a walk, so we could leave a little of Nevada in Nevada. Michael told us not to wander far, since we only had ten or fifteen minutes in the waning daylight. He assured us that we would know when it was time to come back.

We stepped onto the platform. The station was quite plain, like a bus shelter on a concrete platform, the town set in high desert surrounded by mountains. Warm haze and skinny cloud formations refracted spectacular streaks of orange and red against a darkening sky. We walked to the western end of the platform and hopped off, walking on gravel away from the station. Nevada did her business quickly, and we stopped for a moment to admire the scenery and the sunset.

As we began to head back, the train whistle blew twice: *Woooo! Woo-woooooooooo!*

Come back!

We picked up our pace. Near the door to our car, Michael was chatting with another attendant, finishing a smoke. Beyond them a few dozen passengers and crew were strolling in the waning daylight. As we approached the rear of the train, I noticed some people up ahead talking intently. One seemed to gesture toward us, or perhaps toward the gorgeous sky behind us, darkening by the second. He—or she—was holding something like a camera or smart phone. At that distance, I couldn't tell if it was a man or a woman, but I did see a flash of purple before a mob of students walked between us and I lost the sight line.

We hurried aboard.

After our first crowded lunch, we decided it would be better to split up for the rest of our meals, to try to reduce crowding and recognizability. The accuracy of the thugs' description of the three of us in Mendo freaked me out. Add to that a large, extroverted service dog who attracted a lot of attention, and we were pretty easy to find, if they knew where to look.

We decided we would break up our threesome as much as we could, and we would leave Nevada in our sleeper during meals.

In order to use dining car tables efficiently, the attendants seated strangers together in groups of four, which encouraged friendly chatting. For folks like us, who would be on the train for three or four days, getting to know fellow travelers helped pass the time and expand our worlds.

Despite our best efforts, that first night Matt and I were paired for a late dinner with a couple from Manhattan. Tess was in her mid-thirties, even more vertically challenged than Matt, with short brown hair and glasses. She taught creative writing and poetry at NYU and was coming back from a writers' retreat near Sacramento. Philip, her boyfriend, worked in the dean's office at Columbia Law School. He was thin, English, about fifty, and wore a black cap with a button that said "When the people lead, the leaders will follow."

She wrote poems, and he wore a Gandhi slogan. Both sweet, intelligent, and well-traveled. Tess had spent her junior year abroad in Paris and had revisited France and Europe numerous times. I had questions.

"You guys have been on long train trips before. I'm a rookie. Will it be difficult for us to sleep?"

"I don't think so," Tess chuckled. "I always take an Ambien on the train, just to be sure. Where's your sleeper?"

"We're in the last room in the last car, the family room."

"Ah," she said, "so we'll get to Chicago before you!"

We laughed again.

"Seriously, though," she added, "You might find more sway at the back of the train. You know, the Caboose Effect."

"Really? What's that?"

"I don't know. I just made it up. Makes sense, though, doesn't it?"

More chuckles.

Philip had traveled the Trans-Siberian Railway and regaled us with stories from that trip.

"You think the service on Amtrak is bad?" he asked. "Just try to get a decent meal in Siberia, anywhere between Irkutsk and Vladivostok!"

Actually, I thought the service on Amtrak had been pretty good so far.

"As you cross Siberia, many of the facilities are outdated, the showers are marginal or nonexistent, and they boast an on-time record that makes Amtrak look absolutely punctual."

"What do you mean?" I asked.

"They're always late on the Trans-Siberian."

"And on Amtrak?"

"They're not as bad as Siberia, but they have a well-earned reputation for tardiness. Don't ever plan to do anything else on an Amtrak arrival day. You have to assume they'll fall behind schedule."

"Why is that?"

"All long-haul passenger traffic in the U.S. is on Amtrak, but—unlike many of the wonderful train systems abroad—they don't own the rails. They lease space on the tracks from freight train companies like Burlington Northern."

"So?"

"Where there's just a single track, the passenger trains must pull over onto a siding to allow freight trains to pass. Because there aren't sidings everywhere, you can sit waiting for quite a while. Also, some of the tracks are only safe for slower speeds. This can cripple Amtrak's ability to stay on time."

He looked at each of us in turn, though I was playing blind, hiding behind my dark shades.

"Where are you guys heading again?"

Matt answered. "From the Zephyr, we transfer in Chicago to the Capitol Limited to Washington, then a commuter train to Philly. How about you?"

"We're on the Lake Shore Limited from Chicago to New York," Tess said. "It goes through all the upstate cities in New York State. It's a pretty ride."

"How much time do you have between trains in Chicago?" Philip asked.

"Nearly four hours. That should certainly be plenty of

time, even if we're a bit late."

"Ah, we'll see."

Not as bad as Siberia, I thought. *A great slogan for Amtrak.*

I headed back to our compartment and checked the World Series scores. The Giants had pummeled the Royals in Game 4, winning in decisive fashion, 11-4. Again, no homers for either team.

All tied up, at two games each.

Chapter Fifty-Two
FITZ

Aboard the California Zephyr, October 25, 2014

That evening after dinner, even though the hour was late, none of us felt sleepy. As we left Nevada and crossed into the salt flats of Utah, we watched *Fitzcarraldo* on my laptop.

George had seen movies before, and he understood they were plays—artistic works of fiction with scripted lines spoken by actors. But he had absolutely no idea how they were made. He watched the first few minutes and asked some questions. He had seen South America on maps, and he had heard of Peru.

"And this is not right now, Timothy? Am I correct in this surmise?"

"That's right, George. This movie was made more than thirty years ago, and the story takes place in the early 1900s."

"This fellow here with the yellow hair," he said, indicating the lead actor. "His name is Fitzgerald? I know farmers of that name, and some soldiers, too. I believe they tend to be natives of Ireland."

"Yes."

"This fellow, however, speaks English with an odd accent. One I would not attribute to a denizen of that Emerald Isle. And he certainly looks nothing like any Irishman I have met."

"That actor's name is Klaus Kinski. He's German, as is the director."

"Director?" It meant nothing to him.

"The creative force behind the movie. He tells the actors where to stand and how to emote, tells the crew where to put the camera, and arranges all the individual shots together in the final editing session."

He glazed over. Too much information. He knew that cameras made movies, but to George, a camera was anything that recorded an image—like a smart phone. That was all he knew. I persisted.

"The director of *Fitzcarraldo* is Werner Herzog."

In Herzog's opus, Fitzcarraldo wants to become a rich rubber baron so he can build an opera house and one day bring in Enrico Caruso to sing.

Kinski's character is obsessive and somewhat crazed. His brooding, deep-blue eyes project a wildness that bursts forth from his soul. Claudia Cardinale plays his paramour, a happy madam with a profitable brothel, bubbly and upbeat, eager to fund her man's venture.

Assisted by hundreds of indigenous people from the surrounding area, Fitz and his crew eventually do succeed in dragging the intact ship up a steep hill, across a mile of jungle, and into the other river nearby.

At numerous points during the story, Fitzcarraldo plays gramophone recordings of Caruso singing dramatic, operatic arias. It soothes his mood, calms him down, and often serves as a portent of positive events.

"Hearing that music while we watch the ship glide up-river, then slowly slide uphill, reminds me of those Mendo hippies playing 'Dark Star' as she sailed up to Hank's house," I said. "I hope he's okay."

"Me too," said Matt. We brooded silently for a moment, then he added, "You know, there's a similar musical thing in *Apocalypse Now*, in Vietnam, an ominous boat-traveling-up-the-jungle-river scene to the tune of 'I Can't Get No Satisfaction.' To say nothing of that scene of the air strike on the beach, when they play 'Ride of the Valkyries' from the helicopters as they strafe a Vietnamese village. Then they go surfing."

"Hard to get that out of your mind," I said. "Spooky jungle-river scenes cry out for dramatic music."

I had hoped George might take some encouragement from this film.

"This is an overcoming-obstacles story. Early in the movie, Fitz's girlfriend Molly says that 'it's only the dreamers who move mountains.' He dreams of achieving the impossible, and it comes true."

"Partially," said George, warming to the topic. "They do succeed in hefting the boat to the top of the hill, as did our dear friend Hank. But Fitz's plan does not succeed, despite his best efforts."

"He never makes a fortune selling rubber, George, but he does succeed in bringing an opera company to Iquitos to perform."

"Yes, a victory of sorts, I suppose. If one likes opera that much. A sentiment which, truth be told, is beyond my ken. This is not a very satisfying or encouraging story, especially because it is not a story about a war or revolution, but about making riches."

I thought about George and his absence from Valley Forge. The film showed the effect of a strong leader with belief and charisma. But perhaps he was just too crazy, and it was all too far-fetched for George.

Chapter Fifty-Three
BURDEN

The train sped along at a good clip, swaying a bit from side to side, banging at bumps on the rails. Tess was right. The last car was the bounciest.

Michael had made up our beds. The long couch folded into a single bed, with another pull-down bunk above it. Both were more than six feet long, just a few inches short for George and me. But the smaller bunks were kid-size, much too short even for Matt.

We were all exhausted and stressed. A lot had happened since I heard those shots during my dream back in the yurt. We had been on the run all day, our brief stay in Mendocino now just a memory. We were restless, especially Matt.

"I know I'm short, but I'm not a kid," he said. "Why didn't we ask how big the bunks were?"

"Sorry."

"Do you think we can rent another sleeper?"

"I'm not sure we can afford it. Let me nose around.

241

You can take my bunk."

I got up with Nevada and left our family bedroom. Two roomettes on our corridor were occupied earlier but now sat empty. *Maybe I can get forty winks here, and Michael will never know.* The roomettes were unlocked. I let myself into one with Vada, curled up on one of the recliners, and went to sleep.

It started out as a fitful night. I had been playing *Independence* earlier in the day, and it was giving me nightmares. Though I didn't usually remember my dreams, I did recall one spooky image of George standing on top of our double-decker sleeper car as we sped across the Utah desert. He brandished his sword over his head like in the Battle of Monmouth painting, but he was wearing a "Baseball is Life" shirt and flip-flops, riding a train, not a horse. The image was more scary than comical.

I imagined a pretty girl in purple at my side, stroking my arm and nuzzling my neck. My tension dissipated. I began to relax. Finally, my coiled body started to unwind.

I woke with a start. For a moment I didn't know where I was. I couldn't identify the odd sensations I was experiencing or the warm body next to me. Then I realized that Nevada was lying across me, licking me just below the ear.

I sniffed the air. Besides the fact that I needed a shower and sensed the presence of canine saliva on my neck, I thought I could detect a faint whiff of lavender. Wishful thinking. Then I realized that at some point during the night someone had come into the roomette and slipped a pillow under my head. Perhaps it was Michael.

Unable to fall back asleep, I returned to our family room. Matt snoozed on the top bunk. George was awake on the lower bunk, reading the Amtrak timetable.

I sat down on one of the kid-size bunks.

"You can't sleep either?" I asked.

"I have rested for several hours, Timothy," George responded. "That may be all I am capable of at this time."

He leafed through the timetable, marveling over the long list of cities on our itinerary.

"This is indeed a vast and wondrous country. Yet the fact that we can traverse thousands of miles in a few days continues to breathe on my brain."

"Blow your mind."

"Yes, quite so." A master of the idiom.

"Since you're up already ..." I pulled out my laptop and started *Burden of Dreams*, a documentary by filmmaker Les Blank.

"What's this?"

"Another movie. It's about the making of *Fitzcarraldo*."

Matt woke up and watched with us. Director Werner Herzog appeared on screen. He described some of the early problems in mounting his production deep in the Amazon. The boat from *Fitzcarraldo*, the *Molly Aida*, appeared in the background behind him. George was confused.

"Who is this man? Is that not the boat from the movie *Fitzgerald*?"

"Yes. This is the director. This man, and the others we see with cameras and microphones, are the crew making the movie of *Fitzcarraldo*. They are the ones in modern clothing. We also see the actors, in period costumes from about 1900. We are watching an illustrated, recorded story.

"This is not right now, George. It's a complex moving picture with sound. A painting only takes one painter. This film has a very small crew, but most movies take dozens of crew people, working together to capture the actors' performances."

The main challenge faced by the character Fitzcarraldo is also the central struggle of Herzog's real-life production: getting the *Molly Aida* up over the hill. I had shown George the latest Harry Potter movie, so he had seen school kids fly on brooms, fling magic wands, cast spells, and battle supernatural creatures. He was astounded to realize that Herzog was actually hauling a full-size ship over a real hill.

"I had assumed that the ship going over the hill in the movie was one of your magical special efforts," he said.

"Special effects."

"Indeed."

"Nope. They really did it."

In *Burden of Dreams*, George watched Herzog, Kinski, Cardinale, a guy with a camera, and a woman with a boom microphone all interacting in service of a shot. I saw the first bits of understanding glimmer in his consciousness.

"So, this is a movie about a movie?"

"Exactly. It's called a 'behind the scenes' film or a 'making-of.'"

"Ah. Very clever."

In the film *Fitzcarraldo*, the indigenous people agree to help haul the ship over the mountain. Part of the story of *Burden of Dreams* concerns Herzog's real-life efforts to hire them to help build huge winches and then act in the scenes.

Aristotle was right. Art imitates life. Or was life imitating art here?

George was intrigued to see that the movie production utilized additional mechanized means to help haul the ship.

"Aha!" he called out. "They are using a doozer!"

"What's that?"

"A bull-doozer."

"Dozer."

"Yes, like the one Hank and his friends used to assist the *Dark Star* on his hill. Fitzgerald has used one in the movie."

"No, Herzog uses the dozer to help make *Fitzcarraldo*. But he doesn't show it during the movie."

"Ah. If he has a dozer, does that not solve his problem?"

"Keep watching."

The bulldozer breaks down a lot, needs parts, isn't powerful enough. Herzog's engineer urges him to choose a level part of the isthmus.

Herzog, of course, refuses.

"The central metaphor of my film is that they haul a ship over what's essentially an impossibly steep hill. I lose that with level terrain like the Panama Canal."

With four actors and the film crew aboard, Herzog takes his boat down dangerous rapids, filming the climax of the story, where the indigenous people cut the boat free and set it adrift.

The boat is dented after smashing into rocky banks and massive river boulders, and a couple of crew members sustain minor injuries. But the boat survives, and the footage is spectacular. George appreciated the filmmakers' daring in filming this thrilling climax.

Fitzgerald's small victory toward the end of *Fitzcarraldo*: he does sell the boat and use the money to bring an opera company to his Amazon town for one glorious performance.

Herzog's large victory toward the end of *Burden of Dreams*: with heavier equipment and a new engineering plan, Herzog gets the boat up and over the hill and wraps the shoot, nearly four years after the start of pre-production.

Matt looked at me. "Wow!"

I smiled. Herzog was as crazy and obsessed as Fitzcarraldo. The polar opposite of our General. But would George take heed?

He was quiet and thoughtful at first, then looked up. "Thank you, Timothy. Clearly this filmmaking is an effort that takes great passion and energy, strength of character, ingenuity, and organization. Much like mounting a military operation. Inspiring. Overcoming obstacles, indeed!"

Matt added, "I love the part where Herzog says, 'If I abandon the project, I would be a man without dreams, and I don't want to live like that. I live my life, or I end my life, with this project.'"

"I completely understand," George said. "I am caught up in my own dream for our country's future. I cannot be a man without dreams. I refuse to live like that as well."

Chapter Fifty-Four
ROCKIES

I was in a good mood that Sunday, the second day on the train.

Matt read me the breakfast bill of fare before sitting at a different table. I ate with a family from Utah: a dad and two girls, ages ten and thirteen, who had boarded the Zephyr in the wee hours. They were all tired. Dad wore a WWE Raw wrestling T-shirt and a Denver Broncos cap. He was chatty and hungry. The girls were too tired to eat and could hardly keep their heads up.

I wore my dark glasses and had to remember not to look directly at people, but rather to cock an ear in the direction of whomever was speaking. I was good at playing blind, but it took a lot of concentration.

After breakfast, Matt guided me into the observation car, where we spent most of the day absorbing the magnificence of the Rockies. For a while, we sat together with Tess and Philip, the couple from Manhattan, chatting amiably in the swivel chairs facing the huge windows. It was a gorgeous day, rays of sunshine streaking across the terrain and through the car. George sat separately, enjoying the vast expanses of the country he had fathered. Or would soon father.

The Zephyr followed the Colorado River upstream through the mountains. The river rushed across red rock canyons, some rough and tumble, some placid and filled with boats and rubber rafts drifting along in the sunshine. The conductor advised, with a chuckle, that "the rafters like to do the Moon River thing." Up and down the river, young people—mostly men—dropped their pants, bent over, and mooned the train! I was glad I wasn't sitting with George, knowing I could never explain this behavior.

The river valley changed frequently, from scrubby vegetation to conifer forests to scrumbly piles of scree. The autumn sun glinted off the water. It was all fascinating to watch, even as I pretended not to. Matt narrated a running account of the scene for me in a quiet voice. The train crossed back and forth across the river many times, so the best vantage points were sometimes on the left side of the car, sometimes on the right. Other passengers switched sides to keep the river in view, but I stayed put. What did it matter? I was blind. Sometimes the train swooped down low, close to the river, sometimes up high, spanning a deep valley.

Hour after hour went by quickly. We ordered wine, then more wine. Tess regaled us with tales of her wild student days in France, and Philip spoiled too much of the plot of the book he was reading. I was frightfully relaxed, trusting that the cartel thugs had no idea where we were. The car was crowded, but I didn't want to give up my seat, especially with Tess telling us, "That's when I met Jean-Luc, the *Parisien* who took my virginity. A boy, really, a Sorbonne student I met in a café. I wore my 'go-away' café face, but he could tell I was really lonely and talked to me anyway."

At one point, under the general murmur of voices I heard someone hissing, "Why does the blind guy have to take up a seat in the observation car?"

Tacky. Didn't he know that blind people had acute hearing?

After a while I dropped off, lulled by the wine and the movement of the train, still tired from the previous day's desperate flight from Mendo and poor rest since then. When I awoke, Tess and Philip were gone. Matt was on the other side of the car discussing baseball with someone. I stared out at the view, drowsily lost in thought. I felt someone sit down beside me, but paid no attention at first.

Soon I felt I was being watched. Without looking to my right, I said, "Hello."

"Hello," came a female voice. I turned my head slowly to the right, my eyes up to the ceiling. It was a practiced gesture. I tried not to look at the speaker at first, and I made a show of listening. As a kid, I had been fascinated by Uncle Chuck's blindness and spent hours playing blind. I had studied old movies like *The Miracle Worker* and *Wait Until Dark* and could mimic the blind acts of Patty Duke and Audrey Hepburn perfectly. Experience taught me that the correct head tilt early in the game went a long way to faking blindness. First impressions rule.

I knew the woman couldn't see my eyes, so I looked down. Oh my! It was the girl in purple, now wearing a teal shirt and black jeans.

She was cute. Tall, wiry, and athletic, she had dark hair, warm brown eyes, and a broad, inviting smile.

"Hi," she said. "I noticed you the other day in the sleeper car."

Smitten! We really hit it off, talking for hours and hours. Her name was April Lansing, and she was from Portland. She had recently graduated from Oregon State and was on her way to visit family in Cleveland. She liked the Giants and some of my favorite movies. I hadn't talked with a girl—really talked—since Marnie dumped me months before. April was gorgeous. I melted when she smiled.

I told her we were going to Philly to see the sights. I also shared as much as I could about myself without mentioning time travel or the fact that I was traveling with George Washington. I didn't want to sound pretentious. Or ridiculous. Or crazy.

I forced myself to look away often, to continue playing blind, even though I was pretty certain that she had seen me using my sight. If she had, she didn't bring it up. I contented myself with sidelong glances and wished we could make eye contact.

I was still tired and very relaxed by the wine. At one point—I swear I didn't doze off, not even for a moment—I looked over and realized she was gone. The seat to my right was empty, except for a trace of lavender in the air, so faint that I thought meeting April might have been a dream. I groggily looked over at Matt, who flashed a sly grin and a thumbs up and mouthed, "Some babe!"

It wasn't a dream!

A minute later a funny-looking guy with a heavily lined face, owlish glasses, and greasy gray hair sat down next to me and muttered a greeting. He wore a dirty black hoodie and a large cross, and he carried a well-worn Bible. It was time to go. The blind guy didn't have to occupy prime real estate anymore.

Chapter Fifty-Five
199

Matt walked me back to our sleeper, and George followed a short time later. Nevada was happy to see us. Michael brought us lunch from the dining car. I took off my dark glasses and stared out the window. It was a relief not to play blind for a little while.

Now that I was out of public view I could check my phone. The Zephyr didn't offer Wi-Fi, but we passed through wide belts of cellphone service. Of course, I couldn't be seen reading texts or emails. Blind guys don't do that.

Someone had sent me a photo. A text message with no text, from Unknown Name. The photo showed a train bathed in a golden glow, sometime after sunset. An Amtrak train with the number 199 on the first locomotive, parked next to a small station surrounded by mountains. In the background, clouds streaked with orange and red across a warm sky.

Winnemucca. My blood ran cold. I showed it to Matt and George.

"That's our engine, Timmy," said Matt, "but it might not be our train."

"Bullshit."

"They run the Zephyr everyday, in each direction. Whoever sent that pic could have taken it some other time they used this locomotive on the Zephyr run."

"Maybe. But why send this to me? Is someone trying to scare us?" I said.

"It's working, but if the bad guys know where we are, why would they tell us? What's the point of scaring us?"

"Exactly!" I said. "We want to send George back to Valley Forge and his own time. I think they'd try to stop us with force, not convince us it's a bad idea."

"This picture does not seem like a warning," George broke in. "Someone with evil intent would send a threatening image, not this pretty picture of a train and a sunset. I believe it to be an assurance. Other than the three of us, who knows we are on this train?"

"Well, Nevada does," I reminded him.

"Of course."

"And hopefully Chow has figured it out. I sent him a picture of the train depot in Davis. He knows we must return to Pennsylvania," I said. "Hopefully he'll recognize it as an Amtrak station and guess that we're on the California Zephyr. If he checks the ticket sales, he'll find three one-way fares from Davis to Philly in Matt's name and could figure out our route."

"On the other hand," said Matt, "perhaps the deep mole at Homeland Security will figure it out, too. I don't know how they could get their people on this train so quickly, but we are stuck on a long, long ride for three days, with nowhere else to go."

We climbed higher through the mountains, eventually shooting through the Moffat Tunnel under the Continental Divide.

We emerged on the east side of the Rockies. Four thousand feet below we could see in the distance the beginning of the Great Plains: some windmills, lots of farmland, and the city of Denver sparkling in the sun. A very dramatic reveal!

We arrived at Union Station in Denver exactly on time, at sunset on Sunday. So much for Philip and his snarky warnings about Amtrak's tardiness.

The station was a fine old structure, freshly facelifted, with high, vaulted ceilings, a hotel, and a dozen restaurants in the lobby. We took Nevada out for a walk along the tracks, then through the station. I hoped to get a glimpse of April, but she was nowhere to be found.

I called Aunt Rachel for an update.

"Hank is out of intensive care but still in serious condition. Tim, they don't know if he'll ever be able to walk again. They haven't removed the bullet near his spine, and his prognosis is uncertain."

Depressing news.

We headed back to the train. Tess spotted us and waved. Philip invited us to dinner.

I needed the diversion. I enjoyed chatting with smart people. It helped keep my mind off Hank and what he was going through.

Matt ate separately. But by the time George and I got to the dining car after Denver, two strangers were already seated with Tess and Philip. George and I were paired with a couple in their fifties from Reno, Jack Sprat and his wife. Tommy was skinny, jovial but twitchy, with thinning, dyed red hair. He wore jeans and a huge, shiny brass belt buckle bearing the bas-relief likeness of some antlered mammal. Arlene was heavy, blond, blowzy, and outgoing. She wore a sea-foam green track suit. They were on their way to New Orleans for a lodge convention. Both liked to square dance.

They were taking the Zephyr to Chicago, then transferring to the train they called the City of New Orleans. My earlier concerns that we attracted too much attention—that they might ask too many questions—were mitigated by their total lack of interest in anyone else. That was fine with us. Tommy sold Japanese cars, but Arlene preferred American cars "out of respect for my elders," some of whom had worked in car plants in Detroit. Tommy explained—obviously not for the first time—that many foreign-branded cars were actually built in the U.S. with American workers.

Arlene spanked back, "It's not the same."

Meals were included, but just before we paid for our wine and tipped the staff, all of whom were African American, Arlene leaned forward. In a stage whisper she told us that in New Orleans, "The Blacks still sit in the back of the bus." She winked, Tommy laughed, and I hated that they assumed I would share their prejudices. From behind my dark glasses, I caught a glimpse of George, sitting very straight at the table, his long legs folded to the side. His face looked calm, but I could tell he was perturbed. These were not intelligent people.

Dripping with condescension, Arlene told us they had once been the only White folks on a train from Washington to Baltimore. "I guess we probably felt the way they must have in the past, when the trains were mostly White and there were only a few Blacks."

Probably not, I thought.

George and I left soon thereafter.

Chapter Fifty-Six
DIVERSION

We crossed from Colorado to Nebraska that evening and continued to speed across the dark plains.

The Gigantics easily crushed the Royals 5-0 in Game 5. Bumgarner was brilliant, pitching a complete-game shutout. No home runs for either team. I hated missing the games, but when we had cellular service along our route, I could listen to the action on my phone and even watch video highlights when I was alone. The Giants now led the Series three games to two, and the momentum had swung in their favor. One more win would sew it up.

Just before bedtime, the conductor announced that a freight train had derailed up ahead, tearing up some track. Our train had to be rerouted, using tracks that wouldn't allow us to go faster than twenty miles per hour. He estimated the disruption would delay us more than three hours.

At that rate, we would still get into Chicago forty-five minutes before our connection to the Capitol Limited, but the margin of error had suddenly shrunk.

Michael came by and assured us that Amtrak would take care of us, that they would either transfer us to another train or put us up in a hotel. If we didn't make our connection, we wouldn't end up sleeping in the station.

I smiled at him from behind my shades. He was upbeat and helpful, a new employee on one of his first Zephyr runs. This was his second week on his own, after a few weeks of training and shadowing other attendants.

He turned down our bunks. A while after he left, I slipped out of our family bedroom and into the roomette next door, which was still unoccupied. This time I flipped the two recliners down to make a narrow bed, then stretched out. Despite our car lurching, swaying, and bumping at the back of the train, I dropped off quickly.

I awoke some time later to the realization that I was not alone in the bunk. I assumed it was Nevada again, until a long, slender body with bumps in all the right places pressed up against me. I thought I might be dreaming, but the sensation was too real.

It was April. She turned on the night-light, and I realized that the shades on the windows to the corridor were open. I closed them. She rolled on top of me. I wasn't wearing my dark glasses. She held my face in her hands, looked right into my eyes, and stared deep into the windows of my soul.

"Tim." She smiled. "Oh, I like you, Tim."

I melted.

"*Mmmm.*" That was all I could muster under the circumstances.

"I know I shouldn't do this," she said.

"No, you should."

She kissed me.

It was a long kiss, an eternal moment. None of my body parts had been in physical contact with a female human body part for months. A surge of emotion welled up inside me. I wanted to laugh and tear up at the same time.

She smelled great. I kissed her again, laughed again, then kissed her again. And I knew for certain this was no dream.

Eventually we both fell asleep. I woke again hours later. The train had stopped, the shades were still closed. I was alone. I thought I perceived a lavender waft, but honestly, it could have been the air freshener from the restroom just down the hall.

Why aren't we moving? Something feels very wrong.

I slipped out of the roomette, flung open the door to our family bedroom, and snapped on the light. Nevada was stationed at the entrance, eager to get out. But where were the hell were George and Matt? It was four in the morning.

I clucked like a grandma who has misplaced her glasses, but the room was small, and they were clearly not in it. I wasn't sure what to do. Vada leaned hard against my leg, trying to push me out the door, so I decided we should go find the boys. I slipped her into the harness and vest.

I had no idea where to go, but Vada immediately pulled me out of the compartment. The main door to the outside was closed, with a large sign in red letters: "Stop! Do not open door or window. Except employees or in case of emergency." I paused for a moment. Wasn't this an emergency? *Stop! Open the damn door, I've gotta find George Washington!*

I looked out the window. Moonlight, gravel, scrub vegetation. *Are we at a station? Would opening the door set off an alarm? How could I do that and still play blind?*

Nevada sniffed around a bit, pushing on the door of

the shower room. I opened it with trepidation. The outer dressing room was pretty dry, but someone had showered recently, and there was still water on the floor of the stall. Nevada stuck her head in and used her long tongue to lick the floor. I ran the shower to give her another puddle to drink from, happy that she wasn't using the toilet to quench her thirst.

We backed out of there, and Nevada headed for the narrow staircase to the upper level of our car. She was on a mission and bounded up the ten stairs, pulling me after her.

She dragged me along the upper corridor of the sleeper, continuing toward the front of the train. Dim night lights and a gloomy sense of foreboding now replaced the cheery lighting and friendly daytime ambience. Cold sweat and a metaphorical dagger to my heart dampened the warm glow lingering from April's visit.

At the end of the car, I pressed the button and the door slid open. We crossed into the next sleeper, then hurried along to the third. Nevada tugged me along, stopped occasionally to cock her head and evaluate some vibe or scent, then dragged me further. In the third sleeper, she led me down the narrow staircase.

At the bottom we discovered Michael, our sleeping car attendant. The door to outside was open, his small yellow booster step positioned on the gravel.

Chapter Fifty-Seven
SIDING

Aboard the California Zephyr, October 27, 2014

Good evening, sir," Michael said calmly. "Having trouble sleeping? Your companions went outside here to get some air. We only opened this one door. I believe they headed off to the right."

So that's where they'd gone. I was such a nervous nelly! Michael helped me step off the train and onto the track bed. There was no station. We were somewhere in Nebraska, probably a million miles from the nearest town.

I was still freaked out, but his casual tone reassured me.

"We're on a siding, waiting for a freight train," he said. "It's almost here. Probably pass us in a few minutes, so please come right back when you hear the whistle, okay?"

He tried to pet Nevada, but she wasn't having it. She tugged and tugged toward the back of the train. I dropped the leash and trotted after her.

Moonlight guided my footing. Near the end of the train, as Nevada disappeared from sight around the corner, I saw Matt and George standing on the track. The freight train we were waiting for was now approaching. I called out loudly, so I could be heard above the noise of its arrival.

Then I realized Matt and George had their hands up. As I came around the corner, I saw why.

Tess and Philip stood ten feet from my friends, brandishing two big, bad, menacing handguns—black automatics with long metal silencers.

Philip stood at the back of the train, his gun leveled at Matt's heart. Beyond him, little Tess, barely five feet tall, held her gun in two hands and grimly pointed it up at George Washington's head. True to her retriever heritage, Nevada stood frozen, pointing at the two of them with one front paw raised.

I had clomped clumsily into this tableau like a herd of buffalo. Philip and Tess glanced over at me, then back at their targets. Neither seemed puzzled that I didn't appear to be blind.

There was nothing to talk about. They had guns and murderous intent. They were out to kill, not to scare us away from Valley Forge. My arrival had only postponed catastrophe by an instant.

Then everything happened at once.

Our train whistle summoned us:

Woooo! Woo-woooooooooo!

The freight train that had been approaching sped by, answering with a deafening whistle and a loud *clankety-clank, clankety-clank* on the track a few feet away. Boxcar after boxcar, tanker after tanker, dozens of cars hauled by two massive engines.

As I watched in horror, Tess and Philip aimed carefully and squeezed their triggers. Nevada barked a single throaty, once-a-month *woof*, flinging her ninety pounds forward onto Philip's back as he fired, knocking him over and spoiling his aim. Tess fired as well, just as Matt leaped in front of George. I counted five pops from the silenced guns. It was all over very quickly.

George and I stood in shock. Tess sprawled on her back next to the tracks, one leg splayed to the side. A pool of blood spread rapidly on the ground under her head. One of Philip's errant shots had blown away part of her face.

Philip didn't fare much better. The force of Nevada's leap had knocked him off the raised railroad bed, down about fifty feet to the dry ravine below. He didn't move. His black cap lay beside him, the pin with the Gandhi slogan probably face down in the dirt. A short time ago, we had been drinking wine and swapping stories. Now I understood that it had all been a charade.

I was a fool.

How could they do this? Tess was just describing how she lost her maidenhood to that guy on Rue Mouffetard in Paris! I thought we were friends.

Worst of all, Matt lay crumpled at George's feet, a dark stain soaking through his UC Berkeley T-shirt. Another stain appeared in his jeans, near the right hip pocket.

"Matty! Oh, shit!"

George dropped to his knees and looked him over.

"He is alive. I cannot tell how badly he's wounded, but his breathing does not appear to be impaired."

Matt looked like hell, but he was conscious, eyes open.

"I got ya, Matty. Hang on."

"Fuck, this hurts! Timmy, you gotta save George. The train's leaving. You gotta get him out of here. Get him back there." He coughed and winced with the pain.

"We will. But we're not leaving you, buddy."

George balled up Matt's T-shirt and began to apply pressure to the wounds.

At that moment a lanky Asian guy brandishing a pistol ran around the corner, out of breath.

Pierre Chow.

"Found you! Are you all right?"

"No!" I yelled at him. "I am definitely not all right! Those two are probably both dead, and Matt's been shot. I am definitely not all right! And where the hell did you come from?"

"I just boarded the train in Omaha a couple of hours ago," said Pierre, offering me an incongruous fist bump.

Then April came running up, also with a gun.

What?

"It took us a while to figure out how to find you after you left Mendocino," Pierre continued, "but the photo of the Davis station was a good clue."

"Well, it didn't take the cartel's killers too long to figure it out. They beat you here by a lot."

"They did beat me, but I've had an agent on this train keeping an eye on you."

I looked at April. She grinned and winked and waved her pistol. Despite the dire circumstances, I winked back, open-mouthed.

Woooo! Woo-wooooooooooo!

"We can talk more later," Pierre said. "Are you or the General hurt?"

"No."

He scooped up Tess's gun, checked her pockets, and found a smart phone and more ammunition.

He used a flashlight to check out Philip. No movement.

Even if he was still alive, he had to be badly hurt, and we were a long way from nowhere. Pierre pushed Tess's body down the embankment to join Philip, then turned to me and said, "Let's get back on the train!"

George squatted, easily hefted Matt over one shoulder, and rushed back to the train. Pierre followed, loping along the gravel. Nevada started to run after them, then stopped and looked back at me, expectant. Aunt Rachel was right. Vada had come in handy.

I peered over the edge for one last look. No one would find Tess and Philip for quite a while. I wondered if she really wrote poetry, shuddered, and shook my head. April grabbed my arm, and I followed my companions.

Chapter Fifty-Eight
NURSE

The door to our car was now open, and Michael met us there. George climbed aboard, Matt's limp and bloody form on his right shoulder. Chow followed, then Nevada, April, and I.

Ignoring the blood, the situation, and the fact that I could see again, Michael asked, "Is there anyone else still out there?"

"Nope, everyone has come in now," Chow said. "And thank you."

He turned to me. "April has medical supplies and training."

We followed her to the upper level of our sleeper car, to a bedroom compartment with a private sink, toilet, and shower.

The shock of what had just happened started to hit me now. *Tess and Philip tried to kill George and Matt. April works for Chow. What the hell? April lied to me. Is anything she said true?*

With the bunks folded down, there wasn't much room,

so George and I lingered in the hallway, whispering so we wouldn't wake people in the adjoining sleepers. I was worried sick about Matt, but I couldn't help thinking about April, wanting to hold her again, to kiss her and re-create the exhilaration I had felt just a short time ago, before I had waltzed into the gory scene of death and betrayal at the end of the train.

But April and Pierre were working on Matt. In those first few minutes, we didn't know how badly he was hurt—or, even, if he might die. The freight train long past, our train began to move, slowly at first, then picking up speed through the Nebraska night.

After a while, April came out for a moment and urged us to go rest. "I'll take care of your friend, Tim. I'm a nurse. Among other things."

I held her hand, speechless. She wasn't a college girl, she was a federal agent. Playacting.

April squeezed my hand and gave me a knowing smile. "I never lied to you," she whispered. "Well, not too much. Everything I told you was true, including how I feel about you. I just didn't tell you everything. I'm a few years older than I led you to believe, I've been to nursing school, and I'm good with languages. And I do like the Giants."

I smiled wearily. "God, you're beautiful."

She beamed at me, the same smile that had melted my heart just a few hours earlier.

George put his hand on my shoulder. "Come away, lad. Let them do their work."

I needed to know more.

"What happened? How did they get the two of you to go out there?"

George winced. "They fooled us. They had been such

265

charming company earlier in the day. Well spoken, well traveled. And she was so small! I believed them to be who they said they were, academic people from New York."

"Not hit men for the cartels. Or, hit persons."

"They came to our room in the middle of the night, Timothy. You told her we were in the family bedroom in the last car. Tess knocked and said that our light was visible under the door. The train had stopped, and she invited us to come outside for a breath of air and a walk along the track while we waited for the other train to pass. It seemed like a good idea at the time. I detested being cooped up and could not sleep. LaMatthew awoke and began to put on his shoes. Then we realized that you were not with us. Where did you go?"

"I slipped into the roomette next door, as I did last night, in an attempt to give us all more space."

I was reluctant to tell him about April. Maybe it was a mistake. Maybe she was just doing her duty, pretending to like me.

I cleaned up, showered, and put on fresh clothes. I started to feel better, relaxed by the hot water on my back and warmed by the memory of April's smile. Eventually I began to get sleepy, just as the sun broke above the horizon. But I had to check on Matt.

George and I slipped upstairs to April's compartment. Matt was sprawled out on the lower bunk, sleeping fitfully. Pierre was crammed into the top bunk, his legs hanging off the end, snoozing. April rested in the recliner.

"How is he?"

"He's going to be okay, Tim," she told us. "He took two rounds."

"Oh no! Matty!"

"Try not to wake him. One bullet went through his navel, from the right side. It appears to have entered and exited without damaging any vital organs."

"Good. And the other?"

"The second bullet penetrated his *gluteus medius*, also from the right side. It just missed the superior gluteal artery. He must have turned sideways when he jumped in to protect the General."

"Did that bullet also exit?"

"No, I had to go in and remove it, but it wasn't very deep. I gave him a field anesthetic. He hasn't awakened since you left. Fortunately, he didn't lose much blood, and the wounds were actually pretty superficial. He should be fine."

"What is the *gluteus medius*?" George asked.

"The butt cheek," April clarified.

"He got capped in the ass?" I said.

"In a manner of speaking, yes."

"Are we going to get him off this damn train and to a hospital?"

"I don't know. Talk to Pierre."

I squeezed her hand and gazed longingly into her eyes. I hadn't been acting blind for hours. I recalled that Michael, the sleeping-car attendant, had appeared unperturbed by the blood all over us when we reboarded the train.

"Does Michael work for Pierre, too?"

"In a way," April said. "I showed him my Homeland Security credentials when I first got on the train and handed him a fistful of Benjamins."

"Benjamins?" asked George.

"$100 bills."

He scowled. He was still jealous that one Franklin equaled one hundred Washingtons.

"I told him it was all hush-hush," April continued, "a matter of national security. I warned him that people might go missing or he might see blood, but he was to trust me and ignore anything out of the ordinary. I flashed my gun and appealed to his sense of patriotism. He was jazzed to take part, especially when I hinted that I could make trouble for his cousin with the immigration problem."

"How did you know he had a cousin with an immigration problem?"

"I didn't, until he turned green when I mentioned it. He told us where to find you after you left the train."

I turned to George. "Can you give us a minute?"

He nodded and headed back to our room.

I looked at April. I wasn't sure how to feel about her.

"And what about us? Was that all part of the plan?"

"I didn't know much at first. My orders were to watch over you guys. I responded to an emergency call. I was the closest agent, working on a different case in Lincoln, north of Sacramento, and I had to jump quickly once Pierre figured out that you had boarded this train in Davis. I had no prep and didn't know who you were at first, until you made a mistake pretending to be blind."

"In the sleeping car corridor. When I saw you and backed up to let you go by."

"Yes."

"You wore purple."

"Yes. And then when we met, I ... well, I didn't expect to fall for you. I wasn't sure how to proceed. I sent you a photo from Winnemucca, to signal that I was on board to help you."

"That was you? We didn't know what to make of it."

"Sorry." Long silence. "I don't know what's in store.

But my feelings are genuine, and I've never lied to you. Mostly."

Those eyes!

"What's in store? What does that mean?"

"I don't know. We're still in a dangerous position here, Tim. Let's get through this first."

She smiled at me, we hugged, and I left.

Chapter Fifty-Nine
REROUTING

It was still very early in the morning. Back in our room, I lay down and tried to get some shut-eye. George sat up brooding.

The conductor announced that they now expected us to arrive in Chicago four hours behind schedule. We would miss our connection, and Amtrak had rebooked us on a different route.

Our plan had been to transfer in Chicago to the Capitol Limited and head southeast through Indiana, Ohio, Kentucky, West Virginia, and Virginia to Washington, D.C., then to jump on a Northeast Corridor commuter train for a short ride north to Philadelphia. Our new route was on the Lake Shore Limited, which ran east along Lakes Erie and Ontario, across upstate New York, then south to New York City, where we would transfer to a commuter train further south in Philly. Even if we stayed on schedule, the new route would get us to our destination about five hours later than our original plan.

With the new route we also missed the opportunity to show George the city that would be named after him one day, but that was okay. As fascinating as it might have been to see his reaction to the White House, the Capitol, and his monument, I still had mixed feelings about revealing too much of his future to him.

After the attacks at Hank's place and on the siding in Nebraska, we knew we were running for our lives. Every hour counted. The bad guys would not give up trying to stop us.

I was stressed out and bone tired. I slept for an hour or so, until a rough patch of track woke me. The Caboose Effect was in full sway. So to speak.

As I looked around, I seemed to be viewing the train in a new light. Had the cars always been so old and filthy? Were the bathrooms always so crude and untended? On the wall where the familiar Amtrak logo had appeared, it now said *Ferro*.

I grabbed George and had him lead me to the dining car. The menu was in Spanish and included Cubano sandwiches and *hamburguesas*. The front said *El Céfiro*, with a subtitle in smaller print, *Ferrocarriles del Estado de California*; the Zephyr, State of California Railroads.

A tsunami of historical change was catching up with us as we sped across the continent. George Washington's absence from Valley Forge was taking a toll on the centuries of history that followed. The country was devolving into some bizarre colonial nightmare.

Breakfast started out fine, though I couldn't help feeling suspicious of the passengers around me. Were some of them assassins?

In stumbling high-school Spanish, I ordered *huevos rancheros*. We sat with Polly, a pleasant lady in her early forties from New York, and her son Adrian, about nine. Polly was very chatty and wanted to tell us all about their friend in Denver, who developed severe pain during their visit and went to the hospital with appendicitis. Polly felt guilty about leaving while her friend was still in the hospital.

Then things got a little odd, as Adrian began entertaining us with amazing geography facts about the states: the number of miles of coastline, state capitals, and national size rankings.

"Ever been to Kansas?" he asked.

"Yes, I've been to Wichita. And Kansas City."

"Wichita. Capital of Kansas, population 385,577, which makes it the largest city in the state, by either population or area. Also the forty-ninth largest city in the country. Kansas City—"

"Wait," I said. "How do you know that?"

"I'm smart," he said with a sly grin, "and I memorized it!"

He was quite a prodigy—or a savant. But the encounter left me unsettled. How did Adrian know all these facts about some of the United States, when we had signs all around us that the world was degenerating into a new, Washington-less history? How could both exist at the same time?

After breakfast, we took fresh clothes to Matt, who was sitting up in the bunk. He looked better.

"He's been downright perky," April reported. "He's hungry, which is a good sign."

Chow beamed like a proud father. "We're still sending you to a hospital when we arrive in Chicago."

"Oh no," Matt said. "I'm going all the way to Valley Forge. You can't do it without me."

"Matty, that's crazy," I said. "Dude, you've been shot

twice. How are you feeling?"

"Dude, my butt hurts like hell, but that's not going to change if I go to the hospital. I'm going to transfer in Chicago with you, take George to Washington, then on to Philly and Valley Forge to do the deed. I'm from Philly! You need me there."

"As if."

I told him about the new route and checked the Amtrak app, which for some reason still had the original logo.

"We're running about four-and-a-half hours behind."

We were crossing into Iowa. I wondered if there still was an Iowa, despite Adrian's precocious memorization.

"Pierre," I asked, "what's going on? The world seems to be disintegrating toward some alternate, colonial history, but the changes are sporadic at best. The train seems to get more Spanish all the time, but I still see signs of the reality we're used to all around me."

He frowned. "I've heard of this before and sometimes seen evidence of its occurrence. It's a phenomenon we call VTRR."

"Oh no. VTR? Another three-letter acronym? Is that 'videotape recorder'?"

We laughed. Our history and culture might be deteriorating around us, but it felt good to chuckle for a moment, as we sped farther and farther from the two bodies we had left in a ravine, somewhere in the Nebraska night. Gallows humor.

"Four letters, Tim. VTRR. Variegated Temporal Reorientation Response."

"Oh great! Your tax dollars at work! Who thinks this crap up?" My equilibrium was badly shaken, and I couldn't stem the flood of sarcasm gushing from my mouth.

Pierre remained patient.

"When we use the device for a Temporal Vector Displacement, changes we initiate in the past, as you know, can change history. Whatever you think of the name, the butterfly effect is in play here. Small changes can yield massive results, especially over hundreds of years. And sometimes the effects of huge historical reorientations are incremental and take days, weeks, even months to complete.

"Some changes occur immediately, some take longer. We never know what to expect, except we've found that people like us, in close physical proximity to those who have undergone temporal displacements—like George—seem to remember more of the original scenario. But for most people who live through a historic upheaval of this type, the effect is that, for a while, both realities appear to be in play simultaneously, at least in their memories."

"You've gotta be kidding me," Matt said.

"The POA has attempted a few studies into this syndrome, but the results were inconclusive, largely because of the difficulty in reporting massive shifts in historical patterns from a variety of time periods. But it seems clear that most people, unless they interact directly with the time travelers, don't perceive a contradiction between what could be two vastly different versions of remembered history. Their brains play tricks on them and convince them that it all makes sense.

"It's analogous to the way your eye works. The lens focuses images onto the retina, but they are upside down. The brain makes the adjustment, since an upside-down world makes no sense. So your savant kid knows Wichita is the capital of Kansas, even though he appears to be riding into Chicago on a Spanish train."

"Which uses an Amtrak app."

"I would say, Agent Chow," George broke in, "that our world appears to be upside down right now. I am here on a train with you all today, more than 280 years after my birth, and that certainly makes no sense."

"Eventually," Pierre continued, "people who are caught up in these historical typhoons forget the history they have long known and trusted and recall only the new version. Some evidence from our studies suggests that temporal displacement stimulates a tear in the fabric of time—"

"A disturbance in the Force?" Matt asked sarcastically. "Seriously? That's all you've got? That's not how the Force works!"

"I'm saying that close and prolonged proximity to the General might help us remember what's happened longer than anyone else can. Some POA staff receive regular injections of a brain chemical that helps us preserve memories we might otherwise lose."

"A brain chemical?" I asked. "You expect us to believe that?"

"It's something researchers have developed using studies on mouse brains, a protein molecule that helps our gray matter form and hold the folds of memory. The POA staff needs it in order to do our jobs. But for the population as a whole, if we don't change things back to the way they were before, everyone will forget that reality."

Deep stuff.

"Again, we're never exactly sure what will happen. Sometimes when we tinker with history, the results can be unexpected."

"Really?"

"When we are readjusting history to restore a previous version, we're often surprised by how events develop. They don't always return to the way they were before. If we do succeed in sending the General back to 1778, for example, even if he doesn't lose a day in his own time, it's possible he was affected by something that happened during his weeks in California in the twenty-first century—and that everything may not go back to the way it was."

Thinking about that hurt my brain.

"There's something else," said Pierre, after a moment. "I told you the drug cartels were trying to stop our mission."

"Isn't that true?"

"Yes, but it's more complicated than that. The South American drug lords are indeed motivated by their greed to have the largest possible markets for their narcotics. But a U.S. government agency is behind the cartels, controlling and sponsoring their activities in the cultivation, transport, and distribution of heroin and cocaine to many poor urban areas in the U.S. and elsewhere."

"What agency?"

"I can't tell you. But we believe they also control the mole at the POA, who is not some disgruntled tech nerd down the hall, but rather someone carrying out a multi-pronged, ongoing, sophisticated cyberattack—someone we have been unable to purge."

"They sell drugs?"

"They supervise. All in the name of power and control. And they see Washington's revolution as an obstacle."

I took a deep breath and went out into the hall to steal another moment with April. I had my shades on and was playing blind now, in case anyone walked by. But I didn't have to pretend with her. We held hands, and I looked at her.

"I don't know what to think, April. I don't know if I can trust anyone."

"The shooting was pretty traumatic."

"Not only that," I said. "I spent hours with those people and really liked them. I feel utterly betrayed that they tried to kill us. I feel vulnerable, stupid, and naive!"

"I know."

"And," I hesitated. "I don't know if I can trust you."

"You can." She put her arms around me and held me close. "I probably shouldn't have gotten involved with you, but what's done is done. I do like you, Tim."

"You haven't lied?"

"No. As I said, I didn't tell you everything. But everything I did tell you was true."

I had a sudden thought.

"Is April your real name?"

She turned white and looked away. Then she looked back and squeezed my hand. Her eyes were troubled. Her beautiful brown eyes.

"It's not? What is your name?"

"I can't tell you that. I'm so sorry."

"Then how can I ever trust you, if I don't even know your name?"

"Well, I don't suppose you can. But I wish you would."

She headed back to her compartment to keep an eye on Matt.

Confused, I went downstairs to our family room for a nap.

Chapter Sixty
CHICAGO

Aboard El Céfiro, October 27, 2014

The train finally crossed into Illinois, way behind schedule.

George and I occupied separate tables in the dining car. He sat with Peter and Helen, an older English couple. Peter sported a short, white Julius Caesar haircut, plus stylish square spectacles with black rims and red temples. Helen had long red hair and a nice smile. Their third companion was an African American man named Paul, middle-aged, light-skinned, smooth-headed, who kept talking about how "politically correct" Americans tried to be. This term puzzled George, along with Paul's earnest analysis that "Americans relish having a microwave culture. They want everything instantly."

I could hear a little from across the aisle. I wondered if these people bored George, or if he found their very ordinariness to be suspicious. *After our experience with murderous dinner companions,* I thought, *I'm now wary of everyone I meet.*

My own tablemates were odd and a bit unsettling. The

fellow I'd noticed before with the lined face and owlish glasses sat next to me, beat-up Bible crowding the small booth table. Across from us sat a young couple, jammed in with runny-nosed infant and toddler. The mother had dirty blond hair piled on top of her head, one pierced and inexplicably shaved eyebrow, numerous tattoos, cheeks scarred by acne, and cranberry-colored, leopard-patterned leggings, which might have been pajamas. Her mate wore shorts, a Budweiser cap, and a green camo T-shirt that said "My wife, yes. My dog, maybe. My gun, never!"

Mom and dad talked non-stop, oblivious of each other. She ranted on that Obama was a Muslim from Kenya, and hubby gabbed about using assault weapons for target practice and hunting. I choked down my meal.

I felt claustrophobic, emotional, and suspicious. Traumatized by Philip and Tess's betrayal, I couldn't imagine ever again trusting a stranger on a train. Worse yet, *El Céfiro* was nearly five hours behind now and starting to run out of food.

As the light outside waned, George and I hurried back to our compartment, neither of us wanting to spend any more time in public. Who knew what evil lurked in the hearts and minds of our fellow passengers? Or who might recognize George Washington?

As we reached our family bedroom at the back of the train, our sleeping car attendant approached.

"Greetings, gentlemen. How is Mr. Matthew feeling?"

We looked at him curiously. At first glance, this was Michael, the same attendant who had been with us since we boarded the Zephyr in Davis. Same spiky hair, same blue-rimmed glasses, same stocky build. Except this fellow, who seemed to know us, was Latino, not Asian, and his name tag said "Miguel."

As the train neared Chicago well after sunset, we passed through miles of industrial properties and residential neighborhoods. Up ahead the glistening lights of the city suggested prosperity and beckoned us onward. We passed through a dark tunnel, finally coming to rest in the bowels of Union Station.

George led the way off the Zephyr, carrying Matt's duffle as well as his own—and his sword, still wrapped in burlap. I walked with Nevada, following her along the platform and into the huge neoclassical station, resplendent with high, vaulted skylights and stone columns. Chow and April followed behind, assisting Matt, who stepped cautiously and slowly. He had maintained his refusal to go to the hospital. Despite his wounds, he would not be separated from the group.

Many passengers from our train were transferring. We swarmed into the lobby all at once, five-and-a-half hours late, our hive mind focused on re-ticketing our journeys and finding our new departure points. Our group enjoyed being able to walk around freely, though it felt odd to be away from the constant movement of the train.

At the ticket booth, an agent confirmed that we would now be on the Lake Shore Limited to New York. The only sleeper he had was a roomette, which slept two at best and was not available for the entire trip.

"After Cleveland, you'll all be in coach seats. Sorry about that. Since you've paid for sleepers all the way to New York, we're refunding the difference. So there's some consolation," he added brightly. "And while you're here in Chicago, you have access to our Metropolitan Lounge."

The lounge was luxurious, a refuge from the hubbub outside, a calm place to park ourselves and our luggage. Dark paneling, subdued green carpet, large, cushy chairs. Snacks, drinks, coffee were on offer. Dropping our stuff in a clump of chairs toward the back, we all collapsed.

On a large screen, Fox News blared a story about a posting on Facebook: how Steven Spielberg, the great white hunter, illegally killed dinosaurs, and how PETA was up in arms about his poaching. Apparently millions of morons believed it.

"Who is that man," George asked, "and what manner of animal is that?"

"It's a stegosaurus," Matt told him. "It's a kind of dinosaur, an animal that died out on Earth millions of years ago."

"How is that possible? Did he kill it for meat?"

"He's a film director, and the dinosaur was created for a movie. There is no dinosaur. It's a special effect."

"Then how …?" He watched carefully, then his eyes crinkled into a small smile. "So the news is not that he killed the animal, but that people believe that he did." He thought for a moment. "I understand why this is funny."

Chapter Sixty-One
PHONE CALL

Chicago, October 27, 2014

I slipped away to call Aunt Rachel.

"Tim! Where the hell are you? I'm so glad to hear from you!"

"Chicago. Transferring trains. Chow's with us. Some people we met on the train who must have been working for the bad guys attacked George. Matty threw his body in front of him and took two bullets."

"Oh no!"

"He's okay, believe it or not. Flesh wounds. He's been sewn up and refuses to be left behind. Nevada jumped on one of the killers."

"Oh no! Did she get hurt, too?"

"She's fine. I think she loved the action."

"The news from here is a little better," said Rachel. "I've been talking to Maggie every day. Hank is stable. They're hoping to remove the bullet from his back, but it's still touch and go. It's going to be a long recovery. He may have to learn to walk all over again."

"That's terrible, but at least it's progress. How's your knee?"

"Better every day. I'm off the crutches and starting to get more range of motion. The ribs will take a while to heal. They only hurt when I laugh. Or breathe."

"Try to avoid that. Our train was very late arriving."

"Of course, you're on Amtrak Time."

"You know about that? We missed our connection, so now they've rerouted us to a different train, overnight and all day tomorrow, to New York. Then on to Philly."

"I hope you can send George back soon. Somehow. I feel like our culture and history are melting away, day by day. Restaurants, schools, industry, they all seem to be disappearing or changing."

"I'm seeing that here, too."

"But no one around me seems to notice or think it's strange."

I told her about Chow's idea that people could temporarily retain multiple historical narratives during the times of temporal reorientation.

"Interesting. I can't imagine ever forgetting any of this."

"Because you think George is a hunk and you enjoyed kissing him?"

She changed the subject. "Do you think you'll return before your parents arrive?"

"Dunno. Their flight from Rome lands in a few days. I wanna wrap this up soon. But things are more complicated than I was led to believe."

"How so?"

"Pierre says the drug cartels are manipulated by a U.S.

Government agency, which is complicit in trying to control the people through narcotics."

"Are they importing drugs into the ghetto? Is it the CIA?"

"Why do you ask?"

"There may be some precedent for this. Allegations in the press accused the CIA of selling cocaine and heroin in poor urban areas and using the money to sponsor the Contra rebels in Nicaragua in the '80s and '90s. It was a big deal at the time, and the government tried to hush it all up. The CIA maintained these were isolated instances, used to build trust with potential informers and agents."

"I don't know if it's the CIA. He wouldn't tell me."

"Why do they need you there? Why doesn't Homeland Security just take George by themselves?"

"Chow's still battling the mole. He doesn't know if he can trust anyone. There's a lot of that going around lately."

"What do you mean?"

I hadn't intended to tell her about April, but I needed to blurt.

"I met a woman. On the train."

"That's nice, Tim, but is this really the time?"

"I really liked her. I felt she really liked me."

"Past tense? What's the problem?"

"She works for Pierre. She's an agent."

"Oh."

"I felt a connection between us—besides the physical attraction. I think she really likes me, but how can I trust her?"

"You think she was assigned to come on to you? Isn't that pretty cynical, Tim?"

"I've just seen two of my best friends shot. Two charming, urbane people I met on the train—and liked—turned out to be assassins. And I'm traveling with a man who died two hundred years ago. I think I'm entitled to a little cynicism." I paused before adding, "Rachel, I don't even know her real name."

"Why?"

"She introduced herself as April, but when I asked later if that was her real name, she hedged. She said she couldn't tell me. She's a secret agent."

"Oh."

I didn't know what else to say. We were both lost in thought.

"On a happier note," Rachel chirped finally, "how about those Giants!"

"I know! Just one more win to take the World Series," I said. "I wrote them off partway through the summer, but they're survivors."

"A bit like our friend George."

"Oh?"

"Well, history tells us that Washington lost more battles than he won. He decided early that his best play was to outlast the British, to attack and harass them until they grew tired of the effort to keep the colonies and pulled out."

"Really?"

"Of course, he did win a number of decisive battles, but he never held any cities or territory for long. The Americans were outgunned and outmanned for a good part of the Revolution, and Washington realized that a war of attrition was his best bet, rather than major confrontations. In a similar vein, the Giants haven't outhit or outpitched most of their opponents, but they've outlasted most of them by doing all the little things right."

"Hmm …"

"Really. Think about it. Baseball has no clock. As long as you can keep hitting, you can continue the game forever. Time never expires, you just run out of opportunities, always trying to outlast your opponent."

"I dunno, Rachel, your theories are kind of a stretch."

"Tim, you were a history major!"

"Yes, but I've learned more about the Revolution from you and George in the past few weeks than I ever did in college."

"Trust me, there are parallels with the Giants. Tell George what I said. He'll understand," she added with an oddly wistful, almost girly voice.

Trust me. Words to live by, I guess, but who deserved my trust? Rachel, of course, and Matt and George. And Nevada. But murder and betrayal dogged our footsteps. I viewed everyone else as a potential assassin.

What's more, our collective recollection of the Revolution was becoming extinct, going the way of the triceratops, the dodo bird, and the mastodon. Or Spielberg's stegosaurus. I knew that history was rewriting itself, even as we spoke, and I hoped we wouldn't be too late to reverse it. I felt very tired.

"I gotta go, Rachel. I'm beat. I'll call you from New York."

"Go Giants!"

"Yeah, whatever."

Chapter Sixty-Two
LAKE SHORE

Aboard the Lake Shore Limited, October 28, 2014

George woke me from a nap a couple of hours later, and we boarded the Lake Shore Limited. Still groggy, I trudged aboard with the others, one hand on Nevada's harness. The train, which had a normal Amtrak logo and signage, took off for New York around midnight, several hours behind schedule. One long day and twenty stops later, we would terminate at Penn Station in midtown Manhattan.

We looked back. Chicago's skyline appeared dim, diminished, and dirty. The bright lights were gone, as if all the life had oozed out of the Windy City while we were there. It was a depressing sight.

As promised, we had only one small roomette to share. By day it had two facing armchairs, by night two fold-down bunks, which had already been made up. With the bunks down, there was little clearance between the beds and the door, not enough space to stand up. An odd little fold-down toilet and a sink were built into the steps that led to the top bunk.

We put Matt on the bottom bunk so he could rest. Vada hunkered down on the floor under him. I wanted George to take the top bunk, to keep him out of public view, but he insisted I sleep there, at least till they evicted us from the roomette in Cleveland.

"Timothy, I implore you to take the other berth. You look unhealthy, lad, and you must rest. I know this has all been quite a jolt for you."

"I'm fine, George, and I don't want you sitting up in coach class, where someone might spot you."

"Who would know me?"

"You're George-freakin'-Washington, for Chrissakes! Everybody knows you!"

"Indeed. Nevertheless, I recognize the symptoms of shock, and I feel strongly that you must stay here. Consider it an order." He unfolded to his full height and glared at me, not unkindly.

I wasn't in his damn army, but his commanding presence persuaded me to hold my tongue. I could barely keep my eyes open and, in truth, welcomed the opportunity to lie flat. I looked up at him. "Be careful."

"I shall keep my hat on and keep the hood on my sweating shirt fully deployed. I am an old soldier and shall experience no difficulty resting in a comfortable chair."

I fell asleep in my clothes, slept deeply, and awoke the next morning, shortly before we crossed into New York State. I peered over the side of the bunk. Matt looked up at me, smiled, and waved.

Chow poked his head in and beckoned. I met him in the hall.

"What happened?" I asked. "We're out of Ohio and

almost through Pennsylvania. Why didn't we get booted out of the roomette in Cleveland?"

"Amtrak had some last-minute vacancies," he said drily. "Some people decided not to get on the train after all."

"Did you have anything to do with that?"

"Perhaps. I just made them an offer they couldn't refuse," he said, with a sly smile and a fist bump. "Just before boarding, they discovered that they had pressing engagements that would keep them in Cleveland a few more days. Breakfast, anyone?"

"Sure. Where's April? I'd like to see her."

Pierre looked away.

"She's not on the train, Tim."

"What?"

"She didn't board with us in Chicago."

I felt a shiver go down my spine.

"Why not?"

"She was called away. That's all I can say."

"Bullshit. Tell me what happened."

"I guess I owe you that," Chow conceded. "In a nutshell, she had another assignment. When you first signaled me that you had boarded the Zephyr in Davis, we were fortunate that April was a bit further east near Sacramento, working on a different investigation for Homeland Security. The POA is a small group, but we can tap the vast resources of DHS. Since she was the closest agent, I managed to appropriate her on an emergency reassignment, so she could intercept the train quickly."

"What about the bad guys? How did they get on the train so fast?"

"Oh, they are everywhere."

"Thugs for the drug cartels?"

289

"I think it's time you learned who's behind all this."

He took a deep breath.

"The agency controlling the drug lords, sending those thugs after us, nurturing the mole in the POA, it's the FBI. Something that started decades ago. A small brotherhood of a dozen promising young agents were specially selected and mentored by J. Edgar Hoover back in the '60s. Hoover was always looking for ways to expand his power and advance his reactionary, right-wing agenda by spying on and controlling the lives of Americans."

"A megalomaniac."

"Indeed. A number of presidents were wary of Hoover's thirst for power. Nixon was said to be eager to fire Hoover, but feared what scandal might engulf him if a vengeful Hoover released information from his secret files. Harry Truman claimed that Hoover transformed the FBI into his private secret-police force. 'We want no Gestapo or secret police,' Truman wrote. 'The FBI is tending in that direction. They are dabbling in sex-life scandals and plain blackmail. J. Edgar Hoover would give his right eye to take over, and all congressmen and senators are afraid of him.' Despite Truman knowing what Hoover was up to and a number of presidents eying his fiefdom with concern, J. Edgar served as FBI director for forty-eight years, until his death in 1972. He outlasted Truman in office by two decades."

"In his later years," Chow continued, "Hoover learned about the POA time machine and tried repeatedly, without success, to get control shifted from its original home in Defense to the FBI. And the remaining agents in Hoover's secret cadre, most now in their late sixties, still constitute a clandestine directorate to control many FBI actions and policies."

Chapter Sixty-Three
LIFERS

Aboard the Lake Shore Limited, October 28, 2014

But what about the director, all the directors who have succeeded Hoover over the years?" I wondered, shocked.

"You know the director these days is basically a short-term political appointee," Chow explained. "Since Hoover, the directors have been limited to ten-year appointments, but only one has stayed around for a full term. Ongoing Bureau policy, programs, and areas of emphasis are guided by the lifer civil servants—the career people—who never become director but remain the power behind the throne. In the forty-two years since Hoover died, the FBI has had six directors, usually former judges, prosecutors, or U.S. attorneys. Interspersed between them have been six temporary acting directors, all career agents whose missions were to make certain that FBI operations and policy continued, regardless of who was appointed director.

"In particular, the dozen agents in Hoover's cadre were charged with keeping track of the time machine—for many years a daunting task. The POA and our human resources were difficult to penetrate. But as the digital age dawned, as the federal government turned more and more to electronic storage for its communications, resources, and records, the FBI's computer spy network grew more powerful and ready to pounce.

"Ironically, post-9/11 efforts to get all the U.S. security agencies to share information made it easier for the FBI to penetrate our firewalls and gain access to the POA's systems. Once our tech guys figured it out, we began to conduct some operations offline, using burner phones and other untraceable communications. But we can't do everything that way, and the mole—the digital spy in our midst—frequently knows what's happening and moves to thwart our efforts. We're never sure if our communications are being intercepted and our intelligence compromised. They have access to much more of our info flow than you can imagine.

"But here's the rub: the upper echelons of the FBI were trying desperately to find General Washington, and you brought him right into Agent Oreck's office."

"Oreck? What a putz!"

"Exactly. He is a buffoon, so full of his own importance that he's easy to ignore. He didn't grasp the possible significance of what you had brought him and filed a low-priority report about the encounter. He is regarded with such disdain in the Bureau that he hadn't been clued in about the time machine or Washington's disappearance from Valley Forge. Oreck's report was ignored for quite a while, before reaching the higher levels of the Bureau."

"You understood the photo I sent you of the station in Davis?"

"Yes. That's when we poached April from the DHS

and got her on the Zephyr. After she spotted you, I flew out from Washington as soon as I could and boarded in Nebraska. As you know. We were very lucky to have her here."

"I guess."

"Tim, I'm aware that you two appear to have become intimate."

"Nicely put. Wasn't that her assignment?"

"What? No, truly. Her only assignment was to protect you and your companions. Anything beyond that was strictly a personal choice—though I don't think it will make our bosses happy."

I wanted to believe him. All the same, I felt entitled to react in high dudgeon.

"How can I see her?"

"You can't, Tim. She's a field agent, usually undercover. She has a very different kind of life. No digital trail, no involvements, no commitments. Forget her."

Terrible advice. How could I forget those eyes?

"Where's George?" I asked, trying to put April out of my mind.

Chow and I left Nevada in the roomette with Matt and found George in a coach seat two cars behind us. He was listening to my sister's iPod, his eyes closed, face partially covered, and one earbud drooping. I watched him for a few minutes, as he tunelessly mouthed the words to "Ev'ry Time We Say Goodbye" along with Lady Gaga.

It was too much for me. I'm sure he missed his Martha or Patsy or whoever, but I was stuck with the empty feeling that I would never see April again. I turned to Pierre.

"He's in his own world."

"Yes. Hungry?"

Of course I had to play blind again, so we could account for bringing a large dog onto this train. We just made it to breakfast before they closed. I ordered the omelet again. This time, I was seated with a teacher from Chicago—a guy in his thirties leading a Founding Fathers tour—and two of his students, ages ten or eleven. They were headed to Boston, New York, Philadelphia, and Washington, traveling by train the whole way. In Philly, they would visit the Liberty Bell and Independence Hall, but not Valley Forge.

"There isn't really much there," the teacher said. "It's more of a park than a museum."

They seemed perfectly nice, but I was having trouble warming up to anyone. Who else might be following us?

Despite the fact that I slept through all of Ohio and Indiana, it was a long day. We continued to fall further behind schedule. We passed through Buffalo and headed east across upstate New York, through Syracuse, Rochester, and Schenectady, past beautiful farmland mixed with rusty infrastructure, tumbledown warehouses, abandoned factories, and glimpses of red-brick downtowns struggling to gentrify.

Late in the morning I stopped by to see George again. He was furtively thumbing my sister's iPod, and I realized he was binging on Candy Crush again. I left quickly, tapping my white cane nervously as I headed back to our compartment.

As Matt and I contemplated our final railroad lunches, I tried to keep my guard up and trust no one. This menu had changed, too. It was still in English, but instead of the earlier choices of main courses, healthy options, and vegetarian selections, now it all seemed like British pub food. I sighed.

Without Washington's leadership, the American Revolution had failed. Not only was the western part of North America still dominated by Spain and Russia, but eastern North America was still British. We ordered bangers and mash and sat with Robert and Nina, a young couple who were new math professors, both starting their first jobs. They told me that the last part of our route would be scenic, as we followed the Hudson River south to New York City, past Sing Sing Prison, Bear Mountain, and the Tappan Zee Bridge.

Lovely people. I was starting to mellow a little. If Robert and Nina were assassins, they were also first-class actors. Then I thought about Philip and Tess and wondered if the assassin dispatcher for the FBI and drug lords always sent out academic couples.

When we reached Albany, we had a long break and walked the pooch. Vada had been very patient. She needed to run, but we couldn't let her loose in this urban station surrounded by huge railroad yards. We walked her off the end of the platform onto the gravel, so she could do her business in some out-of-the-way place. George and I looked back as the Amtrak personnel divided our train. One of the locomotives and half the cars from the original train were split off to continue east through Massachusetts to Boston. Through the fading daylight, the other half—our section—would turn south and zoom along the scenic route to the Big Apple.

Both trains now bore the logo of British Railways.

Chapter Sixty-Four
BLOWN

New York City, October 28, 2014

We arrived in the City nearly four hours late, missing our connecting train by just a few minutes. New York's Penn Station was even busier than Chicago had been, without the redeeming feature of a lounge. George followed the signs and led us to customer service, where we once again exchanged our tickets for a later train. We had a couple of hours to wait.

"Now what?" Matt asked. He was clearly feeling much better and was even trying to carry his own duffle.

"I'd like to call Rachel again," I said. "And I'm not getting much of a signal down here in the station."

Matt's face brightened, and he turned to George. "Would you like to see New York City? The Big Apple is right up there above us. It'll blow your mind."

George considered this possibility gravely.

"I must impress upon you, LaMatthew, that said mental explosion has already taken place. I believe that blowing commenced when I first encountered you and Timothy, and it has not diminished in the ensuing weeks. But yes, I am curious to see what the future has in store for this most fortunately located of cities. I only wish to clarify why you refer to it as a large item of fruit."

"Damned if I know. Follow me. I used to come here with my parents when we lived in Philly."

After three-and-a-half days—nearly 3,500 miles—in Railroad World, the opportunity to breathe fresh air, to walk on an actual street for a few minutes, appealed to us all. I decided I didn't need to play blind. There was no one here we knew. The other passengers from the Lake Shore Limited had already dispersed.

With a firm grip on Nevada's harness, I followed Matt onto a long escalator, George and Pierre right behind us.

As we ascended, I began to wish I was still playing blind. I really had no reason to trust anyone, though I couldn't imagine any of the folks I'd seen or met on the last train were harmful. Robert and Nina, the young math profs, were both corn-fed bores, bland as Kansas. The teacher leading his charges to Independence Hall seemed above reproach. Adrian's impressive grasp of geographical factoids was unusual but ultimately not threatening. I found the pierced, tattooed mama and her family spooky, but unlikely assassins, given that they had to deal constantly with runny-nosed kids.

Once again, I appreciated how perfectly cast Tess and Philip had been. In an odd way, I missed them. We had made a connection. Or so I thought.

Speaking of which: April.

I tried to put her out of my mind. Chow was right. I should forget her.

The escalator dumped us onto a broad, cracked sidewalk in the heart of midtown Manhattan on a Tuesday evening. But as we looked around, everything seemed off. The huge Hotel New Yorker, one of the largest in the City, loomed a block north, forty dilapidated floors blackened with eighty years of grime. Some windows were boarded up, and many facade stones were broken or missing. Ancient scaffolding blocked the sidewalk. The marquee sagged alarmingly.

"I don't get it," Matt said. "I know they did a face-lift of that hotel a few years ago. We stayed there one time."

A muddy lot diagonally opposite confronted him like a missing tooth.

"That should be a swanky office building."

Across 8th Avenue sat an old, ramshackle, aluminum building with a Royal Mail crown logo on the opposite side.

"That's where that main post office with the stone columns used to be," said Matt. "This is depressing."

It was late enough in the evening that the usual gridlock had relaxed. Cars zigged frenetically across lanes, and taxis zagged everywhere with reckless abandon. A cop in a London bobby's helmet stood on the corner, watching the traffic without interest. Most of the vehicles seemed quite old, the brands only vaguely familiar.

"I feel like we're in a museum," I said. "These cars remind me of pictures I've seen of Cuba, after decades of the American embargo."

"Except these cars are all English," Matt replied.

A small cab pulled up in front of us to drop a passenger.

"Holy cow," Chow said. "It's an old Morris Minor."

"Best-selling car in the world, mate!" called the cabbie, a little guy with a Liverpudlian Ringo Starr accent and haircut.

Three blocks east on 33rd Street, we could see the Empire State Building—or at least a frustrated attempt to create one. The familiar gray stone exterior ended at forty or fifty stories and was topped with a temporary plywood roof and aging blue tarps. Unfinished, perhaps abandoned. Much of the skyline had empty spaces.

"This is awful," Matt said. "It's as if the city's growth has been stunted."

"New York is adjusting, incrementally, to the new history," Pierre said. "No Washington, no victory, no independence, no democracy, no prosperity. The imperialists, as always, suck their colonies dry."

Was there nothing left of our culture and history? Across the street we saw a Starbucks. Down the block, another Starbucks. I had seen one in the station, at the bottom of the escalator. They were like cockroaches. Nothing could kill them.

To our right, perched atop Penn Station, sat a huge arena.

"That's Madison Square Garden," Matt said. "Except, it's not."

We turned a corner and read the sign: "Paddington Garden Arena."

The sidewalk was crammed with people, most of them poor or homeless, a few well dressed and prosperous. The crowd surged toward a police barricade near a loading zone in front of the Garden. We followed the flow gloomily, with Nevada on leash. A young guy near us had his phone out to take a picture. A limousine pulled up.

"Who is it?" I asked.

"I don't know, guvnor."

Another Brit.

A small woman dressed in bright colors emerged from

the stage door and headed for the limo.

The crowd at the barrier roared. "Hey! Come here! Layla! Over here!"

She turned and flashed a big, bright smile, and came to the barricade. As she approached, I could see she was curvy and glamorous, about 5'2", with long, dark hair and honey-colored skin. She worked the line for a minute or two, autographing shirts and photographs, happy to meet her fans. I asked someone who she was. He didn't know, nor did the next guy.

Finally, a woman who looked like she lived in the street told me with great authority, "That's Layla, from WWE."

I had to think a minute. *World Wide ... World Wildlife ...*

"The wrestler?" the woman insisted.

"Oh, of course." I hadn't watched wrestling since middle school.

George stood there, flabbergasted.

"This little lady, Timothy, is a wrestler? A grappler? How is it possible for a member of the weaker sex to engage in such a masculine sport?"

"Ouch, George, don't let my Aunt Rachel hear you say stuff like that. Weaker sex, indeed."

"Is this woman perhaps more masculine than feminine? I have heard of such people."

"No, look at her," Matt said. "Hottie!"

"A very athletic hottie. Besides, George," I added. "Professional wrestling is more entertainment than a sporting competition."

"You are aware, of course, that I find your beloved San Francisco Gigantics entertaining?"

I knew now that he was just saying "Gigantics" to jerk my chain.

"Of course they're entertaining. But they and other baseball teams are truly competitive. In professional wrestling, the outcomes of matches are more controlled."

"You mean, they cheat and take unfair advantage?"

"In a way, but it's all theatre. Their bouts are scripted, including the outcome. What's particularly troubling to me, though, is that pro wrestling—which is pretty lowbrow on the culture scale—is one of the vestiges of American culture to survive the ripple in history caused by your absence from Valley Forge."

"That and baseball," Matt said. "So far."

The cute lady wrestler waved to her fans, slid into the limo, and was off.

"I'm calling Rachel," I told Matt, as I moved across the sidewalk with Nevada to a less crowded spot. I felt disoriented and stressed out, like a character in a dystopian story, caught up in huge changes beyond my understanding. My nerves were jangled.

Her phone rang twice, then she answered.

"It's me."

"Hello? Tim?"

"Yes!"

"Where are you? Did you get my message? Can you come for brunch?"

"What? Aunt Rachel, I'm in New York."

"What are you doing there?"

"Are you okay? You knew I was coming here. We just got in, and we're waiting for our train to Philly."

"You're going to Philadelphia?"

Had she forgotten? What was happening?

"Who's with you?"

"Matt and George."

"George?"

"And Nevada."

"Nevada? Why would you take her to New York?"

She didn't remember a thing. Either my dear aunt was going senile before her time, or her brain—in response to unrelenting evidence around her—was forgetting her time with General Washington and accepting the nightmarish, alternate reality created by George's absence from the Continental Army. The same reality that had a major foothold everywhere else. Seeing Manhattan brought that home to me. The nightmare was happening everywhere.

We had to get him back to his troops. There was no time to lose.

Chapter Sixty-Five
LUGGAGE

I rang off with Rachel, disturbed by our conversation. From my corner of the sidewalk, I could see the top of the long escalator we had ridden from Penn Station far below. As I watched, I noticed Jack Sprat and wife getting off the escalator and looking about—Tommy and Arlene, the passengers who had gleefully described their sick racism during our meal together on the California Zephyr.

What were they doing here? They were going to New Orleans and should have transferred at Chicago. It was comforting, in an odd way, to see familiar faces, and I almost called out. But they thought I was blind, so I held my tongue. They walked purposefully across the sidewalk, toward the crazy traffic.

As I watched from a distance, skinny Tommy with the dyed red hair began to rush forward, his shiny, antlered mammal belt buckle reflecting even the gloom of this underlit, underdeveloped New York. I couldn't comprehend what was happening. My confused and overloaded brain felt like I had nothing but open space between my ears. Tommy was running across the broad sidewalk, quick and light on his feet, right hand extended, as if offering a handshake.

Arlene, in a pleasant mauve pastel track suit, followed closely, surprisingly agile for her size. Apparently it was her job to handle the luggage. She was pulling a bright-teal, hardshell, upright "spinner" suitcase. On top of the spinner she had a red tote and, around her neck, a heavy blue duffle. She and Tommy were heading right at George. He was looking the other way, standing with Pierre at the curb.

Tommy raised his hand higher as he got closer. It almost seemed like a friendly gesture. Almost.

Suddenly I understood.

He had a gun. A small gun.

I panicked, the blood rushing to my head and blocking out all sound.

Nevada pulled on her leash. I yelled at the top of my lungs, but no one heard me over the crowd. Tommy pointed the gun at George's head. Arlene scooted the spinner with the red tote toward the legs of the Father of Our Country and prepared to swing the heavy blue duffle at his head. Clearly she intended to use their weight and forward momentum to push George into the traffic if Tommy's pistol attack failed.

I glanced over at the cop in the bobby helmet. He was facing away, chatting with a pretty girl in a short tartan kilt.

The crowd roared again as another wrestler exited to a waiting car. George and Pierre turned to look, only to be confronted by Tommy brandishing a firearm and Arlene brandishing luggage. Chow, who was closer, sprang lithely forward into Tommy's path, grabbed him by the lapels, and flung him to the ground with a jiujitsu hip throw, his head banging on the ground.

George sidestepped the suitcase assassin, pirouetted gracefully, and fell to one knee, swiping at Arlene's legs with the burlap-wrapped sword. She staggered and stumbled, her momentum carrying her into 8th Avenue, where an out-of-control, yellow, London-style cab in a hurry to get uptown knocked her ten feet in the air. She landed with a splat and lay still. The teal spinner suitcase rolled into the street and was hit by a second cab, sending clothing and undergarments across three lanes of traffic. A large pair of pink bloomers landed on the windshield of a black sedan, blocking the driver's view. In the ensuing chaos, several vehicles sideswiped and rear-ended each other. Finally, a delivery van ran over the blue duffle Arlene had swung at George, which apparently contained, among other things, a large watermelon.

Matt and I ran up with Nevada. Tommy lay unconscious on the sidewalk. Chow and I dragged him into a dark corner behind a decrepit newsstand and took his pistol. It was just a small revolver, which probably accounted for his reluctance to shoot until he got close to the target. That reluctance had been his undoing.

We looked around. No shots had been fired, and the crowd on the sidewalk focused its attention on the street, where the cabbie who hit Arlene stood nervously beside her limp, lumpy mauve form on the pavement. Other drivers honked and yelled as they tried to get around the multi-car pileup. No one noticed us. Chow quickly bound Tommy's hands and legs with cable ties, then searched him.

"No phone."

He unloaded the pistol and stuck it back in Tommy's pocket.

"He took a pretty good crack in the head. Assuming he hasn't got a permit, he should get in trouble when they find him with this gun. New York City has strictly regulated handguns for over a hundred years, since the Sullivan Act. But we've gotta get out of here."

Rather than take the same escalator, Chow led us down 33rd Street to an office building, talked to the security guard for a minute, and flashed his badge. Soon we were dashing across the lobby, then into an elevator to head down to the trains.

Chow pushed a button for the lower level, the door closed, and nothing happened. He pushed the button again, then the Down button, then the Door Open button. We weren't going anywhere. Finally he hit the alarm, and a loud *whoop-whoop-whoop* sounded throughout the lobby.

The security guard showed up quickly, shut off the alarm, and yelled, "I have a key! Stand by!"

George looked at me. "Does this happen often, Timothy? Now I understand why your mother dislikes elevators."

He was sweating through his shirt and starting to peer about with the haunted look of claustrophobia. "This does feel a bit like that freight train," he said, in a flat, worried voice.

I put a hand on his shoulder. "It's okay, George. This elevator won't zip you away across the country."

"Quite so."

Nevada sensed his anxiety and nuzzled George's rump with her head.

We heard the guard fiddle with the key, then drop it.

"Hang on!" he called. Then metallic rattling, then the key fell again. Then more rattling.

"It's stuck," the guard yelled. "The key isn't working, but I've got another idea. Uh, wait there!"

Wait there? Where would we go? It was hot and airless

in the elevator, our lives were in danger, and this guy was practicing his stand-up routine.

A better problem-solver than comic, he soon returned with a metal rod, which he poked into the crack between the elevator doors. A couple of minutes later, he had pried the doors open and sprung us free.

Chow burst out of the elevator first.

"How else can we get down?" he demanded.

The guard led us across the lobby to a fire exit, and we scampered down three long flights of steel stairs to the main level of Penn Station. Once there, I put on my dark glasses, and Vada and I played blind again. We melted into the crowd of travelers.

We still had to wait for our train to Philly, so we slipped into a TGI Friday's on the main concourse. The host rushed forward to stop us when he saw Nevada, then noticed the blind harness and service vest and backed off.

The restaurant was very deep, three large rooms. We hunkered down at the back, ordered beers, steaks, and salads, and kept looking over our shoulders. Even though we were all tired of railroad food and the steaks smelled great, we found it difficult to eat after another violent confrontation— further evidence of the disintegration of our once-proud nation into the depressing depths of dependent colonialism.

My brain was working overtime. What had just happened? Were Tommy and Arlene hired assassins, attempting to pull off a momentous murder of startling historical consequence with a small pistol, a spinner bag, and a watermelon?

When our train was announced around 11:00 p.m., we slipped out of Friday's and down the stairs to our platform.

The last leg of the journey was a Northeast Corridor commuter train to Philadelphia. Rain sprinkled the windows as we sped through the night. Ninety minutes later, we pulled into 30th Street Station in Philly and detrained. The ornate clock near the schedule board in the lobby read 12:34. By now it was pouring outside.

"That's a good omen," Matt said. "1-2-3-4 means a good start."

"Lame-o, Matty. Never heard that."

"We'd better separate from here," Pierre said.

I was happy not to play blind anymore.

"We reserved a hotel near the airport," I said. "We'll rent a car out there. How about you?"

"Another agent is meeting me. We'll rendezvous with you at Valley Forge as soon as possible. I'll be in touch in the next day or so, as soon as the weather clears up."

"You mean Einstein's precious time machine doesn't work in the rain?" I was tired, scared, and sarcastic.

"It's very delicate. Einstein never got around to weatherproofing it."

"George can't just get into it and close out the rain?"

Chow looked sheepish. "It's not like that. You'll see. It's a device, not a vehicle."

"So we might get rained out."

"Yes. Correct. Sorry, but this is delicate technology. We don't want to lose George somewhere between here and there."

"Of course," I said, "but things are rapidly going to hell here, and we've gotta get him there ASAP."

Chapter Sixty-Six
PHILS

Philadelphia, October 28, 2014

Outside the station, there was one cab left. The driver, an Indian fellow, fussed over us, concerned about fitting three guys and one large dog, plus luggage, into his Austin Mini taxi. We got soaked as we loaded our gear and piled in.

George got the front seat, as usual, puzzled that "shotgun" was on the left side of the car, since they drove on the left side of the road here, in the British manner. Matt and I tussled with Nevada for legroom in the back. Somehow we all squeezed in.

The taxi took us to a car rental agency near the airport, where we rented a Hillman Minx sedan that looked as if it had been built in 1963. It took me a minute to figure out the gear shift. Then we got lost and circled endlessly on poorly marked loop roads around the airport. Tired, wet, and stressed from driving on the wrong side of the road, we eventually found our hotel.

Our room was a small suite, with a queen bed, a rollaway, a pull-out couch, and a kitchen with a minibar and snacks. We took hot showers, ate, fed the pooch, and replenished our precious bodily fluids with transfusions of alcohol. Best of all, we had modern telecommunications. Heaven.

Matt fired up the laptop, and I flipped on the TV, both with a common quest—what had happened in Game 6?

The first thing I saw was a news report from New York about a crazy lady who had stepped in front of a taxi near Penn Station. A crude, shaky cellphone video captured shots of the pileup of cars on 8th Avenue, including a pair of bloomers on a windshield, a teal suitcase, a pile of mauve clothing that used to be Arlene, and a smashed watermelon. No mention of a skinny guy with a gun, bound in cable ties.

It had been a bad night for the Giants. Kansas City shut them out 10-0. The Royals bagged fifteen hits and showed no mercy. The momentum had flipped in their favor going into Game 7. But who would pitch for the Giants? Madison Bumgarner had already started two games in the World Series and was too gassed to start another. Their other pitchers had been iffy lately. Perhaps Mad Bum could throw an inning or two in relief—if it came to that.

It was very late by the time we dozed off. I dreamt of April snuggling close to me in the Zephyr roomette and woke up at one point to discover Nevada crowding me off the couch.

We slept late. I had put out the Do Not Disturb sign, so no one bothered us. We roused at noon, hungry and achy after days of sitting on the train. Outside was dark and rainy. We grumbled around the room for an hour or so. The weather dampened our spirits, because the time machine didn't work in the rain. I walked and fed Vada again, then we decided to go for a drive and get some food.

We feasted at a Panda Express a couple of miles from

our hotel. Cheap grub, generous portions, with comforting doses of starch and protein. George in particular liked his Kung Pao Chicken. He found it a bit spicy, but the peanuts intrigued him.

"I have observed few farmers growing this crop within my state of Virginia. Prepared as they are here, these legumes can provide tasty and scintillating stimulation to the senses."

The nuts were definitely scintillating. Our release from the confinement of the train added to our appreciation of the world around us. I couldn't imagine how George had survived a cross-country trip on the floor of a boxcar, but he was a pretty tough dude.

Matt mopped up the last of the black bean sauce with a moo shu pancake.

"Let's go to the Phillies ballpark," he said. "The season is over, and there won't be a game, of course. But we can walk around, maybe peer through the fence and think about hot dogs!"

We all smiled.

"What's your favorite ballpark dog, Matty?"

"The Texas Tommy at Harry the K's. A big dog, with bacon, cheese, and chili."

"Heartburn!"

"Yeah, but so worth it."

"Cheesesteaks, too?" I asked. "Aren't they a Philly thing?"

"Sure. Cheesesteaks at Tony Luke's!"

George looked amused. "It seems your early baseball memories are primarily tied to your stomach, LaMatthew."

"Yeah. Before we moved to Berkeley."

"Do you remember any games?" George asked. "Or only the food?"

"I remember a lot of frustration when I was a kid, because the Phillies rarely made the postseason. And then, three years after we moved away, they won the damn World Series! I gloated from afar, even though no one around me in the Bay Area gave a shit. Two years after that, the Giants beat the Phils in the playoffs, but by then I'd become a San Francisco guy. The Gigantics"—he winked at George—"won the World Series that year, as you know, and again in 2012."

"They're on schedule to win this year, too, another even-numbered year," I said. "Tonight's the last game, each team with three victories. It should be exciting—if baseball is still happening. Maybe we can watch it at the hotel."

"I'm excited about visiting the ballpark," Matt said. "They have these cool old sculptures outside, huge statues, which they moved from their old ballpark. Generic, stylized ballplayers, much larger than life. They honor baseball as an art form, rather than showcasing any individual. I loved climbing on them when I was a kid."

After Panda, Matt directed us down a road a few miles east of the airport, and his face fell.

"It should be right there."

Though I'd never been to the Phillies ballpark, I had watched them play the Giants on TV many times. I knew roughly what to look for: large, asymmetrical grandstands, red brick and steel, new-looking but old-style.

What we saw instead as we drove up was a run-down sports stadium made of old, gray cinder blocks and rickety wooden stands, none too clean, of uniform height, and perfectly circular. We came upon a worn wooden sign:

Barclay's Cricket Oval
Philadelphia Phillies

"Oh no!" Matt said. "It's named for a British bank now.

And they don't play baseball here."

A temperamental neon sign flashed:
Today's Championship Test Matches
Postponed for Rain

Massive, stylized statues still stood outside the Phillies park, but they were no longer the baseball players Matt remembered. Gone was the blank-faced, lean, muscular guy of Matt's memory, in baseball cap, knickers, knee socks, and jersey, sliding into base as another impassive player attempted a swipe tag with the ball in his glove. Instead, one stone sculpture froze a cricket bowler in mid-hop at the end of his run-up, just before releasing the ball with an overhanded windmill motion toward the batsman. Another showed a tableau of players in white flannel: a padded, gloved, helmeted wicketkeeper knocking over the wickets on a cricket pitch, as a padded, gloved, helmeted batsman with a flat bat was "stumped," unable to get back in time. Most of the statues had been targeted by birds, some were missing a finger or two. All were stained from many years of weather and neglect. None were about baseball.

We parked in the empty lot. Stepping around puddles, we then walked up to the back of the circular ballpark and peered in through a cyclone fence. We could see the oval cricket field. On the near concourse, huge banners showed players in full cricket action. Some were familiar Phils names in an unfamiliar sport—bowlers Cliff Lee, Cole Hamels, and Jonathan Papelbon, and batsmen Grady Sizemore and Chase Utley. All Caucasian. No Black players, no Latinos, no Asians. I wondered if anyone of color played for these Brit Phillies or anywhere in the cricket league.

We could see two of the food concessions, Covent Garden and Leicester Square. On their menus: steak and kidney pie, bubble and squeak, fish and chips, spotted dick, and devils on horseback. No Tony Luke's, no Harry the K's. No cheesesteak, and not a Texas Tommy or a Bratwurst in sight.

"English food," I muttered. "We are losing more than 200 years of American art, history, and culture, and we are left with English food!"

"I learned to hate cricket when we lived in England for a year," Matt said. "How can you trust a sport where a 'leg break' is a type of throw, a 'pitch' is a place, 'over' is a noun, and 'innings' is singular? Let's get out of here."

Chapter Sixty-Seven
INDEPENDENCE

Philadelphia, October 29, 2014

The next day I drove us downtown, with Matt navigating from the back seat. We were aghast. Philly was a wreck.

"I recognize some of these buildings," Matt said, when we got a good view of the skyline. "But many of the ones I remember are gone. Or perhaps they were never built. This is so messed up!"

Many of the freeways were missing, so we took city streets toward the heart of town.

Matt was confused.

"Turn right here, Timmy. Now, turn left. No, don't. Turn right again. Man, what is going on?"

"What's the trouble?"

"Independence Hall. It's just … not there. The whole complex. The State House, Old City Hall, and Congress Hall. Gone. And," he whirled around and looked out the back. "the Liberty Bell used to sit in a separate building in the park in front of Independence Hall. That's all gone, too."

This was upsetting news to George. Independence Hall was the site of the First Continental Congress, which he had attended as a Virginia delegate, and the Second, when he had accepted his commission as Commander in Chief. The Declaration of Independence was signed there while he was in Massachusetts with the army. Years in his future, it would also serve as the venue for the Constitutional Convention.

We parked and walked around.

"A lot of these old brick houses are still intact," said Matt, "but the neighborhood has gone to seed. It's run-down and dirty, downwardly mobile. Not the sparkling, well-preserved historical icon and tourist destination I remember from trips here as a kid."

"Where was Independence Hall?" I asked. "I mean, where should it be?"

"Right here on Chestnut Street, between South 5th and 6th."

A British Petroleum gas station and a tumbledown warehouse now occupied the site. On one wall of the warehouse was a neglected old brass plaque, darkened and pockmarked with age. I used spit and an old bandanna to clean off the grime, so we could read it:

On this location stood the former Pennsylvania State House, site of an infamous, treasonous rebellion against the Crown in 1776, put down with great dispatch in 1779 by the King's Own Regiments, His Majesty's Marine Forces, the Royal Artillery, and the Royal Cavalry. Buildings destroyed by fire in 1814. Plaque placed here in 1923 by the Pennsylvania Loyalist Brigade.

Treasonous rebellion? That was one view, I guess. We hoped George could reverse that history, inspiring new births of freedom around the globe for centuries. If only Einstein's time machine had been built to be waterproof, we might have

316

been able to send George back already.

I thought about the teacher from Chicago leading his students on a Founding Fathers tour. I wondered how many historic locations would still be intact when they got there, and how many would just be a few wrinkles in our collective memories.

I wondered about the weather forecast, if we would be able to use the time machine before it was too late, and where Pierre was, what he was planning.

Then I thought of April. Again.

I've got to forget her.

We headed back to our hotel, depressed and annoyed.

When the rain let up, we left Nevada in the room and walked to a nearby restaurant. We were impatient to finish our task, but we hadn't heard from Chow yet. So we tried to enjoy a good meal and a bit too much wine, after days of travel, stress, and violence.

As we paid for dinner, the rain began to come down in sheets. George thought of the drought we had left behind in California.

"Such a vast and varied country, Timothy! I appreciate having the opportunity to travel across it with you and La-Matthew."

"Uh, sure. But right now, we just have to get back to our room."

A flash of lightning lit up the night sky, followed almost immediately by a deep clap of thunder. The lightning was very close. I hesitated for a moment.

"Are we afraid of our shadows, gentlemen?" George asked.

"Hey," I said, "You first. You're the famous explorer, adventurer, and general. I'm just a grad student."

George laughed. "Come, lads, there's naught to fear. Follow my lead!"

What the hell. Despite my fear, after the wine, I felt a bit immortal. Not good. In a lightning storm, delusions of divine protection might induce cockiness. George had survived many battles and never been wounded. I wondered if he had ever challenged the gods of lightning.

It was too wet and slippery to run, so he trudged off in the direction of our hotel. We followed as closely as we could, dodging puddles, as thunder exploded around us and lightning traced jagged streaks across the sky.

I considered dashing from tree to tree but couldn't remember if standing under trees in a lightning storm was a good idea. With a great deal of splashing, we scampered across a couple of parking lots—about 200 yards of open ground—before we slipped into the side door of our hotel. In our room, we found Nevada, that big, brave defender of our liberties, in a tight spot between the sofa and the coffee table, cringing from the thunder. She bellowed a single, deep *woof!*—very glad to see us—and wouldn't leave my side for the rest of the evening.

For the second time in two days, we were soaked. We put on our last clean clothes and dried a load at the hotel laundry. Then Pierre texted me.

TMW7AMGWHQVF

"What is that?" George asked eagerly. "Is it a code?"

"Yeah," Matt said. "A cipher for simpletons. 'Tomorrow, 7 a.m., George Washington's Headquarters, Valley Forge.'"

"He refers to the residence of Farmer Potts, which has served as my living quarters and the office of the general staff."

"I guess he thinks the rain is going to stop," I said.

"So it would appear, my boy," said George. "So it would appear."

Chapter Sixty-Eight
SERIES

I was nervous about the rendezvous at Valley Forge. George watched me pick up a control stick and illuminate a large looking glass in our hotel room. I pushed tiny buttons on the stick, and the pictures changed.

"Let's find the World Series," I said.

"Do you really think baseball's still happening?" Matt asked. "So much is changing. The Phillies are now a cricket team!"

I clicked past talking newspapers and movies displayed devoid of color, then found the game.

"Is this right now?" George asked.

"Yes," I said. "This is a live broadcast from Kansas City. It's the deciding game of the Series."

George had learned to read the info at the bottom of the screen. For our Giants, Panda Sandoval had scored, followed by Pence (one-hundredth of a George). Then the Royals scored a pair as well.

The Giants went ahead, 3-2, in the fourth. The TV picture wobbled, swelled on the screen, flickered, shrank suddenly, and reverted to static. Then back to normal, followed by a repeat of odd behavior.

In the bottom of the fifth, Madison Bumgarner, the Giants ace starter, came into the game as a relief pitcher. Manager Bruce Bochy had hinted for the past several days that Bumgarner might be used in relief in Game 7, but no one knew how long he could pitch. How much more would they ask of him?

"He's a farm boy, grew up in North Carolina," I said. "I'm sure he's still got life in that arm, but the Giants would be lucky to get an inning or two from him."

The TV picture faded in and out, swelled and diminished, then turned to static.

I tried different channels, stopping when I came upon an odd scene. In an enclosure somewhat like a boxing ring, several scantily clad women jumped around and knocked each other down, yelling and appearing to fight.

George quickly understood what he was seeing.

"Is this the grappling competition of which you spoke earlier?"

"Wrestling," I said. "And it's not a competition, really. The winner is predetermined."

"Why do audiences watch if they already know the outcome?"

"The audience doesn't know who's going to win, and it's fun to watch," said Matt. "Check it out."

Four women wrestlers occupied the ring, both inside and at the edge, along with a male referee in a striped shirt. One of the wrestlers climbed on the ropes, then flipped over backward and landed on top of her opponent, flat on the floor.

"Oh my!" said the General.

Another wrestler performed a double bounce off the ropes and finished with a kick to the head of another. Or so it appeared.

"Watch this slow-motion," I said. "Notice how the woman getting kicked actually jerks her head back a split-second before the kicker makes contact. It's playacting."

"Quite so. Yet it is, as you say, entertaining to observe."

"See the one on the right, shorter than the others, powerful and agile?" I pointed to a woman in a pink top, with a bare midriff, short shorts, high boots, and a wide, jeweled belt. Curvy and strong, with long, dark hair, she had skin the color of honey. "That's Layla, the one we saw in New York. At Madison Square Garden. Or whatever they call it."

"I had almost forgotten that encounter, in light of the dreadful events which followed. She is, indeed, the same lass?"

"She is, indeed, a hottie," said Matt, not for the first time.

"Most wrestlers are men, huge guys with enormous muscles who act heroic or mean and throw each other around the ring," I said. "These women wrestlers are all amazing athletes."

Layla smashed her opponent into a corner, then flipped over and hung from the ropes upside down, appearing to use her own weight to choke her opponent on the top rope.

"Acrobats, really. Some of these moves would make any gymnast proud," I added.

"But tell me, Timothy, why do they yell at each other so?"

"It's scripted, like a play," I told him.

We watched two men with pumped-up, bulging physiques yell at each other in a prelude to the next match.

"They have writers who invent feuds and grudges, develop story lines about jealousies and hatreds, and write scenes for them to perform. Unlike baseball games. They're entertainers, actors in a very physical drama. Only no one really gets hurt."

"They do have accidents and injuries," Matt said.

"Sure. That's inevitable, with the number of bodies flying around."

"I am still a bit shocked by the display of so much flesh, by both the men and women in this sport," said George. "And the size of the men's muscles is, somehow, disturbing. These matches are, nonetheless, not unpleasant to behold, and I do find this spectacle quite entertaining."

"Yeah, yeah," Matt said. "Now, can we please go back to baseball?"

Chapter Sixty-Nine
BUM

I switched back to the Series. The TV picture came back but kept wobbling.

I was disturbed.

Why are we getting such poor reception on the channel with the Series, but wrestling is clear and crisp? Maybe it's not about the reception. Perhaps, as the world around us devolves into dystopia, baseball is fading into obscurity, but professional wrestling is surviving as a beacon of American culture.

I shuddered at the thought. The picture straightened itself out. Madison Bumgarner, on only two days' rest, gave up a hit to the first batter he faced in the fifth inning, then dispatched the Royals without further ado. He surrendered no more hits and no runs in the fifth, sixth, and seventh. After starting and winning two games earlier in the Series, surely no one could expect more of him.

The Giants clung tightly to their one-run lead. To our amazement, Mad Bum came out to pitch the eighth inning. Three up, three down again. But the Giants' bats were cold, too, and they didn't score again.

Bumgarner walked out to the mound to pitch the ninth,

his fifth inning in relief that day, trying to protect the Giants' one-run lead.

"That's leadership by example. Deeds out-trump words," I said.

Maybe Mad Bum's charisma will inspire George when he is back with his army. If he gets back. But who knows what could happen tomorrow morning at Valley Forge?

In the ninth, Bum induced the first batter to strike out swinging. The second fouled out. With two outs, down by a run, and facing an imminent, tough World Series loss, Alex Gordon of the Royals looped a fly ball to the outfield. Gregor Blanco, the Giants' usually sure-handed center fielder, came running over, got fooled by a crazy bounce, and allowed the ball to scoot past him. The left fielder chased the ball all the way to the wall, then kicked it himself. As he finally ran it down, Gordon was heading toward third. For a breathless moment, I wondered if he would try to score and tie the game.

Gordon rounded third. To our amazement, the Royals' third-base coach waved him home, a surprising, gutsy move. The Giants' left fielder threw the ball to the shortstop, who hesitated, then relayed a great throw to catcher Buster Posey. Gordon slid into home. Posey caught the ball out in front of the plate and executed a swipe tag. In a very close play, Gordon hooked around the outside part of the plate and appeared to elude the tag.

I leaped off the couch. "Oh no! No!"

But the home-plate umpire called him out—the third out of the ninth inning. The Giants had won!

Or so it seemed.

As Matt and I had explained to George earlier, this was baseball's new era, the first year of instant replay challenges.

As the Giants jubilantly poured onto the field, Royals manager Ned Yost ran out of the dugout, protesting loudly. Of course he would challenge the call. He had nothing to lose. The championship was on the line. It ain't over till it's over.

The umpires conferred with their headquarters in New York. The new system had been in effect all season, with mostly good results. I thought about Pierre and wished he could conjure up a positive outcome here.

The ruling came in less than a minute. The slow-motion replays were clear. The umpire's decision on the field was overturned. Posey's tag had missed Gordon. He had slid around it and was safe at the plate.

The game was now tied in the bottom of the ninth, and the Royals had one more out. The Kansas City crowd went wild. At last they had something to cheer about.

The next Royals batter, Salvador Pérez, had hit seventeen home runs during the regular season. He was the backbone of this team, the big, iron-man catcher who led with his glove and his bat. He stepped to the plate.

Mad Bum looked tired now, but Bochy left him in the game. He didn't even have anyone else warming up.

The first pitch sizzled on the inside corner for a strike. Pérez watched it go by. Second pitch, inside corner, same place. No balls, two strikes.

"What will he throw next?" Matt wondered.

"Won't he make the same pitch again?" George asked.

"That's what he wants them to think," I said. "He's got Pérez set up to worry about getting another inside strike. But let's see what he does."

The third pitch was a slider on the outside corner. No one but the guy at the plate expected it. Pérez was waiting for it, his arms extended. He drove the ball deep down the left field line, a frozen rope that cleared a low fence and landed in the box seats for a home run. The Royals had won the game and the World Series.

"He was laying in the weeds!" George said. "He knew what was coming, but the pitcher didn't know that he knew. If you know what's coming, you can attack at will. That batsman must have discerned that they did not plan to continue bowling inside to him."

Bummer! I was more annoyed than saddened by the Giants' loss. They had come a long way, barely making the playoffs, then winning every round, dragging out their amazing season until the very last inning of the last game of the last series. But now it was over, and they were losers.

We switched off the TV. The rain and lightning had stopped by now, so I walked and fed Nevada. We only had about a day's worth of dog food left, and our cash was running low. If Valley Forge didn't work out tomorrow, I wasn't sure what would happen. We had enough money to get home, but not enough to prolong the mission.

"My butt hurts," Matt said. "I'm gonna crash."

We drifted off to bed. I could hear George humming softly to himself.

If things worked out the way we hoped, this could be our last night together.

Chapter Seventy
H Q

Valley Forge, October 30, 2014

We set out just after six the next morning. Our first problem was getting there.

Matt recognized some of the buildings and streets, but the freeways and some of the roads were badly marked or simply didn't exist. Potholes and detours abounded, and of course we still had to drive on the left side. My iPhone freaked out every time I tried to use the GPS. The navigation app still functioned, but the landscape and maps seemed to be in a constant state of flux. At a stoplight, I watched as a road map on my phone undulated and reconfigured itself.

We eventually arrived at King of Prussia, the town nearest Valley Forge, and stumbled around till we found Gulph Road. Matt recognized the street name, which should have led us through the site of the Continental Army encampment. We arrived just before seven, about a half hour before sunrise. As the sky slowly brightened, gently rolling hills, brilliant and green, watered by the recent rains, peeked through the low clouds. A clear, pre-dawn sky promised love-ly fall weather, and a red glow to the east hinted at the start of an auspicious day.

"This is so weird," Matt said. "No signs, no national park, no visitor center."

We drove through some trees, then emerged beside a grassy knoll.

"This used to be the Anthony Wayne statue. It's not here. Nor is the von Steuben memorial."

"Memorials? Statues?" George was incredulous. "General Wayne and the Prussian I have yet to meet?"

"Well, yes. And you, too, of course," Matt said.

Don't tell him too much, I glared.

"I'm pretty sure that if we follow this road, we'll get to Washington's HQ," Matt added.

"What is HQ?"

"Headquarters," Matt clarified, before adding, "Is that it?"

We drove up to a decaying two-story farmhouse made of fieldstone set in white mortar. George looked dismayed. Several windows contained shattered glass, a number of stones were missing, the porch sagged, and the paint on the doors and trim was peeling. Tall grass surrounded the house. A large barn in even worse condition stood nearby.

"This was so tidy when we came here on field trips," Matt said. "It's so wrecked now."

"Twenty people lived and worked here?" I asked. "It doesn't look big enough for that, or solid enough."

"Indeed, Farmer Potts's home appears to have deterio-rated greatly. During our encampment, we added a two-story log addition in the back of the main house, which I fail to see here. The kitchen had an additional floor in my day, and the house has a full cellar and a large garret room. My man Billy Lee sleeps in the attic."

"Oh yeah," Matt said. "You're fighting for freedom with your slave by your side. If you win your freedom, will he get his?"

George eyed him warily. This would not be settled in the few minutes we had left, but clearly Matt's message about slavery was starting to get through.

I wondered if George felt nervous about going back. I wouldn't be surprised if he did, considering the drama of our flight across the country and the possible consequences of his return.

We parked next to a black van, the only other vehicle around. Nevada was eager to get out. George wore his full Revolutionary drag—long coat of buff and blue, with waistcoat, brass buttons, gold epaulets, ruffled white collar and cuffs, dark cloak, and black, three-cornered hat. His long legs were housed in tan breeches tucked into tall black boots, his shoulder-length reddish-brown hair, showing more gray than ever, neatly tied in a tight cue with a black ribbon. The curved hunting sword with the silver-and-green-banded handle hung in its leather scabbard along his left thigh, its burlap wrappings discarded.

He hadn't worn the uniform since the day we returned to Point Isabel. I had grown accustomed to seeing him in running shoes, khaki shorts, and sports jerseys. Once again I was impressed by his stature. Though I was an inch or two taller, he carried himself with a bearing and air of confidence that inspired trust. George's physical presence, twenty years younger than the stony-faced figure on the dollar bill, conveyed a broad-shouldered, big-boned power and command.

Pierre was in the black van with two other guys. He

greeted us with a brief smile and introduced his companions. "This is Wesley, and that's Kenny."

They nodded to us, unsmiling. Both had short hair, athletic physiques, and wore dark windbreakers with suspicious bulges under their arms. If they were impressed to meet George Washington, they didn't show it.

Pierre looked at us. "This is it, gentlemen. We've come a long way for this."

"Indeed," George said. "My thanks to you all. Agent Chow, I deeply appreciate all your efforts and perseverance in getting us to this point."

Pierre smiled. George turned to Matt with a dignified air.

"LaMatthew, you are indeed a credit to your people."

"My *people*? Which *people*, George? I told you I'm Black and I'm Jewish. Which people get the credit for me?"

George smiled. "Please excuse my clumsy words. You represent the *American* people quite well. I shall never forget your heartfelt pleas against slavery. And it is clear to me, beyond a shadow of a doubt, that I owe you my life." He offered a hand.

Matt looked up at George, nearly a foot taller, met his gaze for a long moment, then shook his hand solemnly.

George turned to me.

"Timothy—"

"General," Pierre jumped in, "we must start to move to the site of our procedure. We are planning to use the same jumping-off point as the last time we were here, over near the track."

He opened the van, to reveal a half dozen black travel cases.

"What are those?" I asked. "And where's the time machine? How can it fit in a few cases?"

"This is it," Pierre said. "These contain the Temporal Vector Displacement device. Grab a case and let's go."

We followed him and his men north from the head-quarters house, up a low hill. The grass was still wet, and a fine day was dawning. Nevada ran ahead, ecstatically inhaling the bouquet of sweet smells released by the rain.

This was nothing like the *Time Machine* movie based on the H. G. Wells book. That time machine—my main reference for what one should look like—was an odd, Victorian, steampunk contraption with brass control levers, mechanical date-selection dials, spinning flywheels, and rotating silver umbrellas that defined a circular force field for travel through time and space. But maybe all time machines were different. In the movie *Hot Tub Time Machine*, the time machine was, well, the hot tub. Obviously there was some wiggle room, in fiction, anyway, where the realities of physics are no impediment to the imagination.

But this situation was much too real. This wasn't a time-travel story we were talking about. This was my life.

Chapter Seventy-One
BAKELITE

The wind picked up as the sun crested the horizon. We followed Pierre and his men to the top of the hill, a railroad embankment. Here we found two sets of train tracks and a run-down station. North of the embankment, the Schuylkill River ran choppy and rough, engorged by the downpours of the past couple of days.

"This station was well preserved when I was a kid," Matt said. "It was a museum."

"And it does not exist yet during our encampment," George said. "Of course, there are no railroads at all."

"Were. There *were* no railroads at the time of your encampment."

"Timothy, at this moment, under the circumstances, the choice of correct grammatical tense presents a quandary beyond my ken."

"And no doubt it's the least of our problems," Matt growled.

We crossed the railroad bed to an abandoned, broken

concrete boarding platform on the north side of the tracks, covered with ivy, slick with moss, reverting to nature. An ancient stairway appeared to lead to a tunnel beneath the tracks, unused since passenger service had been discontinued. No trains stopped here. We set down the black cases on the platform. A stand of trees separated us from the river.

"This is where we need to be," Pierre said. "This is where we dispatched von Steuben, causing the General's temporal bounce." He turned to George. "You must have been quite close to this spot when it happened."

"I did stroll up this hill in the snow that night to watch the aurora borealis."

"Are we too late?" I asked Pierre. "So much has changed already. Philadelphia is only half the city it used to be, the Phillies now play cricket, and New York seems like an exploited, long-neglected colony."

"And yet, some things are still the same," Pierre said. "I have received reports that other areas of the country are changing more slowly than here in the heart of the Revolution."

"The damn World Series still took place on the West Coast and in the Midwest," Matt said with a note of bitterness. "The damn Giants still lost. They couldn't pull it out this time, in an even-numbered year. I guess Bumgarner isn't Superman, after all. But the games did go on as scheduled."

"Not a positive outcome, Pierre. Can we do anything about that?" I asked.

He smiled. Clearly he'd been asked to change the outcome of a sporting event before.

"Remember," he said, "sometimes, when we restore history with a temporal vector displacement, the results are unpredictable."

"Yes. But why?" I asked. "And how far off will the new reality be?"

"There's really no way to tell. As I mentioned, small reversals we initiate in historical events can play out differently than expected, especially when their consequences are magnified over hundreds of years."

"The butterfly effect," I said.

"Precisely. And sending the General back could be a *huge* change with epic consequences. We don't know exactly what will happen. Unpredictable results often cluster around particularly nettlesome problems—triumphs of human emotion over rationality, decisions which could easily go one way or the other. A temporal vector displacement reversal can influence events in surprising ways."

We all paused to contemplate what we were doing: trying to re-create a cherished past—and possibly an uncertain future—to replace our bleak present. Pierre and his men set out the black cases in a line and began to open them.

Sun streaked in from the hills to the east. The dewy, verdant landscape glowed and glistened in the warm light. A sense of well-being overcame me as the sun warmed our bodies. We had traveled thousands of miles to get here, in just a few days. Hopefully George's return to his own time would bring an end to the dark reality devouring our world. I watched him gazing through the trees at the river rushing below. He turned to me and smiled, the end of our journey near. Our efforts would soon come to fruition.

Pierre showed us that one of the cases held the monitoring module for the Positive Outcomes Authority's Temporal Vector Displacement device. Wesley and Kenny lifted it out and carefully set it on the ground. It looked as if the unholy spawn of an old Jaguar dashboard had mated with the control panel of the *Spirit of St. Louis*. Clusters of circular vintage gauges in several sizes mounted in polished walnut, connected to panels of polished, patterned stainless steel holding rows of old toggle switches. Two large, bulbous glass displays dominated the module: one a green oscilloscope tracing that looked like the sonar on an old submarine, the other a vintage DuMont television with sharply rounded corners. It had been new when Eisenhower started building freeways.

I looked at Pierre. "You've gotta be kidding me."

"Einstein didn't have today's electronics available to him. We've reworked parts of it, but much of the monitoring module is original." He opened another case. "This holds the temporal vector engine."

The engine was mounted on panels of molded black Bakelite, that early plastic used in transistor radios and Brownie cameras. An old-style toggle switch on the side said ON/OFF.

"I see it has large air vents. What needs so much ventilation?"

"The tubes. It has two fans."

"Vacuum tubes?" Matt asked.

"Yes, and they are getting harder and harder to find. Tubes were state of the art in Einstein's day, but now they've grown obsolete. I wish we could redesign and rebuild this device with modern components."

"Why don't you?"

"We have, well, constraints."

"Homeland Security has a time machine capable of altering the course of history many times over, and you have budgetary limits?"

Chapter Seventy-Two
SADDLE

Another case held the control module—black dials, red on-off buttons, adjustable sliders, and mechanical, alphanumeric displays.

"Historically, we used this to set the EDA, the arrival date," Pierre explained.

"Can you set the time of day as well?" I asked.

"Yes, but the mechanical time control is regrettably inaccurate. Since we must avoid overlap—we don't want there to be two General Washingtons roaming around Valley Forge, do we?—we'll set his arrival time for several hours after the time he left."

He pulled an ancient laptop out of a shoulder bag.

I was incredulous. "A Mac PowerBook 100?"

"Yes. The legacy system was substantially updated in the early '90s with the addition of a personal computer."

"Really?" I squealed. "Obviously, you found this in a cave somewhere, along with the Dead Sea Scrolls. Did God use it to write the Ten Commandments? Or did he have newer hardware?"

He winced.

Kenny broke in, "Agent Chow, we really need to move this along."

Pierre nodded. "We do have a newer controller, but we still use the PowerBook to establish a constant sync pulse during temporal vector displacements. A drifting sync pulse could scramble the molecules of a person undergoing displacement, and we certainly don't want that, right?" He grinned.

I remembered *The Fly*, the old Jeff Goldblum horror flick where a scientist attempting teleportation inadvertently merges with a common housefly at a molecular-genetic level. I shuddered. "Certainly not. But where does he sit *during* the displacement? Or stand? Where's the damn time machine, Pierre?"

"We're getting to that."

There were now two cases left: a long, narrow one and a large cube. The long one contained a stand of some kind, like a sleek sawhorse, which Pierre and his men unfolded and set up. It looked as if someone could sit on it. But something was missing.

They opened the final case. Inside was a large, well-worn leather saddle, tan, edges tooled in a floral pattern, with silver buckles and a saddle horn wrapped in rawhide.

George gaped. "A Spanish war saddle!"

"We call it Western," Pierre said. "I know you're accustomed to riding English style, General, but this is the original seat wired for the device."

Wesley and Kenny picked up the saddle, placed it onto the fold-up stand, and strapped it into place.

"In Einstein's original plan, the seat was placed on a

low wall or on wooden sawhorses. The problem is, there isn't always a wall around when you want one, and sawhorses don't travel well. This lightweight aluminum stand makes the whole device more portable. It's one of the newer parts of the system." Pierre seemed quite proud of his time machine.

I was perplexed. "But why a saddle?"

"That's what H. G. Wells put in his story," he said.

"No, he didn't. His time machine had a brown leather seat like a dentist's chair and shiny, whirly things that rotated around it."

"In the movie. But in the book—in the original story—his time machine had a saddle."

"Guys," Matt broke in, "it doesn't matter. That's all fiction. Wells didn't invent a time machine, Timmy. He just wrote a clever story."

"True," Pierre said, "but a saddle turns out to be a good choice. The leather is easily embedded with magnetic sensors that maintain close contact with the rider's legs. Feet in the stirrups and hands on the pommel complete the circuit."

"What's this?" Matt asked. "It looks like a GoPro camera, mounted to the front of the saddle. Don't tell me Einstein invented the GoPro, too."

"No, that's one of the latest modernizations of the system. When we activate the device, the occupant of the saddle is transported to the destination era, but the saddle itself and the rest of the equipment remain here. Through years of experimentation, we discovered that a camera mounted up front can see briefly across the years during the displacement of the temporal vector."

"So we'll be able to see Valley Forge 200 years ago?"

"Hopefully. At best, only for an instant, a very short window. We shoot a burst of high-definition video at the moment of displacement. If we're lucky, we can record and recover a usable frame or two from the destination era. In this case, we have positioned the saddle and camera to point down the hill toward the headquarters house.

He turned to George. "There are no reins. Think you can handle a Western saddle?"

"I believe I am prepared for the challenge, Agent Chow, though I have not ridden or even seen a horse for some months now."

As Chow and his men connected and warmed up the TVD device, George placed a hand on my shoulder. "Much has happened since that afternoon we met at your dog park. Providence has blessed me. I was so fortunate to meet you."

He turned to include Matt. "You lads have taken care of me and struggled to determine what to do, how to restore me to my own era and effect a return to the destiny we believe to be just and true. You have also introduced me to baseball, which I shall miss terribly."

"George—" I said.

"You began our adventure together with reluctance," he interrupted, "yet you have risen nobly to the occasion. You are loyal and capable and earnest. Given different circumstances, I would be proud to have you serve on my staff. You both possess keen judgment and passion, similar to my military aides in the Revolution."

"I'm not very military, George," Matt said.

"Shut up, Matty," I whispered. "He's honoring us, comparing us with Alexander Hamilton and the Marquis de Lafayette."

Chapter Seventy-Three
BALLERINOS

Nevada had wandered off a while ago. I could hear her now, unsubtly galumphing through the verdure at the river's edge. She did love to swim, but the current looked strong, and we had no towels. I hoped she wouldn't jump in.

I heard a booming *woof,* followed by more crashing through undergrowth. Then two more *woofs*, distant and echoey, the first time I could remember three *woofs* so close together.

She flushed out some big game. Chased by my large, black puppy, three men stumbled up the stairs from the dark, abandoned tunnel beneath the tracks. Shielding their eyes from the bright sunlight, they ran toward us, wildly firing automatic weapons.

Of course, the men were after George. Matt and I, closest as they advanced, rolled off the sides of the slippery concrete train platform. Wesley and Kenny pirouetted with the poise of primo ballerinos and whipped out machine pistols from under their windbreakers. Dropping to their knees, they returned fire.

Their bullets stopped two of the attackers, whose guns sprayed into the air as each of the men was hit. I looked up to see George still standing, reaching for his sword, advancing aggressively against the attack. *No, no, no*, I thought, *move away from them. Pride goeth before a fall, General. Get the hell out of the way! We need you to go back to your own time and undo the perversion of history we're living. Let Pierre's guys take care of these goons!*

The third would-be assassin tried to scramble past me, firing his weapon while facing into the sun, his feet losing traction on the slick surface, Nevada nipping at his heels. I grabbed his ankle and held tight. In the blink of an eye, George unsheathed his curved saber and slashed upward viciously. The killer's torso split open. Blood poured from a huge gash across his chest, as the powerful blow knocked him from his feet.

As he fell toward the edge of the platform, his face frozen in an astonished grimace, I noticed his eyes were odd, maybe different colors. Creepy. He rolled down the embankment and through the trees, probably dead before he hit the water. The swollen river swallowed his body and carried him downstream.

George stood there, his chest heaving, anger clouding his brow. He looked down at the river, then poked at the other two assailants with his boot. No signs of life. He looked around grimly. "Timothy?"

"I'm good."

"Me too," Matt said. Wesley rolled the bodies of the other two gunmen off the platform and into the river.

George cleaned and sheathed his sword. We noticed blood on the front of his jacket.

"It's not mine, lads. It's his. They haven't injured me."

I wiped the blood with my sleeve, vainly trying to tidy him. Two fresh holes in the coat bore witness to the famous Washington luck.

"I did hear bullets whistling past me," he said with a tight smile. "But I had no idea they were so close."

Indeed, they must have just missed his chest.

But we hadn't escaped unscathed. Wesley and Kenny huddled over Pierre, who lay flat on his back on the mossy platform.

Pierre was conscious, though in great pain. He had taken a bullet in his side. Wesley opened Pierre's shirt and applied pressure to the wound, then butterfly dressings and bandages from a small medical kit to stanch the bleeding. Kenny kept his weapon at the ready as Wesley stapled the wound and stuck a syringe in Pierre's side.

"For the pain," he said.

"We must get you to a hospital, Agent Chow," George said.

"We must get you to your encampment, General Washington. That is our first priority." Pierre's breathing was labored. "We can finish here quickly. We owe it to our posterity. Those men were professionals, and there could be others."

"These guys weren't as low-rent as Tommy and Arlene, that couple that tried to kill you in New York with a peashooter and a suitcase," I said. "These guys were prepared."

"Exactly," said Pierre. "Please allow us to ready the device."

George thought for a moment, then bowed to him and gave way. With Wesley's assistance, Pierre sat up, drank some water, then got to his feet, swaying unsteadily.

"Steady there, buddy," I said, grabbing his arm. "Let me help you."

The lanky agent moved slowly down the platform.

"Chow," Wesley interrupted impatiently, "gotta do it." Both he and Kenny now had their Uzis out and scanned the area with suspicion.

Pierre clutched his side, caught his breath, then turned to George.

"General, please mount the device."

With great dignity, George Washington walked toward the saddle, firmly strapped and clamped down to its newly designed, lightweight aluminum frame. He stopped for a moment to lengthen the stirrups, placed his left boot in the left stirrup, grabbed the saddle horn, and gracefully swung his 6'2" frame aboard. The man really knew how to sit a horse, even an inanimate, stationary, time-travel high-tech sawhorse like this.

While Kenny continued to keep guard, Wesley flicked switches on the monitoring module and turned rotary pots on the control module. The whir of the temporal vector engine's cooling fans grew louder, as the machine reached its running speed.

I had a thought.

"George," I called out. "The iPod!"

He looked puzzled.

"The little looking glass. And the ear buds."

He nodded, reached into his uniform jacket pocket, pulled out my sister's iPod Touch and headset, and tossed them to me with a smile.

"Have you preset the temporal parameters?" Wesley asked.

"Yes, right here," Chow replied, brandishing an iPhone. "Tim, I told you, there's an app for that. It's proprietary, of course. You can't get it at the App Store for any price. But it makes life simple for us and bypasses a lot of this crude old legacy gear. It also remote-starts the GoPro recording."

He showed us the time and date setting on the smartphone screen: 7 a.m., February 23, 1778. The morning after George had disappeared.

With a flourish, Chow touched a green Activate button, and the iPhone emitted a loud, rhythmic *ribbit-ribbit-ribbit* frog sound. For a few seconds, nothing else seemed to happen. Then the engine began to hum. The cooling fans started to run faster and grew louder, fighting the ancient vacuum tubes' tendency to overheat. Wesley reached for a panel of toggle switches and looked at Chow, who nodded. Wesley flicked four of the switches down, then studied the oscilloscope's display. Squiggly green lines traced across the screen. "Looking good," he yelled above the noise.

The ground began to shake beneath our feet. Nevada whimpered and leaned against my legs. George looked over at me. We locked eyes, and I grew melancholy. After we had come so far together, the moment had finally arrived.

He spoke, but I couldn't make out the words.

"What?"

He yelled, "O brave new world, how many goodly creatures are there here! How beauteous mankind is! O brave new world, that has such people in't!"

I choked up, my eyes filled with tears. I turned to Matt. He looked at me quizzically.

"It's *The Tempest*, Matty. He's quoting from *The Tempest*."

Chapter Seventy-Four
PATSY

Valley Forge, February 23, 1778

The General felt his body go limp, as if his bones had melted into a puddle, his mind shattered into thousands of shards. He experienced a great sadness. All went white. Consciousness fought exhaustion, both mental and physical. Then all went black.

He awoke sometime later, flat on his back in a snowbank. Every part of his body ached and throbbed, and he was chilled to the bone. To the east, a cold dawn struggled to illuminate the winter landscape. The railroad was gone.

A soldier came running up the hill.

"General! Your Excellency! Where did you come from? We have been searching. He is here! The General is here!"

The soldier put down his musket, knelt on the ground, and helped Washington to his feet, brushing the snow from Washington's coat and gathering his cloak around him. Others came running. Soon young Alec Hamilton was at Washington's side, helping him walk—unsteadily at first—back to the stone farmhouse. Lafayette ran up to assist.

"*Mon Général!* We have been looking for you all night! Where have you been?"

"I have been ... out for a walk."

"A walk? All night?"

"Yes. What have I missed?"

"Your Excellency," Hamilton replied, "The Prussian general we have been awaiting, Baron von Steuben, arrived in camp quite late last night."

"Yes? What is your impression of him, Colonel Hamilton?"

"He has interesting ideas about rigorous, standard training and drilling for our troops. He believes we can garner some advantage from this miserable winter. Perhaps we can gain strength with his methods, transforming our stout-hearted rabble into a unified fighting force, despite losing soldiers to the ravages of disease and climate."

"I completely agree, Colonel. When can I meet him?"

"As soon as you care to, Excellency. As soon as you have recovered from your ordeal."

"Ordeal? As I said, I went for a walk, and we shall speak no more of it. I shall return to HQ to greet Lady Washington and change my clothes. Then you can bring the Prussian to me."

"HQ, sir?"

"Headquarters, Hamilton. Headquarters."

They approached the Potts house, which looked as the General remembered it, the newly built wings intact and well-tended. His manservant Billy Lee emerged, the enslaved human who had served him for twenty years.

"Billy, please take care of this," Washington said, removing his uniform coat. "There are blood stains to be cleaned."

"Blood, General? Are you injured, sir?"

"It's not my blood, thank you, Billy. There are also some bullet holes to repair. And please keep it to yourself."

He looked Billy in the eye with the barest hint of a twinkle. "In particular …"

Billy smiled. "I'll keep it away from Miz Washington, sir."

Billy had always supported him with energy, intelligence, loyalty, and understanding. The General stared. Billy met his eyes, then looked down.

"Something else, General?"

"Ah. Not yet, Billy, not just yet. But thank you."

Washington touched his slave on the shoulder, then walked past him and up the few steps into the house to see his wife. Martha had just been roused from bed, demurely donning a warm bathrobe and white bonnet.

"Pappa!" she said with a relieved sigh and a warm smile. His heart swelled.

"Patsy, my dearest. A very lovely good morning to you."

Chapter Seventy-Five
TVD

Valley Forge, October 30, 2014

The ground shook for a minute or two, pounding like a pile driver. George appeared to be completely at home mounted on the saddle, elegantly draped across the artificial horse of the time machine. In his eyes I saw eagerness, the joy of going home, a flinty determination, and a bit of merriment. *We did have some good times together*, I thought. The corners of his mouth curled slightly upward.

Then he was gone.

A white flash. I flinched away from the TVD device. The pounding in the ground slowed for a few seconds, then stopped completely.

As promised, the saddle and its mount were still there. So was the GoPro.

Pierre came up excitedly. "Cool, huh? Let's see if we got any images."

Wesley manipulated dials on the monitoring module. What had appeared to be an old television set mounted in the console revealed itself to be a high-def monitor. He pulled the SD card from the camera and inserted it into a reader that plugged into an added-on USB port on the PowerBook 100.

"We've modified the computer over the years," Pierre said. "None of this old legacy gear is what it seems. This PowerBook has a custom, updated MacBook Pro processor and modern connectivity inside that ancient shell." He turned to Wesley. "Get anything?"

Wesley scanned through the few minutes of video shot during the displacement. The footage showed Matt and me watching George, then cringing away from the white flash, followed by a few garbled images and the two of us after it was over.

Wesley went back to the seconds just after the flash. These frames appeared to be corrupted, but he ran them through a file-recovery system, added enhancement, and produced two fairly clear color frames taken during the brief window when the GoPro could see the destination era through the device.

From the train platform, the camera had captured a snow-covered valley. The cold light of dawn revealed frozen fields and leaden skies. The train tracks, station, and tunnel were gone. A couple of men with muskets, in three-cornered hats and long cloaks, trudged up the hill toward the camera. In the background, we could see the HQ farmhouse.

"It looks like he got back there. Do you have a way to verify?" I asked.

"Not really. Let's see what happens."

Wesley and Kenny quickly packed up the gear and shuttled it to the van.

Kenny came up to Pierre. "Let's get you patched up properly, Agent."

Chow nodded. He looked wan and strained as the exhilaration ebbed and the pain injection wore off.

Matt and I helped him down the hill to the black van and eased him into the back seat. He bumped my fist.

"Go home now. Pick up your lives again. I'll be in touch soon."

"Assuming George got back okay, and assuming things work out, how long will it take for things to get back to normal?" I asked.

"I don't know. It's quite unpredictable."

"It took a few months—since we found George Washington—for the world to deteriorate into this subservient colonial existence. Is it likely to take as long as that to fix itself?"

"There's just no way to tell. It could happen overnight. Or it might drag out for months. And everything might not go back to the way it was before. Whatever 'before' means. And assuming we remember all this."

Chow had said that POA agents received regular inoculations of "brain chemicals," protein molecules that helped them retain memories of past events that had been changed. I couldn't imagine that I would ever forget our summer with George.

Kenny revved the engine on the van. We closed the side door, stepped back, and waved goodbye.

Matty and I stopped at a pet store and bought a dog crate big enough for Nevada. The next morning, we caught a United flight from Philly back to San Francisco.

It was weird to be without George. The airport seemed normal enough, with a few concessions selling English food, several hot dog stands, and a Cinnabon. And three Starbucks, of course. Some things never change.

I could have brought Vada on board as a service dog,

351

but I just couldn't pretend anymore. Playing blind reminded me of April. Now that George was gone and the tension had dissipated, I kept thinking of her on the train. Smiling as she passed me in the hall. Lying with me in the roomette and staring deep into my soul. Running back into the train together after the bloody confrontation on the Nebraska siding. Hugging me outside her room, as Matt lay wounded inside.

All I had left were memories.

PART THREE
Forgetting

"It breaks your heart. It is designed to break your heart. The game begins in the spring, when everything else begins again, and it blossoms in the summer, filling the afternoons and evenings, and then as soon as the chill rains come, it stops and leaves you to face the fall all alone."

—A. Bartlett Giamatti, Commissioner of Baseball,
A Great and Glorious Game

Chapter Seventy-Six
PARADE

San Francisco, October 31, 2014

We landed at SFO in the late afternoon and dragged ourselves off the plane. I was dead tired. Matt complained that his butt ached. I bought a *Chronicle* and stuck it under my arm to read later. The airport appeared as I remembered it, filled with places selling sourdough bread, clam chowder, paninis, burgers, sushi, and cappuccinos. Apparently world history was correcting itself very quickly.

We collected Vada at baggage claim, dragged her and our luggage to the curb, and called an Uber for a ride home. I sat on the sidewalk, legs crossed, hunched over, head to my knees. My parents were back from Italy and waiting for me at home, and I was eager to see them. But I missed George. And April.

The driver picked us up in a Ford SUV, threw the crate and our duffles in the trunk, and sped away from the airport. Nevada sat up on the back seat, eagerly supervising the drive home. I slumped down and soon started to doze. The driver headed north toward San Francisco.

"I can go through City now, guys, because parade over already." He spoke with a Russian accent.

"Parade?"

"Yes, earlier in day I *vould* go other *vay* from airport and take other bridge. Too many people come to parade."

"I'm sorry, what parade? Halloween?"

"No, mister. Giants. *Vhat*, you live under rock? Giants *von Vorld Serious*."

I opened the *Chronicle* I had bought. It was nearly all in English.

The banner headline on the front page read "DYNAS-TY. Giants Take World Series from K.C. in 7 Games."

Chapter Seventy-Seven
REPLAY

Berkeley, October 31, 2014

Y ou went to Valley Forge with Matt? Why there?" Mom was curious.

"Well, you know, history major and all."

"Sure, Tim, but I've never known you to be particularly interested in the Revolutionary War."

"I've recently become fascinated by Washington."

"What about it?"

"George. I've developed an interest in George Washington."

"Oh. What about him?"

"I read an article," I lied, "about how the winter at Valley Forge was a major turning point in the Revolution. Even though there were five more years of war afterward."

"So you wanted to see it for yourself," my dad said. "How was it?"

"Not much there. Valley Forge was an encampment site. No battles were fought there. No battlefields. We did see

Washington's headquarters, though. That was a thrill." I was desperate to change the subject. "How's Hank?"

They looked puzzled. "Fine, I guess," said my dad. "I got a call from him just after we got home. We'll probably go up there next week and hike with him and Maggie."

"Hike?"

"Yeah, we're planning to meet in Hendy Woods and walk around those ancient redwoods."

"He can hike?"

"Sure, Tim, why wouldn't he?"

I didn't know what to say. The last I had heard a few days before, he had a bullet lodged near his spine and might never walk again.

"How about them Giants!?" I croaked through my incredulity.

My folks broke into big, goofy smiles.

"I know! We've been so excited," said my mom. "Even though we were gone for most of the season, we still followed along. Watched a lot of game highlights—"

"When the Wi-Fi was working in the apartment in Florence," my dad interjected.

"Yeah, but what happened in the last game?"

"What do you mean?"

I paused, not certain what to ask. We had discussed their sabbatical time in Italy, and clearly they were unaware of any vast historical changes in geopolitical power structures. Either the unraveling of our culture that we had witnessed had failed to reach Europe, or, more likely, my folks no longer remembered the changes. I couldn't tell them too much about our summer: meeting George, fleeing cross-country, and sending him back with a time machine invented by Einstein. I just didn't think I could sell that kind of how-I-spent-my-summer-vacation story.

"Do you want to watch game 7?" my dad asked. "I have it on the DVR."

"Okay. I'll text Matty."

Matt came over and greeted my folks, then gratefully tucked into some nachos and guacamole as we watched the game.

Most of it unfolded as before. Once again, Bumgarner came into the game in the bottom of the fifth, the Giants clinging to a one-run lead. Again, he held Kansas City to one hit and no runs for four innings. Again, with two outs in the ninth, the Royals' Alex Gordon hit a looping fly ball. Again, Giants center fielder Gregor Blanco booted it, and the left fielder kicked the ball and chased it to the wall. Again, Gordon was around second and headed for third as the left fielder retrieved the ball and threw it in. And again, for an excruciating moment, I was sure the Royals' third-base coach would wave Gordon home, again, to tie the game.

This time, though, out of an abundance of caution, the coach held Gordon at third. My jaw dropped. I looked at Matt, who was likewise astounded. Pierre had warned us that things didn't always revert to their previous form. What butterfly had caused this effect? Had the George Washington we'd sent back varied enough from the "original" to change baseball history in some small way that was then magnified over centuries? What else would be different?

The Kansas City crowd went wild, despite the fact that the Royals were still behind. This was their first hit in five innings, and they had a man on third, just one run down. The hometown fans had been sitting on their hands all evening. Now they had something to cheer about. Many turned their hats inside out to make rally caps.

Salvador Pérez, Kansas City's big, iron-man catcher, came to the plate looking determined, as his fans cheered and whistled and applauded. Matt and I knew he was a dangerous hitter. We had already seen him homer to win this very game.

Pérez stepped into the batter's box. Bumgarner looked tired now, but the Giants had no one warming up in the bullpen. Bum threw nothing but high fastballs. Pérez swung at and missed two, let two go by for balls, and fouled one off. On the sixth pitch, Pérez popped up to Giants third-baseman Pablo Sandoval, the Panda, who caught it in foul territory. With a huge smile, he fell onto his back like a stranded turtle, pumping both fists in the air.

Un-be-lievable! The Giants won the game, 3-2, and the *World Serious*, four games to three. Matty and I jumped up and danced around, whooping and hollering, as if this were the first time we had seen this outcome. Of course, it was.

Despite coming in second in their own division during the regular season, the Giants had extended their phenomenal record of postseason success, winning championships in 2010, 2012, and now 2014. It was an even-numbered year, after all.

Chapter Seventy-Eight

LIBERTY

George returned to Valley Forge, met Baron von Steuben, and bought into the Prussian's suggestions for standardized training, organization, and drilling. That spring, the revitalized Continental army defeated the British at the Battle of Monmouth, as depicted in the painting at Doe Library. Under George's inspirational leadership, his army schlepped its own figurative ship up and over the hill and down the other side. The Americans won the war against one of the world's greatest military forces, and their quest for independence inspired similar liberty movements elsewhere. Colonialism eventually failed around the world, and the Spanish, British, and Russian empires curtailed their colonial ambitions in North America.

My world quickly returned to normal. Mostly normal. The *Chronicle* went back to English only. The run-down empanada joint on Solano Avenue was replaced overnight by a high-end, fancy, deep-dish pizza place. My friends David and Daisy reappeared with the old menu at the Burger Depot.

The new Spanish dishes disappeared, except for the Madrid sandwiches, which had proven quite popular. I thought about *el nuevo David*, proprietor of the place when it was *La Estación de Hamburguesas*, and I wondered where he was in this newly re-altered reality. I mean, he had to be somewhere, didn't he? Or had he just never been born? Too many mental gymnastics for my brain.

Rachel had completely forgotten meeting, scheming, hanging out with, and kissing George, as well as holding his hand. She did remember being hit by a car after a Giants game. Eventually her injuries healed, though she continued to walk with a slight limp.

The Giants ballpark never became a bullring, but not everything changed back to the way it had been. The *Banco de España* stayed in our neighborhood, the Wells Fargo Bank gone for good. The piroshki place and some of the Spanish restaurants stayed. The national train system reverted to Amtrak but showed no improvement in on-time performance. Starbucks continued to proliferate.

With the advent of late autumn, I missed baseball. The Giants' championship, of course, was a huge story in the Bay Area. Only Matt and I remembered any different outcome.

After weeks of negotiation, Pablo Sandoval, the beloved Kung Fu Panda, left the Giants, signed a massive contract with the Boston Red Sox, then turned on his former team in an interview, saying the Giants had disrespected him and his agent—despite their offering him $95 million to stay—and that he had few friends on the team.

Ludicrous! I took the news hard, snatched up my orange-and-black panda hat, and took it out back to burn in the barbecue. But I kept seeing George in my mind, wearing the hat at the Giants' ballpark, and I couldn't do it. I tossed the hat in the back of my closet.

A few weeks later, David and Daisy retired and closed the Burger Depot. I was disappointed. If only they knew how hard I worked to get them back!

In an unrelated development, Layla retired from pro wrestling.

I wondered if I would ever see April again. I despaired over our apparent lack of a future, or even a present. I missed George and continued to study his paper trail. Apparently he missed baseball, too. According to a soldier's diary, on May 4, 1778, just two-and-a-half months after he arrived back in Valley Forge, General Washington "did us the honor to play Wicket with us." I wondered if he taught them the value of laying in the weeds.

Speaking of weeds, George's diaries, published long after his death, contained a notation that one year he "began to separate the male from female (hemp) plants rather too late … Pulling up the (male) hemp. Was too late for the blossom hemp by three weeks or a month." The blossoms and buds had no value for making rope or fiber. The Father of Our Country was taking Hank's advice, cultivating the high-THC female plants for the maximum intoxicating buzz. Some historians speculate that Washington at times used cannabis to deal with his ever-worsening tooth pain.

After returning to Valley Forge, he ran several different spy rings to gather information on British troop strengths and movements, supply lines and strategic plans. He employed techniques he learned in his time with us: his Culper spy ring used dead drops, where one agent left documents with vital military information in a field or tavern or hollow tree for another person to pick up, eliminating the danger of being seen together. Much like the thumb drive in the alley behind the Burger Depot.

Washington and his spies developed a sophisticated code for messages, using numbers from one to 763 to substitute for words, just as George imagined after we saw *The Imitation Game*. In his code, sixty-eight through seventy-two stood for brigade, business, battery, battalion, and British. 727 was New York, 728 Long Island, 732 Staten Island, 733 Boston, and 711 General Washington himself. A few handwritten copies of the codebook were made. Four have survived to this day.

The Americans also used disappearing ink on written messages, though not our crude Cub Scout lemon-juice trick. Sir James Jay, a physician who dabbled in chemistry and brother of Founding Father John Jay, developed a clever invisible-ink system with two chemicals. The sender used the first chemical to write the message, which disappeared when dry. The recipient applied the second chemical to bring out the hidden text.

George also proved expert at planting misinformation, false intelligence about the Colonial Army. After the war one British general was famously quoted as saying that the Americans hadn't outfought the Brits, they had outspied them.

George lived more than twenty years after we sent him back. His family's relationship with slavery traced an erratic path. Two trusted house slaves, Martha's maid Ona Judge and the family cook Hercules, ran away during George's presidential terms in Philadelphia, years after Pennsylvania banned slavery. Exhibiting unfathomable arrogance, both Washingtons resented the disloyalty of their enslaved servants.

By the time of George's death in December 1799 at age sixty-seven, the laws of Virginia had changed to allow manumission by a slave owner.

More than 300 enslaved people lived at Mount Vernon by then. Matt was delighted to learn that, in his will, George declared that all 123 slaves belonging to him would be freed after his beloved Patsy died. He provided for the education and training of slave children, as well as homes for their sick and elderly.

Billy Lee was the only slave George mentioned by name in his will. In return for his service during the war, the General granted Billy immediate freedom and provided him a pension and permanent home at Mount Vernon. Disabled by horse-related injuries to both knees, Billy Lee learned a cobbler's trade and outlived George by decades, making shoes. He was known to enjoy visiting with Revolutionary War veterans, including Lafayette, who came to pay their respects to the memory of the charismatic General who had led the War of Independence.

Most of the other Founding Fathers owned slaves at some point. None of them freed their slaves the way George did, en masse and designed to make a powerful statement.

Distraught over George's passing, Martha never again slept in the master bedchamber they had shared at Mount Vernon, staying instead in a garret room on the third floor. She outlived him by a couple of years. During that time, as George's slaves jubilantly awaited their impending freedom, she feared they might hasten her passing in order to achieve it. So she freed them herself, signing a Deed of Manumission at the end of 1800.

After her death in 1802, the 153 Custis dower slaves, descendants of the enslaved people that had come from the estate of Martha's first husband four decades before, fared less well. George was right not to trust his family. Within a short time after Martha's death, her grandchildren had sold or split up most of these slaves, breaking up families, separating children from parents, and continuing their bondage indefinitely into future generations.

Chapter Seventy-Nine
FIONA

Berkeley, January 4, 2015

Over the next few months, I enjoyed being at home with my folks and preparing for my graduate work in history at Stanford.

I stopped playing *Independence*. Video game conversations with George Washington paled compared to memories of my real conversations. I had no patience for the bizarre scenarios in the game. Watching our own world fall apart around us had provided more than enough heinous alternate reality for a lifetime.

Matt was back in grad school, but we enjoyed hanging out and rehashing our summer with George. We chuckled over his responses to toilets, baseball, elevators, the sailboat, hot dogs, ganja, and more. We whispered our recollections of George's coolness in the face of harrowing events—carrying Matt, capped in the ass, back into the train that night in Nebraska; spinning gracefully on the sidewalk in front of Penn Station as his berserk attacker, armed with a rolling suitcase and a watermelon, ran herself into oncoming traffic; and slicing open the third assassin on the train platform at Valley Forge.

We could talk to no one else about this. Rachel never did regain any memory of George. When I called him later, Hank was in fine health and remembered that Matt and I had visited around the time he dragged *Dark Star* up the hill. But he didn't recall that we had brought a friend with us, or that he'd nearly died of gunshot wounds. It was too bad, really. Hank and George had really connected over farming.

Only Matt and I remembered it all. And Pierre, of course. After healing from his bullet wound, he looked in on us every now and then to help ease our transition back to normal life.

"You guys are heroes, you know," he said on one of those visits. It was nice to hear, though no one else would ever know about it. Soon I would be a grad student accumulating huge debts, living month to month, worried about money. I told him so.

The next time I saw him, Chow handed me an envelope stuffed with Benjamins.

"The POA wants to pay you back for all the cash you laid out during your trip back East," he said. He didn't have to ask twice.

On another visit, he told me that they had eliminated the mole.

"We got some valuable info from the numbers on Tess's cell phone. We figured out who was running her, and from there we found links to the FBI's mole at the POA."

"Who was it?" I asked.

"Don't ask. If I told you, I'd have to kill you," he said with a grin, then realized he was being scary and offered a friendly fist bump. "Just kidding. It's no one you know. Recently we figured out that the digital trail left by the mole's IP addresses led back to a small, specialized FBI office in Virginia. Don't ever underestimate their hacking skills. A number of agents have earned advanced degrees in computer science. They were a real threat to our operations."

"Were? What's happened to them?"

"They've had their systems dismantled, on every level, technological and personal. I'm pretty certain we've stopped their digital incursions and neutralized their attempts to get the time machine. FBI leadership has forced the retirement of the remnants of J. Edgar Hoover's cadre of loyal senior agents, who had controlled the Bureau so thoroughly from behind the scenes."

One day just after the dawn of 2015, I walked to the new pizza place on Solano Avenue to sample a pesto-chicken pizza and have a couple of beers. As I ambled back down the block toward my parents' home, I noticed someone sitting on my front stoop. Someone female—tall, wiry, and athletic, with dark hair and beautiful brown eyes that glowed warmly in my direction.

My jaw dropped. I walked closer. The girl in purple now wore royal blue and yellow. She took my hand, and we strolled down the street past my house. I didn't know what to say. I knew I had a goofy grin on my face.

April squeezed my arm and broke the silence.

"I really did grow up in Portland and go to Oregon State. I really do have family in Cleveland. I tried not to lie to you."

I thought for a moment.

"What about the Giants?"

"I do love the Giants. Tim, they're taking me out of

the field."

"Who is?"

"Homeland Security. They want me to write an emergency first-aid manual and teach conversational Mandarin at a Department school in Monterey."

I couldn't stop smiling. "You speak Mandarin? What else haven't you told me?"

"I'm pretty good with languages."

"So I gather. And you've been to nursing school."

"Yes."

"Funny how none of that came up when I first met you."

"You were pretending to be blind, and you didn't tell me you were traveling with George Washington."

"Mmm, no. But you knew that already. Wait a minute—Monterey, California?"

"That's what I'm trying to tell you, Tim. It's a good job. Less stress. No danger. More money. And I'll be nearby."

"Oh."

"And I won't be undercover anymore."

"Wait—you mean?"

"Yes."

"Oh!"

"Yes. We can be together."

I didn't know what to say.

"I mean, we don't know each other very well," she continued. "But I felt something, and I know you did, too. Now we can be together—or not—as much as we want to, as long as it works between us. I want you to trust me."

We stopped walking, embraced, and gazed at each other. Her hair smelled faintly of lavender.

"Unless," she said, "you don't want me. Or there's

372

someone else."

"There's no one else." I could easily get lost in those eyes. "And yes, of course I want you."

"One more thing you should know," she said shyly. "My name isn't April."

"Shocker. Is your name actually May June?"

"No." She chuckled.

"Augusta September?"

"No, I'm not a month." She laughed, looked away, and closed her eyes. Opening them, she stared deep into my heart and said, "My name is Fiona."

"No."

"Fiona Merryweather."

"No!"

"Yes."

"Really? What are you, a hobbit?"

We laughed.

"No, Tim," she giggled, sounding nothing like a government agent. "I am definitely not a hobbit. I'm much too tall to be a halfling. And I don't have big feet or furry toes." She wrapped her arms more tightly around me.

We laughed and kissed and embraced for a long while, unable to let go. I began to shudder, the last anxiety of our summer with George finally leaving my body.

I wondered, not for the last time, if Pierre had a hand in her change of assignment, as a way of expressing his gratitude to me. For, you know, saving the world.

It didn't matter. For the first time, we had a future.

Chapter Eighty
EPILOGUE

Stanford, March 28, 2016

Wake *up, Tim. Wake up, Tim.*

The alarm purred rhythmically as it gently tugged on my t-shirt.

I pulled up the blanket to cover my face. I was struggling to retain a dream, to bring it forward into my consciousness. Something fantastically important had transpired, in my mind's eye, something elaborate with swords, a saddle, and voluptuous lady wrestlers on trains. But the dream faded as I woke.

The tugging continued. I opened one eye. A warm, brown, female eye lay inches away, gazing into mine. It crinkled in a smile. I opened the other eye and smiled back.

"Cool. I was hoping to wake up next to a beautiful, sexy woman!"

"Well," said Fiona, "you're stuck with me."

"Oh, you'll do just fine." I flung one leg over her and wriggled closer.

She pulled me to her bosom. I loved snuggling against her body, bumps in all the right places. She hugged me tightly, then rolled away and jumped out of bed. It was six in the morning. I lunged at her.

"Nice, warm woman. Don't go!"

"Sweetie, you know I've gotta dash. Throwing on clothes and heading out. See you Thursday."

I nuzzled her chest as she stood next to the bed.

She smiled and kissed me. Then she was off. I knew I should get up, too, but I lolled in bed for another fifteen minutes before getting ready for class.

We wanted to live together, but our separate pursuits took place too far apart. Fiona came up from Monterey on Thursdays, spent the weekend at my little, ivy-covered cottage on College Terrace near Stanford campus, then took off again early Monday. She had scheduled all her classes in the early part of the week, so we could have four nights a week together.

This was the best we could do for a while. We were crazy in love and craved being together, but having a few days apart every week gave us each space to work on our specialties. Fiona taught at some government school and was writing a book, and I was more than a year into my graduate program in American history. I nurtured an intense interest in the Revolutionary War, though I couldn't recall exactly when it had started. I had attacked the subject hungrily when I arrived at Stanford—drawn, for some reason, to the leaders of the Revolution, like Hamilton, Lafayette, von Steuben, and especially Washington.

Fiona and I were very happy together. We had met on a cross-country Amtrak train a few months before I started school. She was on vacation, heading to Cleveland to see family, and I was on my way with Matt to tour historic battlegrounds in the East. For some reason, we had decided to bring Nevada. I was a bit vague about which places we had visited, though I was sure we had gone through Pennsylvania.

I dressed and headed out, picking up a latte at Starbucks. I paused as I stuffed the change into my wallet. Gazing at the old, grim visage on the one-dollar bill, I wondered, not for the first time, what he had looked like when he was younger.

I was excited. Baseball season was about to begin, and next week we had tickets to see the Giants. Even though they had tanked in 2015, 2016 was another even-numbered year.

It was the first week of spring quarter. I had dawdled, not yet in rhythm with the early mornings, and now I was late for my eight o'clock class. As I hurried across Main Quad, a slim, athletic-looking, Asian-American man approached. He reminded me of someone.

I continued to walk. The man strode alongside and offered a tentative fist bump.

"Tim?"

He looked me in the eye.

"Yeah, that's me, dude, but I'm late for class. Can't stop."

I sidestepped him, then brushed past. There was something vaguely familiar about the guy. I couldn't put my finger on it. Perhaps he resembled someone in my dream.

I stopped to look back. He smiled, then walked away.

I watched for a moment, shrugged, and hurried off to class.

AUTHOR'S NOTE: WHY WASHINGTON?

Warning: here be spoilers!

I grew up fascinated by the presidents, Washington in particular.

George became my touchstone for trying to understand the alluring technology of my mid-century boyhood: aviation, photography, trains, cars, rockets, satellites, television, movies. I frequently asked myself: how would I explain this to George Washington, if he were to come back to life right now?

So, why not bring him back to life and find out?

In recent years, there's been renewed interest in Washington, especially since the publication online of his voluminous personal papers. George, of course, is a major character in the Broadway smash *Hamilton*, and a number of new biographies attempt to educate our history-deprived population in the complexities of his life and the War of Independence.

I researched the historical background carefully. IRL, history mostly did unfold as presented here. But what about the science?

Early on, a fellow writer advised me about time travel. "Don't get too technical," he said, "or people will just pick it apart. Instead, focus on what it does and how it's used." Good advice. No flux capacitors here, though there is an occasional vacuum tube.

I originally thought of this as a comic, fish-out-of-water story, but as I learned more about my subject, I realized there was more to it than that. The story couldn't be as simple as I had envisioned. George was a charismatic leader, but a soft-spoken, uninspiring orator. A courageous man, who endured the burden of dental pain throughout his life. He was a powerful, ambitious man, but a kind, gentle husband and stepfather. A 6'2" giant, at a time when most men were much shorter. A skillful horseman, a graceful dancer, a man's man who enjoyed the company of women.

Perhaps most significantly, like most of the Founding Fathers, he was a slave owner. History establishes that Washington, privately, had at least a dawning awareness that slavery was evil and immoral. But both George and Martha (aka Patsy) felt betrayed when two enslaved people ran away from their Philadelphia household during his presidency.

George did attempt to free his slaves, or some of them, in his last will and testament, but ... it's complicated. For many, the result was tragic, as detailed in the narrative.

Full disclosure. A few times, I bent time and space for dramatic license. At the time George disappeared from Valley Forge, the Battle of Rhode Island (where an all-Black regiment distinguished itself) had not yet happened. We don't think of Pennsylvania as earthquake country, and it's not that far north, but both a scary quake and a bright display of the northern lights really did occur in the Philadelphia area the same winter George was at Valley Forge—though I have moved them a few weeks later. Layla the wrestler did appear at the real Madison Square Garden in 2014, but in July, not October. The Giants game Tim and the gang attended in San Francisco the night the Dodgers clinched the pennant actually took place in Los Angeles.

On the other hand, Baron von Steuben did arrive in Valley Forge the day after George's birthday in 1778, whether you believe my version of how he got there or not. Einstein did postulate about time travel in his relativity theories. And, I can tell you from experience, the California Zephyr is often late getting into Chicago.

With the exception of the game mentioned above, all the baseball history is accurate as well, including the outcome of the 2014 World Series. One of the outcomes, anyway.

I mean, it could have happened this way, right?

Bill Zarchy
Albany, California
November 2020

ACKNOWLEDGEMENTS

Many people helped shape and improve this book.

First and always, thank you to my wonderful family, who have supported me in all ways:

My parents, Jeanette and Harry Zarchy, who raised us with love, respect, and a high regard for books and education.

My wife Susan, who has always believed in me and actually let me read this book aloud to her—twice.

Our kids: Razi and Leah, Danny and Ashley. Talented writers all, who have provided cheerleading, inspiration, feedback, and baseball gossip for years.

Sue and Craig, Nathie and Jeanette, and a slew of cousins, nieces, and nephews. And Norm (who always told me I should write a thriller).

Thanks also to:

My hybrid community of dear friends, filmmakers, colleagues, bowling buddies, travel pals, writers, storytellers, and former students.

Larry Habegger, friend, teacher, and mentor, who read and guided this book in its earliest and very latest stages, along with members of his writers group: John Dalton, Bonnie Smetts, Jacqueline Yau, Jenn Baljko, Dana Hill, Yvette Zhu, Jacqueline Collins, Barbara Robertson, Carol Beddo,

Kimberley Lovato, and Michael Sano.

My other early readers: Pete Beaven, Hue Freeman, John Nash, and John Nutt.

Folks at the Book Passage Mystery Writers Conferences, who read pages and encouraged me to pursue this book idea: agents Amy Rennert and Kimberley Cameron, and authors George Fong, Tim Maleeny, and David Corbett.

Matthew Félix, who handled the final stages of editing, design, and publication.

Besides book research, I rode Amtrak from California to Philadelphia, visited Valley Forge, Independence Hall, the Liberty Bell, Mount Vernon, Colonial Williamsburg, the Smithsonian National Museum of American History, the Washington Monument, New York City, Mendocino, the Doe Library at UC Berkeley, Citizens Bank Park in Philadelphia, and AT&T Park in San Francisco. I am grateful for the assistance of Mary V. Thompson, Research Historian at the Fred W. Smith National Library for the Study of George Washington at Mount Vernon, who answered a number of questions for me about Washington's voice, accent, demeanor, and relationship with Martha.

BOOK LIST

These books served as invaluable resources during research for *Finding George Washington*. Many thanks to the authors for their scholarship, insight, and imagination.

Timothy B. Allen, *George Washington, Spymaster*

Applewood's Pictorial America, *George Washington 1732-1799*

Ron Chernow, *Washington: A Life*

Mary Higgins Clark, *Mount Vernon Love Story: A Novel of George and Martha Washington*

Alexis Coe, *You Never Forget Your First: A Biography of George Washington*

Charles Dickens, *A Christmas Carol*

Joseph J. Ellis, *His Excellency: George Washington*

Newt Gingrich, William R. Forstchen and Albert S. Hanser, *Valley Forge: George Washington and the Crucible of Victory*

James Gleick, *Time Travel*

Phil Hornshaw and Nick Hurwitch, *So You Created a Wormhole: The Time Traveler's Guide to Time Travel*

Hugh Howard, *The Painter's Chair*

Paul Johnson, *George Washington: The Founding Father*

Brian Kilmeade and Don Yaeger, *George Washington's Secret Six: The Spy Ring That Saved the American Revolution*

Stephen King, *11/22/63*

Len Lamensdorf, *The Ballad of Billy Lee: The Story of George Washington's Favorite Slave*

Mark Lardas, *George Washington: Leadership, Strategy, Conflict*

Jack E. Levin, *George Washington: The Crossing*

Carla Killough McClafferty, *The Many Faces of George Washington: Remaking a Presidential Icon*

Joseph Plumb Martin, *Memoir of a Revolutionary Soldier*

Ellen G. Miles, *George and Martha Washington: Portraits from the Presidential Years*

Sarah E. Mitchell, *Men's Clothing 1760-1785*

Paul J. Nahin, *Time Machines: Time Travel in Physics, Metaphysics, and Science Fiction*

Paul J. Nahin, *Time Travel: A Writer's Guide to the Real Science of Plausible Time Travel*

Audrey Niffenegger, *The Time Traveler's Wife*

Official Guidebook, *George Washington's Mount Vernon*

Gary Paulsen, *The Rifle*

John Thorn, *Baseball in the Garden of Eden: The Secret History of the Early Game*

Mark Twain, *A Connecticut Yankee in King Arthur's Court*

George Washington, *George-isms*

George Washington, *The Journal of Major George Washington*

George Washington, *Quotations of George Washington*

H. G. Wells, *The Time Machine and Other Works*

Henry Wiencek, *An Imperfect God: George Washington, His Slaves, and the Creation of America*

ABOUT THE AUTHOR

Bill Zarchy filmed projects on six continents during his forty years as a cinematographer, captured in his first book, *Showdown at Shinagawa: Tales of Filming from Bombay to Brazil*. Now he writes novels, takes photos, and talks of many things.

Bill's career included filming three former presidents for the Emmy-winning *West Wing Documentary Special*, the Grammy-winning *Please Hammer Don't Hurt 'Em*, feature films *Conceiving Ada* and *Read You Like A Book*, PBS science series *Closer to Truth*, musical performances as diverse as the Grateful Dead, Weird Al Yankovic, and Wagner's Ring Cycle, and countless high-end projects for technology and medical companies.

His tales from the road, personal essays, and technical articles have appeared in *Travelers' Tales* and *Chicken Soup for the Soul* anthologies, the *San Francisco Chronicle* and other newspapers, and *American Cinematographer*, *Emmy*, and other trade magazines.

Bill has a BA in Government from Dartmouth and an MA in Film from Stanford. He taught Advanced Cinematography at San Francisco State for twelve years. He is a resident of the San Francisco Bay Area and a graduate of the EPIC Storytelling Program at Stagebridge in Oakland. This is his first novel.

billzarchy.com
findinggeorgewashington.com
showdownatshinagawa.com

Made in the USA
Middletown, DE
15 February 2021